# How to Walk like a Man

## by Eli Easton

# Acknowledgments

Thanks to my beta readers Kate Rothwell, Jamie Fessenden, Nico Sels, Pam Ebeler, and Veronica Harrison. It would be very difficult to do this job without you!

Cover by the talented Reese Dante.

Dedicated to Lola, Lucy, and Livy, our fabulously funny bulldogs.

# Also by Eli Easton

*From Dreamspinner Press*

Superhero

Puzzle Me This

The Trouble With Tony (Sex in Seattle #1)

The Enlightenment of Daniel (Sex in Seattle #2)

The Mating of Michael (Sex in Seattle #3)

A Prairie Dog's Love Song

Heaven Can't Wait

The Lion and the Crow


*From Eli Easton*

Before I Wake

Blame it on the Mistletoe

Unwrapping Hank

Midwinter Night's Dream

How to Howl at the Moon


www.elieaston.com

# Readers Love Eli

**For "Unwrapping Hank"**

"Queen of the sexual tension, she makes us wait for the love scenes.... When the sex arrives it's always hot and deliciously satisfying and in my opinion all the more sizzling for the delay." - *Sinfully Sexy Book Reviews*

"Easton masters effective and persuasive writing, her style natural and smooth. Dialogue is realistic, the story doesn't linger inside people's heads for too long, and the narrative grabs you until you find yourself turning pages, unwilling to stop until the very last line." – *Joyfully Jay*

"I love Eli Easton's books and this one is just the right book to sit with the Christmas tree and lose yourself in. Funny, endearing, happy, loving, and it left me smiling like an idiot." – *author RJ Scott*

**For "The Mating of Michael", Rainbow Award Winner for Best Contemporary Gay Romance 2014**

"Hot, sexy, and emotional.... DAMN, Eli Easton just NAILED this one and she nailed it HARD!!" – *My Fiction Nook*

"I couldn't put this story down. The characters were richly developed, and the story was well thought out and enjoyable." – *Swept Away By Romance*

"The story just plucks at every darn heart string and leaves you with a huge smile on your face, after you've gotten done crying, of course." *The Kimichan Experience*

**For "Blame it on the Mistletoe", M/M Goodreads Group award winner**

"I got hooked on the story and could not keep that goofy smile off my face." – *Head Out of the Oven Blog*

"This is a wonderful little gem of a holiday story. I enjoyed every moment I got to spend with these beautiful boys." – *Gaylist*

"The genuine fondness, admiration, and eventually love that these two feel for each other really jump off the page. I was hooked from beginning to end" – *Mrs. Condit and Friends*

## Published by Pinkerton Road

Pennsylvania, USA

First edition, November, 2015

eli@elieaston.com

www.elieaston.com

How to Walk Like a Man

# 1

## The Imminent Threat Of Tangerines

"Now Roman, remember. You're going to have to stay very conscious about not exhibiting any dog-like behavior during this meeting. We can't afford to raise suspicion."

"Yes, sir. I'll be on my guard."

Roman didn't need to be reminded. He knew humans were unaware that dog-human shifters, called the quickened, existed. But he could tell Lance was anxious, and his chatter was down to nerves. Sweat beaded on Sheriff Lance Beaufort's upper lip as he steered the car and—Roman sniffed as subtly as he could—Lance smelled wary, suspicious. Roman's inner dog wanted to whine at the unease of his pack leader, but Roman swallowed it. *No dog behavior.*

They were driving to Fresno in Lance's white sheriff's department SUV for a big regional law enforcement meeting. The DEA was giving a presentation, and Lance had asked Roman to go along. He probably just wanted company on the long drive, but Roman had been thrilled. Since he'd become a full-time deputy with the Mad Creek's Sheriff's Office, he had a purpose in life again, and he liked being included in Lance's plans. Besides, he loved to ride in cars! It was even better when you didn't have to drive and could roll down the window and stick your hand out, feel the wind buffet your skin.

With the window rolled down, a scent caught Roman's nose on the warm September air. He turned his head as they zipped past endless pine trees. There was something dead out in the woods—something small, like a groundhog. If he were on foot, he'd go find it just for the fun of it. But not today. Not today.

He smiled and looked at his hand as he tried to catch the wind. Today he was a man, and it was still amazing. *Hands* were amazing. Lately he'd been finding his own body more fascinating. He'd been quickened for two years now, but sometimes he felt like he was just now wakening from a dream—only to find it wasn't a dream at all.

"I think it's very different," he said, wiggling his fingers. "Being quickened from birth, like you were, and getting it later in life, like me. Living as a dog first."

"I'm sure it is," Lance agreed. "Incredibly different."

"I'm glad I was who I was. That I had that time in Army K-9. With James."

Lance said nothing, and Roman felt a pang of self-doubt. Maybe he was talking too much in an 'un-human-like' way. Lance was pack, but he was also Roman's boss. He cleared his throat and rolled up the window. "So. What do you expect to happen at this meeting today?"

"I don't know." Lance frowned at the windshield. "I'm hoping it'll be good news, but—"

"We haven't had any trouble. Not since that night those drug dealers shot up Tim's house."

"I know. But I have a sense something's coming, like... a prickling on my neck. I've had a bad feeling for days."

Roman didn't have any such 'bad feeling', but he didn't say it out loud. As a border collie shifter, Lance worried about his territory obsessively, more than Roman or any other quickened. So if Lance sensed something, he was probably right.

Roman's heart beat a little faster. "Do you want me to carry my weapon, sir?"

Lance laughed. "No, I don't mean I expect trouble at this meeting. Coffee and donuts and a lot of ass-kissing is probably as dangerous as it'll get. But the DEA's presentation... This is the first time they've called us all together for something like this. I'm assuming it's not going to be good news on the war-on-drugs front. I just hope whatever's brewing out there, it has nothing to do with Mad Creek."

"Because that would be bad." Roman knew Lance's philosophy: fly as under-the-radar and away from human things as possible. Mad Creek was in the middle of nowhere for a reason.

"Yes, Roman. Because that would be *very* bad," Lance said darkly.

\*           \*           \*

There were at least a hundred sheriffs, deputies, and other law enforcement personnel at the meeting. Roman stayed by Lance's side, said 'hello' when he was introduced, and otherwise kept his mouth shut. He also refrained from scratching his ears or visibly sniffing people. He adopted the stoic military stance that was so familiar to him from his time in the Army. There was a

10

lot he didn't know about being human, but he knew how to imitate a soldier.

In fact, it felt like the old days being around so many people in uniform, though most of them were older and not as lively or fun as the soldiers in Afghanistan. Still, there were jokes Roman didn't get, lots of backslapping and, yes, coffee and donuts. The ones with the white icing and raisins were Roman's favorites! He ate six of them before a warning glare from Lance reminded him to slow down.

After the donuts, it was time for the presentations.

The Forest Service went first. An older man with gray hair and a pot belly spoke. "Last year, we found over four hundred illegal marijuana farms in California. Three hundred of those were in the Sierra Nevada Mountains."

The man showed pictures of razed dirt areas among trees and big water ponds sheeted in plastic. "The worst part of all this is the extensive destruction of public lands and animal habitat. These illegal farms use heavy pesticides. They cut down trees. They set out poison for animals. They create irrigation ponds, siphoning off hundreds of gallons of water that starve the area of moisture, and rob water from the cities downstream."

11

Lance had been right. It wasn't good news. Roman felt the hair on the back of his neck stand up as he looked at the slide show. He loved the woods around his cabin, loved to run there, both as human and dog. It was beautiful and it was full of life. He'd be so angry if someone did that to *his* woods.

"Besides the environmental impact, it's a danger for hikers and campers who might stumble across these things. There were twelve murders last year for exactly that reason. And it's a danger for our Forest Service officers, who aren't trained, and don't have the bandwidth, to do this extensive policing. So we've asked the governor, and the governor has asked the president, for resources from the DEA."

The man from the DEA—the Drug Enforcement Agency—talked next. His name was Dixon. He had silver in his brown hair, but he was trim and tough-looking. He wore blue jeans and a black T-shirt that said "DEA" on it in gold letters.

"I guess I don't have to tell you that this is a huge problem," Dixon said. "It's mostly marijuana farms in California, but in Arizona and Texas we're seeing an increase of meth and opium labs in wooded parks like these too. Fortunately, we've gotten the funding we need to make a concerted effort here in the California mountains."

Dixon put up a list of town names. Mariposa, Oakhurst, Briceburg, and Coulterville were on the list, among others. And there, in black and white, was the name Mad Creek. Lance started vibrating with tension in the seat next to Roman's.

"The new operation is called Operation Green Ghost. We're funding a full-time agent in each of these towns for at least the next twelve months. These DEA investigators will be based out of your offices and will form a coordinated web under the control of the DEA. We've got—"

Lance shot to his feet. "Excuse me!"

Dixon looked at Lance warily. "Yes?"

"As the sheriff of one of the towns on your list, I think we should have a say about this. We don't need any extra manpower. We're overstaffed as it is, and I can promise you, we haven't had any trouble with the drug trade anywhere around Mad Creek."

Lance was in his most intense mode. His voice made Roman shift in his chair uncomfortably, even though it wasn't

13

directed at him. But Dixon just narrowed his eyes. "Mad Creek? Are you Sheriff Beaufort?"

"I certainly am."

Dixon nodded. "Well, Sheriff, I'm afraid you *don't* have any say over this. This is a federal operation, and we've chosen the locations for this task force strategically." He brought up another slide showing the Sierra Nevadas with circles over every town he'd listed and lines interconnecting them. Mad Creek was one of the towns most distant from all the others, so it was clear to Roman they held a key position. Maybe it was clear to Lance too. He sat back down, his blue eyes bright with worry. Roman's instinct was to rub his arm and shoulder up against Lance, to soothe him. But that was dog behavior. He remained still.

Dixon went on. "I'll be running the operation from here and coordinating with the Forest Service. The DEA task force members located in these towns will report to me. They'll work fairly independently day to day, but there may be times when they'll need your assistance. For example if they need to investigate a suspicious site. We hope you'll—"

Lance popped up again. "Excuse me! If we have to have an additional staff member in our office to coordinate with this

14

'Green Ghost' task force, can we be allowed to hire them ourselves? I have several candidates—"

"Sheriff Beaufort, these will be specially trained DEA agents, on *our* payroll. No, you will not be hiring them or interviewing them or picking out their clothes. They're our agents and they will be assigned to your town. They will sit in your office, if you would be so accommodating, but they will not report to you. Is that clear?"

Dixon was losing patience, and so were the other people in the room. Some turned in their seats to give Lance begrudging glances. Maybe, Roman thought, they also wanted more of those donuts with the white frosting and raisins, so they wanted the presentation to hurry up and end.

But Lance didn't care. He was a good-looking and charismatic man with his thick black hair, tight compact build, and turquoise blue eyes. For a long moment, Lance stared at the DEA man, his shoulders high and tight in a warning. Dixon stared back. No human being on this earth could out-stare Lance Beaufort, so the man gave up first. He went back to his slide show and continued to talk, ignoring Lance. Lance sat down.

Roman could feel the anger coming off Lance in waves. He understood why Lance wasn't happy. He didn't want a stranger in Mad Creek, not a stranger like this, an investigator who'd be looking down every dirt road, who'd be sitting in their office. Roman pushed down a growl. He didn't want that either. He loved the sheriff's office in Mad Creek, where he had his very own desk in a room he shared with Charlie. There was even a little sign with his name on it and everything! Everyone who worked in the office was quickened. They'd have to be so careful with a stranger around.

Dixon went on to discuss the details of Operation Green Ghost. Roman did his best to listen. But he was too aware of Lance's anger, too aware of the fact that all this spying would be over the homes of people he knew and land he loved. It made him feel edgy and threatened.

Mad Creek was a safe haven for so many souls—good souls, trusting souls, sometimes lost souls. He should know. He'd been lost himself.

After the meeting broke up, Lance pulled Roman aside in the hall. "Stay here. I'm going to go talk to the district supervisor, see if I can't do something about this." His blue eyes burned so bright it almost hurt to look at them. He kept his voice low so only Roman could hear. "I can't push too hard, though, or I'll just draw more attention to Mad Creek. Goddamn it. Just don't talk to anyone. And don't do anything... weird. Okay? I'll be back."

\*　　　　　\*　　　　　\*

Roman waited in the hall.

The Fresno County Sheriff's Office was a low stone building. There were wooden planks on the walls and they were covered with pictures, certificates, and maps. Roman kept his back to a wall, standing in parade rest. In his deputy's uniform—green pants, green tie, khaki shirt, and badge—people passed him with barely a glance, like he was security, like he belonged there.

They didn't guard their tongues either. He heard a few men complain about Lance, wondering what his issue was, if he was just a control freak or had something going on 'up there'. Lance was right. If they protested too much, people would get suspicious. An older woman in uniform was telling stories about drug crimes in her area and others talked about their budgets or bad knees. The people all smelled of too much coffee and fast food—a slightly rancid oily smell. Roman stood still, waiting.

The hall emptied as people made their way outside. Lance still hadn't returned. Roman's gaze darted down the hall where there was the door of a men's room. He sure would like to use the bathroom before the long drive back to Mad Creek. Should he wait for Lance to ask permission?

Would a real man wait to ask permission? Probably not. Lance was his boss, not his master. And it wasn't as though Roman was guarding anything. He was just waiting.

He sharply turned on his heel and headed for the bathroom door.

He pushed it open and turned the corner. There were three urinals on the white tiled wall, two stalls, and some sinks. There was also a man already in the room. He was in the process of peeing into a urinal.

Roman's eyes snapped away, but not before he registered the black DEA T-shirt stretched across broad shoulders and the slender waist. The man was young, fit, had a soldier's build, and dark brown hair that was short in the back but longer on top. The scent of the man's urine was ripe in the air as Roman moved to the urinal closest to the door—and farthest from the man. He knew to keep his distance even though everything inside him itched to get closer, smell deeper.

Human ways were just plain baffling sometimes. A dog's instinct was to size up a stranger by sniffing their scent. That made so much sense! His brain stored smells very precisely. He could remember if he'd smelled that creature before, if he'd found its urine on a tree or in the grass. He could even tell if it was sick and what it had been eating recently.

But humans hated it when you sniffed their crotch as a dog. In human form, well, it was so far out of line, it would land you in a fight. Roman should know. He'd gotten in a few fights for that very reason when he was still young enough not to understand.

Roman stared down as he took out his penis and held himself over the basin. He hesitated another moment, though, unable to resist testing the pure urine smell in the air one more time, reading what it had to tell him... *male, excellent health, at reproductive peak, hasn't eaten sugar lately, faint traces of beer.*

He could also smell the man himself—warm and faintly sweaty, a frustrated sweat, like he'd done something unpleasant recently.

Satisfied he knew the score, Roman let himself go. He didn't look up. When he finished and zipped his pants, he was surprised to see that the guy was still standing at his urinal. He was trying, with his right hand, to get the button at the top of his pants through the hole. His left arm was in a sling. Immediately images of dogs and men, broken and limping, came to mind along with a wave of pity. *Afghanistan.*

The man glanced at Roman, his eyes bright with frustration. "I'm left-handed, of course. Son-of-a-bitch pants."

Without a second thought, Roman crossed the space between them in one stride and dropped to his knees. "I can do it."

He grabbed both sides of the man's waistband, tugging them together and slipping the button through the hole. Above him, the man tensed and slowly moved his right hand out of the way. Roman grabbed the zipper and put his fingers inside the waistband to hold it still as he moved the zipper up.

"There." As he released the pants, his fingers brushed across a soft-hard bulge that was growing under the canvas fabric. At the same moment, a musky scent rose up, perplexing Roman. He frowned, still on his knees. He couldn't resist—his nostrils flared as he tried for another whiff, staring at the bulge in the canvas. It smelled like... musky tangerines, like when a tangerine is past ripe and is just starting to go moldy. Roman liked the smell. A lot.

The man took a step back. "Thanks, I... wow. That's an, uh... interesting technique."

Roman got to his feet and looked at the man's face. He was very good at reading faces and the expression he saw there confused him—mouth slightly open, eyes evaluating him in a warm and curious way that he'd never seen before. Then the man's expression changed to one of surprise.

"Oh my God! You're that guy!"

Roman saw it too and everything clicked. He knew this man. This was the DEA SWAT soldier that he'd gone after during that drug bust several months ago. In all the tension and confusion of the drug raid—the one he and Lance were *supposed* to be merely watching—Roman had seen this man get shot in the distance and had snapped. Something about the way his square jaw and the shape of his nose had looked in the dim light.... Roman had been convinced in that instant that the man was James. He'd run right into the firefight, endangering Lance, endangering himself, and the mission.

No one had been hurt, and Roman had managed to drag this man to safety, but that was mere luck. The mistake had been one of the most humiliating moments of Roman's career—either as a man or a dog.

Unsure how to respond, Roman ducked his head and went to the sink. He turned on the water to wash off the scent of the man, and his own scent, from his hands.

"You're the guy who pulled me out of that fire fight in Coarsegold." The man was at his side by then, only a few feet away. Roman met his gaze in the mirror. The man had large, brown eyes with long lashes, and his square jaw did make him look a little like James. His expression was excited. "That's where I—my arm. It was shot up pretty bad."

"Sorry." Roman's gaze dropped to the man's arm where it was bent and flush against his chest in a black sling.

"Eh, modern medicine, you know? PT and all that shit. It's coming back. Anyway, I'd probably be dead if you hadn't pulled me out. But man, that was some crazy-ass stunt. You could have been killed!"

"I know." Humiliation burned in Roman's chest. He shut off the water and grabbed a few paper towels. He hadn't thought about that night in many weeks now. It was not a good memory. He tossed the paper towels and turned, not having much choice. The man stood there watching him. His gaze was too sharp and observant. Roman felt nervous.

"Hang on a sec." The guy reached around Roman to wash his right hand and dry it. "There." With a sheepish smile, he stuck out his hand. "I've been wanting to shake your hand, but I figured I should wash first. Not that you weren't just practically touching my junk, but it's only polite."

There was a sharp lilting bite to his words that Roman recognized as humor, even if he didn't quite get why it was funny. He shook the man's hand.

"I'm Matt, Matt Barclay. I thought about you, you know. Sort of wanted to try to find you and thank you, but I thought you were a civie. You're a sheriff's deputy?" He looked at

23

Roman's badge, his hand still clasping Roman's. Roman didn't pull away. He liked Matt's strong-gentle grip. He missed being touched.

"I am now. Deputy Roman Charsguard. Mad Creek."

A complicated series of expressions moved over Matt's face, and he dropped Roman's hand. "You're... Mad Creek, huh?"

"Yes, sir."

Matt looked away. "Of course you are," he muttered to himself. With his good right hand, he ruffled his own hair and huffed out a bemused laugh, though Roman didn't have the first idea why. "Well, Roman... Are you as unwelcoming as your sheriff?"

Roman wasn't sure how to respond to that. He didn't always understand the subtleties of human communication, but he got the feeling the man didn't like Lance. Roman didn't want to say or do anything against Lance, so he said nothing.

Matt shook his head and started for the door. "Right. Well. Anyway. What I said before—thank you."

Roman knew he'd disappointed the man and was sorry. He didn't dislike Matt. In fact, he thought Matt's military bearing and short hair were very nice. He reminded Roman of the old days. And he had a pleasant face too.

"Good-bye, Matt Barclay," he said. "Maybe we'll meet again."

Matt gave him a funny smile. "Oh, you can count on it."

# 2

## Who Will Watch The Watcher?

### *Dogma #1*

The first strong memory Roman had was of the day he met Sergeant James Pattson.

He was in a kennel. It was clean and roomy, but he still disliked the strong metal wire that kept him from the green grass he saw in the distance. His muscles itched to run—run as far as he could, until his lungs burned and his legs gave out. He was lonely too. Men came into the kennel to give him food and, on good days, a few strokes of his fur. But they always left again.

Until James. James walked up to the kennel with another man, both wearing green T-shirts and the green-and-tan pants with all the spots on them. They came inside.

"Hey, buddy." James bent down on one knee.

"His name's Roman," said the other man, sounding tired. "This is the only dog you haven't seen yet. And, personally, I think he's the best of the bunch."

26

"Hey, Roman." James's hands were strong and felt so good as they rubbed Roman's ears and neck. He smelled good too—like bright light and warm blankets and the tang of sweat in the hot sun. James looked Roman over, big hands running over his hind legs. Roman let him pick up one leg and flex it at the knee, touch the pads on his paw.

"He's from great stock," said the other man. "One hundred percent German shepherd. Three generations of military service dogs on his paternal side, and his mother's a show champion."

"He's a damn fine-looking dog," James muttered.

"He's young, though. You'll have to start him from scratch, Sergeant."

James said nothing, but he took Roman's head and looked him in the eye. In that moment, Roman sensed he was being judged, like James was looking right down inside him to his heart.

"Are you a good boy?" James asked him, his voice kind. "Are you a brave dog?"

27

Roman leapt up to lick James's face, knocking him in the nose. James laughed. "I guess the answer is 'no' to the first and 'yes' to the second. This one's got something special. I'm not sure what it is, but it's definitely something."

He rubbed Roman's ears, his lips in a wide smile. Roman suddenly wanted to go with this man more than anything. And he did! When James left the kennel, he clipped a leash to Roman's collar and took him along.

Roman could still remember the sensation he'd felt that day of total, blazing joy. He was sure life had finally come for him. He belonged to James—and James belonged to him. He didn't know where they were going, but he knew it would be exciting. He couldn't wait!

*   *   *

"Dad, I told you. Luci isn't moving in with me. She's just staying here for a few weeks because she lost her place."

"Now that's the dumbest thing I ever heard. If that's not a sign from God, I don't know what is. Perfect time to get married—you're starting in a new town, and she needs a home.

28

For God's sake, Matthew, do the deed! What are you so afraid of?"

"I'm not afraid of anything, Dad." Matt spoke as calmly as he could. "We're just not there yet. I'm not sure how long this assignment's going to last and Luci wants to finish her degree—"

"She can't do that if you're married? Don't be an ass. Your mother finished her bachelor's while you and your brother were running around the sand box with your weenies hanging out. You're taking advantage of that girl. You need to man up and—"

His dad went on. Luci walked through the living room of Matt's newly rented cabin, carrying boxes. She looked at Matt and gave him a cross-eyed grimace. He pretended to hang himself with a noose, making garbled noises. She laughed.

"What's that you say?" his dad asked, shutting off his diatribe.

"Oh, that was the neighbor's dog. Hey, Dad, I need to go. I want to go in to the sheriff's office and make sure everything's set up for Monday."

There was a heavy sigh on the other end of the line. If there was one thing that could get General Thomas Barclay to shut up, it was the idea that he was interrupting Matt's work. Work came first, always.

"Fine. I suppose you already know my opinion on the subject. Think about it. This is a new start for you, son. And now you've got Luci living with you. You know I don't approve of that kind of monkey business before marriage. You need to treat that girl with honor."

"I'll discuss it with Luci, Dad. Okay? Gotta run."

"Stay sharp." His dad hung up, his voice still unhappy.

"Ugh!" Matt groaned. "I knew you coming up here would cause a shit fest with the General."

"Sorry," Luci pouted. "I really do appreciate it, though. It would be a pain to find another apartment for just two months. And if I stayed with any of my cousins, I'd be at the mercy of the Hernandez mama brigade."

"I know. It's fine."

Luci was starting her first year of law school in January and planned to stay with family from Thanksgiving through the New Year. But Matt understood that any more 'family time' than that was likely to send her stark raving mad, so he'd offered a haven.

"Besides, these mountains are to die for. All the fall leaves and crisp air! I feel like I'm at summer camp. I swear to God, I have such a craving for s'mores."

Matt let out a shaky breath. He hated those conversations with his father. *Hated them.* "Okay, but we're going to have to orchestrate a breakup at Thanksgiving. He's getting downright irascible on the subject of marriage. Now he's shaming me because I'm 'taking advantage of you' and 'not honoring you'. *God.*"

"Your dad put the 'I' in 'irascible'. He can't help it."

"True."

"Also the breakup might need to come an eensy bit sooner. Before my mother has the entire wedding planned."

"What?"

Luci looked guilty. She bit her lip. "You know how conservative my papa is! I couldn't tell them I was staying with

you for the fall and not, sort of, kind of, hint that we were...
engaged?"

"Luci! Oh my God!" Sometimes the lie that was his
heterosexuality felt like a black hole that kept sucking more and
more into it.

"Don't worry! Engaged is not married. Engaged people
break up all the time. It's fine."

"Your dad is going to kill me."

"Not if your dad kills you first." Luci grinned at him and
winked.

Luciana Hernandez had been his good friend—and
beard—for a year, since they met in a criminal justice class at
Berkeley. With her thick black ponytail and glasses, she was on
the adorable side of brainy. It suited Luci, too, that everyone
thought they were dating. Her parents were very traditional.
While they tolerated their daughter's quest for a law degree, and
were even proud of her in their own way, they never stopped
harping on the husband and children thing.

Ugh. Engaged. It was getting so fucking complicated. *Lying always does.* He didn't want to deal with it right then. He had other fish that needed a nice batter and a swim in hot oil.

"Well, like I told my dad—which actually wasn't a lie for once—I'm going to drive down to the sheriff's office and check in."

"It's Saturday, *cariño.* I thought you didn't start 'til Monday?"

"I don't, but I want to see what dark hole they're going to tuck me into and get my desk-slash-cardboard box set up. And if there're going to be open hostilities, I'd rather get it over with."

"Such an optimist!" Luci said drolly.

To say he was not looking forward to working out of Sheriff Lance Beaufort's office was an understatement. Apparently, Beaufort's objections hadn't ended in the meeting down in Fresno, but had been reiterated afterward and had made it up the line fairly far before being nixed. It had made Matt's boss, Dean Dixon, suspicious there was something shady going on in Mad Creek. Matt hoped that wasn't the case, because having to rat out his new office mates would not do his career, or his blood pressure, any favors. It was Matt's first job as a full-fledged DEA investigator, and he was determined to do it right.

Compared to all of that, this situation with Luci was a cake walk.

"Maybe he won't even be in today, that sheriff that hates you so much," Luci said.

"Maybe."

Her eyes narrowed. "Oh, no, wait! It's not the sheriff you want to see, it's that hottie deputy, right? The one who saved your life?"

Matt shifted uneasily. He was not going into the office today hoping to see Roman Charsguard. Definitely not. "I told you, Luce. He's hot but kind of strange. I'm not sure what to make of him."

As if running into a firefight for a stranger weren't enough, there was the whole doing up Matt's zipper in the men's room, and then looking blank, as if he didn't have the first idea why Matt thought it was a come on. Guys didn't do things like that. At least, not in the bathroom of the Fresno County Sheriff's Office, they didn't.

Strange or not, Roman Charsguard was a walking wet dream. He was big—at least six two with shoulders that blocked out the sky, and he was incredibly fit looking, with big hands, big feet, a long face, the gentlest eyes, dark stubble, and thick dark hair in a regulation crew cut. He had ears that stuck out from his head, and his right ear had obviously taken shrapnel because it was torn up on the edges. The ears sealed the deal for Matt. They were both dorky and, thanks to the scars, gave him a badass warrior vibe at the same time. Matt had a slight military kink, or maybe a not so slight one. Roman Charsguard rang that bell hard.

"Sure," Luci said. "Not hoping to see the hot military guy. Gotcha. I'll unpack your kitchen while you're gone, okay? Because that's the kind of friend I am."

"And because you want to fix yourself lunch?" Matt guessed.

Luci laughed. "So untrusting, Mattie. You should work on that. Don't forget to stop on the way home and pick up some graham crackers, chocolate bars, and marshmallows. Oh, and pumpkins!"

"It's barely October," Matt grumbled.

"Hey, I'm in the mountains. I'm enjoying this fall to the fullest!"

Matt only wished he could be so lucky. He had a feeling *his* fall was going to suck ass.

\*                    \*                    \*

Matt parked his red Jeep Cherokee in front of the sheriff's office on Main Street. He got out of the car and looked around. The town had a simple, unassuming look. Unlike a number of other towns in the California mountains, Mad Creek had not put up those fake Western facades, and there was no ice cream parlor, McDonald's, or motel on the main drag. It was almost as if they didn't want tourists. The buildings were mostly brick and sturdy but unadorned. There were no window boxes full of colorful flowers. There was a town park—a four block long section of green right along Main Street, and people actually roamed in it, even though the day was overcast and chilly.

Despite its lack of pretentiousness, or maybe because of it, the little town had a pleasant feeling about it. It felt... alive, Matt thought. Besides the unusually large number of people that

36

were taking advantage of the park, there was a cheery-looking restaurant called "Daisy's Diner" with a red neon sign. Through the window, he could see booths that looked fully occupied. And there were people on the sidewalks too. At the post office, a man with a heavily-receding hairline and big ears chatted enthusiastically with a plump man. And here and there were groups of two or more people just standing and talking and—

Okay, that was weird. A young man with glasses crossed paths with another man on the sidewalk and they rubbed up against each other as they met. Matt squinted. It didn't appear to be sexual. The two men were woefully mismatched, the man in glasses being at least twenty years younger than the other. But they rubbed against each other's chest and side—the man with glasses actually turning and doing it again—then they stood and talked as if nothing had happened.

Was it a new version of a 'high five'? Somehow, those two didn't seem like the types who would be sporting the latest 'homey' signs. Secret handshake? Huh.

It was not, however, Matt's problem at the moment. He was procrastinating. With a shake of his head, he turned toward his torture chamber for the next twelve months. The Mad Creek

Sheriff's Office was marked with a woodsy brown sign out front. It was a one-story brick building with big windows that had half-open white exterior blinds. Matt steeled himself and opened the door. A small bell tinkled overhead.

Inside, the room was cold, as if they hadn't turned on the heat. There was a central desk facing the door with a woman seated behind it. She had long, blonde, extremely fluffy hair and makeup that wouldn't have been out of place in the 80s. She could have been any age from twenty-five to forty. She had big brown eyes, a pleasant face, a long nose, and a happy smile. Her name tag said 'Leesa'.

"Hi there! How are you?" she asked enthusiastically.

Matt looked around behind him to make sure she wasn't talking to someone else. "Um… I'm good, how are you?"

"I'm really great! What can I do for you?"

"I was wondering if—" *Sheriff Beaufort. Sheriff Beaufort.* "—Deputy Charsguard or, um, Sheriff Beaufort is around?"

"They sure are!" Leesa continued to smile at him.

He nodded. "Okay. Good. Could you tell..." *damn it* "...Sheriff Beaufort that Matt Barclay with the DEA is—"

Simultaneously, two doors beyond Leesa opened. Sheriff Beaufort and Roman Charsguard appeared in adjacent doorways, and they both stared at him. Christ, he hadn't been speaking *that* loud.

Sheriff Beaufort was a strange one. He was a fairly young man and damned good-looking. He had black hair, blue eyes, and wore clothes tight enough to see muscle definition. In another life, Matt might have found him attractive. But Beaufort's bristling attitude put a guy right off. He was glaring at the moment, as if Matt were some vile graffiti that had been painted on the window. *Mad Creek sucks*, perhaps, or something with the words 'Beaufort' and 'motherfucker'. As for Charsguard, it was hard to tell what he was thinking. He was perfectly still and watched Matt with no expression whatsoever.

His eyes were golden brown. They were not unfriendly. Maybe 'curious' was the right word. Fuck, the guy had the broadest shoulders.

Matt tore his eyes away and addressed the big boss. "Sheriff Beaufort? I'm Matt Barclay. I'll be your DEA investigator. I know I'm starting Monday, but I thought I'd come in and introduce myself. Get my desk set up, if that's possible."

Beaufort was far enough away that Matt didn't feel compelled to reach out his hand for a shake, and Beaufort made no move to get any closer.

"Excuse me," Beaufort said, low and tight. "I need a word with my deputy."

He looked at Roman, tilted his head toward his office, and they both went inside and shut the door.

Matt blinked. Well. That had gone... about as bad as he'd expected.

"Want some broth?" Leesa asked cheerfully.

"What?"

"Broth! We've got beef broth or chicken broth. So so good! Or there's coffee if you like that better!"

"Uh... I'd love a cup of coffee, thanks. But I can get it myself." There was no point in getting off on the wrong foot with Leesa, since she seemed to be the only person in the office happy to see him. In Matt's experience in the military, and then the

DEA, there was nothing a female hated more than being expected to get you coffee.

"Oh, no! I don't mind at all!" Leesa got up and skipped, literally *skipped*, down a hall, which presumably led to the coffee and… broth.

Matt had been in Mad Creek for only an hour and already it was the strangest place he'd ever been.

\*                    \*                    \*

Lance paced in his office, a glower on his face. "I've tried every way I know how to get out of this. Looks like we're stuck with Matt Barclay for at least a year." He stopped pacing and looked thoughtful. "Unless we can get him to turn tail and run."

Roman didn't like that idea or the look in Lance's eyes. "You said yourself, if we push too hard it will only make them suspicious."

"Too late," Lance muttered.

"Maybe it won't be so bad having Matt here. We're stretched too thin with just you, me, and Charlie. We haven't been able to keep up with our drug patrols the way we should."

Roman had started with the sheriff's department last spring, when Lance was concerned about marijuana growers moving into the area. Roman had set up road patrols with some volunteers from the pack. But since becoming a full-time deputy a few months ago, there always seemed to be other things that needed doing, someone in the pack who wanted help or just a drive-by to make sure they had what they needed, roads washed out, wildlife in the wrong place, or strangers in town Lance wanted watched. Roman liked the chance to see the pack members regularly and be useful. But that meeting in Fresno had him worried again about drug growers. They had thousands of acres of wilderness around Mad Creek to protect, and right then, they weren't doing it.

Lance rubbed his forehead. "It's not that we couldn't use help. But having a trained investigator around the town 24/7.... He'd have to be an idiot not to figure out the truth. At least he's inexperienced. His records show he was in SWAT until recently. Let's hope he's better with target practice than he is at snooping."

"You told me it's hard for humans to believe in us. They think changing form is only possible in stories."

Lance shot him a look as he paced. "True. Hopefully Barclay is the skeptical type. Maybe we can convince him we have a lot of eccentrics. The problem is, there are so many young quickened in town right now. No matter how much we repeat the warning at the pack meetings, we can't expect them to behave perfectly all the time. They're just not there yet."

"No, sir." Roman remembered what it was like after he'd been quickened, how many mistakes he'd made, how people had stared. There were a million tiny details about being human that you didn't know until you *were* one. "How can I help?"

Lance stopped pacing and grasped Roman's arms. "Here's what I'm thinking. I'll get a photo of Barclay today, tell him we need it for our records. Then we'll have a pack meeting tonight. Make sure everyone knows him on sight and understands how important it is to not engage with the man, and to watch their behavior when he's around."

"That's smart."

"Even so—the more we can keep Barclay out of town, the better. He's supposed to be here looking for illegal marijuana farms, so let's make sure he does that *all the time*."

"How can we do that?"

Lance gave a feral grin. "As of today, your job is to shadow Barclay. Understand? You'll act as his local guide. Drive him around, give him new places to look—places that are *uninhabited*. Got it? Keep him as far away from town as possible. And when he is here, he'll have his desk next to yours and his back to the window. We'll move Charlie into the spare room for now. That way, if Barclay calls someone or write emails, you can get the gist of it. You'll know if he starts getting suspicious."

Roman nodded. It was a big responsibility, but he was glad Lance trusted him. "What about my other duties, sir?"

"Charlie and I will handle what needs to be handled. Barclay is the first priority. If he figures out about the quickened, God help us." Lance ruffled his hair in frustration. "I'm sorry to put this on you, Roman, but it seems like the best way. You'll have to be careful, though. It will be challenging to be with him so much and not give yourself away. Do you think you can do that?"

"Yes, sir!" Roman said the words with absolute determination, and he meant it. Mad Creek had given him a home and a purpose in life when he'd been utterly without hope. Now the pack needed his protection. He would do everything within his power to keep Matt Barclay from learning the truth.

# 3

## Puberty Bites

### *Dogma #2*

"Come on, Roman. You can do it. I know you can do it!"

Roman shivered. There was cold rain coming from the sky in buckets and his fur was soaking wet. Water ran into his eyes from the top of his head. He panted, sitting on his hind legs in the mud, tired and so desperate to quit.

He lifted one leg, starting to shift to lie down in the mud. He needed to lie down. But James was there, looking at him, waiting. He couldn't lie down when James wanted something from him.

James squatted down to better look in Roman's eyes. "I know it's cold and wet, pup, but we may see worse conditions than this in wartime. I don't give a shit if the course is wet—you can do it. Roman? Do you hear me? You can do it!"

Most of James's words were *blah blah blah* to Roman then. But he understood the encouragement and the force in James's voice, and he knew what he was supposed to do. The obstacle course was second nature by now, but they kept making it harder all the time—raising boards, adding new things. This one had a building, and he had to jump onto the roof from a barrel. The roof was steep and slippery in the rain. He'd already fallen off it four times and it frightened him. His hip hurt and his legs trembled.

"Roman! Look at me."

Roman's gaze left the building's roof and shifted back to James's face.

"Come on. One clean run-through and we can go inside. I'll give you a nice hot bath and look..." James took something out of his pocket—a tin. Roman whined. He knew what was inside tins with that shape on the cover. Fish. Tasty, yummy little fish in greasy oil. The potent smell of them was almost as good as the taste. They were Roman's very favorite thing!

"See this? Give me one clean run-through, bud, and it's yours. You can do it. Just go fast. Go fast and fly over that tile. Come on! Be my brave boy!"

James's voice was so strong and sure. Roman's muscles itched to respond. With a deep sigh, he got up. He and James jogged to the start of the course and he tensed, waiting for James's signal.

James made a swipe with his hand. *Go!*

Roman ran. He went up a wooden ramp and across a narrow board. All the time, the rain beat down, and James was next to him on the course, giving commands and using that pitched voice that made Roman want to fly.

He leapt through three hoops that were normally burning with fire, but they weren't today, then slunk through two walls where moving rods above him could catch him if he wasn't belly-to-the-ground. There were very loud noises here too, *rat-a-tat-tat.* He ignored them.

"Go, Roman. Up, up!"

It was time for the roof. Roman jumped onto the box, then the rusty barrel. He braced himself, gathering energy, then leapt as far up onto the roof as he could. His nails scrabbled on the wet tile, but he was all forward momentum and he made it to the top of the roof and over.

Down the other side, slipping and sliding, but landing on the ground safely. Then there was a wooden ladder he'd done lots of times, and a platform with sharp rocks and a ladder down. The next part was where James told him to duck, and he shouted out the order now. Roman ducked, crawling into a long, tight tube.

When he came out the other side, James was crouched there waiting for him.

"You did it!" James grabbed Roman and hugged him against his chest. James didn't usually show affection like this when they were working, but he did at night, when they were in the barracks and done for the day. Roman slept on James's bed every night. Everything he ate was given to him from James's hand—except for the treats other soldiers snuck to him even though they weren't supposed to. He never left James's side.

But they must be done with the course, because James hugged him then. It felt so good. Roman rested his tired head on James's shoulder. He was so happy he'd been strong and that James was pleased. Joy and pride filled his chest like he'd swallowed a warm ball of happiness.

"You're the best dog in the world, you know that?" James's voice was low and rumbly as he hugged Roman tight. There was heavy emotion in his voice—love and sadness all mixed together.

And Roman... understood him. The words sunk in, and he understood. James felt bad for pushing him so hard, even though he had to, and he was grateful to Roman for coming through. Roman licked James's ear to show him it was okay.

Just then he had an odd stroke of clarity. He suddenly saw that he and James were a team, they were working together. He was a dog and James was a man, his handler. And he thought that he was very lucky to have an important job and such a good handler as James. He loved James with all his heart, and he would do anything for him—*anything*—if it was within his physical ability to do it, and maybe even if it wasn't.

It was Roman's first spark of unusual self-awareness. It wouldn't be his last.

         *                       *                       *

On Monday morning, Roman waited for Matt to arrive. He stood stiffly by Matt's desk until he walked in. "Sheriff wants me to take you out today and show you around the area. I coordinated drug patrols around Mad Creek before. I can show you what I did."

"Yeah. All right. Great." Matt was wearing a suit, tie, white shirt, with a black arm sling for his left arm. He had a canvas bag over one shoulder and a thermos cup in his good hand. "I was just going to check my email. And I thought about grabbing breakfast at the diner. It's not even seven yet."

Roman held up a brown bag. "Daisy made us egg sandwiches. My truck's out front. Let's go."

There was no one on Main Street when they got into Roman's truck. It was a white pickup with the gold sheriff's logo on the side. It was an older model, Lance had said, but Roman didn't care. He loved it to death. He was always happy to drive it, and he felt relieved that he was getting Matt out of town so early.

The thing Roman liked best about the truck was the electric windows. He liked to play with them while he was driving. But Lance had told him it was 'not normal human behavior', so he couldn't do that when Matt was in the truck.

"Um… so what exactly did you have in mind for today?" Matt, strapped into the passenger seat, was trying to sip what smelled like coffee from his thermos cup.

"I brought a map." Roman nodded his head toward the backseat. "There's a ridge where you can see all of the valley. It's a good place to show you what we've done and haven't done."

"Is it a hike in to this ridge?"

"Only about four miles each way."

Matt's eyes grew wide. "Eight miles round-trip? We'll need to stop at my place first. I'm not dressed for it."

Matt gave Roman directions to the cabin he was renting, as if Roman, Lance, and Charlie, as well as all the quickened who'd attended the pack meeting over the weekend, weren't aware of *exactly* where he lived. Roman wasn't very good at pretending, so he followed Matt's directions with a blank face. He waited outside while Matt went in to change.

When Matt came out, he was wearing gray pants in some high-tech fabric, a plain white T-shirt, a thin jacket, hiking boots, and a stained tan arm sling.

As he shut the passenger side door, he smiled. "Well, that suit lasted about an hour. Can't say as I'm sorry."

"You look much better in those clothes," Roman noted politely.

Matt gave him a funny look, and Roman didn't know why. So he kept his mouth shut for the next half hour, until they reached the dirt road, and the faint trail he was looking for.

"I'll take the maps on my back so I can show them to you at the top." Roman pulled his backpack out of the truck.

"Nice backpack. I thought about bringing mine, but it's buried in a box somewhere. I filled up my pockets, though." He showed Roman a water bottle he had in one pocket of his jacket and a camera and phone in the pockets of his pants. "Good thing I don't have to carry a Bowie knife, or I'd probably be singing soprano tomorrow."

Roman didn't know what singing had to do with anything, but he felt he needed to say something too. Roman's backpack had been abandoned at the diner and adopted by the sheriff's office. It was a rusty orange color, and as he looked it over now, he supposed it was 'nice'. He put it on.

"I find it very convenient to wear things on my back."

Matt laughed, as if surprised. "O...kay. Don't forget the egg sandwiches. I've been smelling them since we left the office. Should we eat them first or hike them in? I'm pretty hungry."

"Let's eat first."

It was almost eight a.m. then. The sky was getting brighter, but there was still that smell of fresh wet grass from the dew. Roman loved that smell! He could also smell the leaves turning—a slightly burnt smell of a million green things withering at the tips. Soon they would be crunchy underfoot. He loved that!

Matt leaned against the hood of the truck and ate his sandwich, so Roman did too.

"This hardly feels like working," Matt commented. He had a voice Roman liked. There was a word for it he'd learned in Lily's class—melofelous? Maloderous? Something like that. It had strength and deep vibrations but also a trace of humor almost all the time, as if his voice was a secret smile. It made Roman's ears perk up and his chest tingle.

"We are working," Roman said. "You're supposed to keep illegal operations out of the woods. So we have to look in the woods."

"I know. Believe me, I'm not complaining. I'd much rather be here than in the office. After my arm got me booted from SWAT, I thought I was doomed to a desk belly." He patted his flat belly, crumpled up his wrapper, and stuck it in the bag. "Come on, Roman. Let's do this."

Roman had been trying to eat his sandwich delicately, instead of swallowing it in two huge bites like he usually did. He finished off the last of it, carefully licking each finger. Matt stared at him while he did that, so Roman hurried, then he locked the truck. The two of them headed up the trail.

The trail was rough and tight in places. It was more of an animal trail than anything. About a mile in, Matt commented on it. "How'd you find this trail anyway? It doesn't appear to be used much."

"I was looking for a way to the ridge we're going to. Found this."

"Huh. That's impressive. You don't worry about getting lost?"

"Lost? What do you mean?" Roman couldn't imagine it. Even in the most remote places, the wind carried sounds of the distant town, or a high point would give him a view to see where he was. Streams pointed the way downhill. And, worse case, he could always follow his own scent back to the truck.

"Oh, it's one of those mere mortal things. Never mind. Hang on a sec." They were going up a steep hill, and Matt was breathing hard. Roman, who was hiking in front, stopped and Matt stopped too.

"Is your arm okay?" Roman asked, hoping he hadn't hurt Matt.

"Yeah. It's not painful anymore unless I overuse it, like after PT. The sling reminds me to lay off, but I'm about ready to ditch the damn thing." He took out his water bottle with his right hand and drank some. "Jesus, you're fast. I thought I was a strong hiker. You're in badass shape."

"Thank you." Roman preened a little. He had a flash of memory of the old days, James or another soldier saying how

Roman looked in great condition, and petting him as they said it. But Matt wasn't going to pet him. Too bad. Roman had an ever-present hole inside where he missed that loving touch.

"You really know the area. How long have you been in Mad Creek?"

"Two years."

"That's all?" Matt seemed surprised, like Roman had said something unlikely, but he couldn't figure out what, so he just shrugged.

"Where were you before you came here?" Matt asked.

"In the army. Afghanistan."

Matt nodded like he understood. "I went into the Marines, but I only lasted two years. Wasn't for me."

"Why not?"

"Personal reasons. My Dad... well, let's just say I grew up a military brat. I was expected to enlist right out of high school, so I did. But ultimately I wanted more privacy and freedom than you get in the service. So—"

Roman felt like he should say something. "I see."

"What about you? Why'd you leave the army?"

Roman had a vivid memory of James lying on the ground, bleeding out. Before he could stop himself, a whine left his throat. Humiliated, he followed it with a hard cough. "We'd better get moving. Long way to go."

Fortunately, Matt dropped it. They hiked on, this time with Matt in front so he could set the pace. It took them about an hour and a half to reach the ridge. There was some scrambling up rocks at the end. Roman tried to help Matt, getting in front and reaching down a hand, but Matt just laughed.

"Hey! Kiss my ass, Mountain Man. I may have only one good arm, but I can still get my butt up some rocks."

He said it good-naturedly, the way the soldiers had teased each other in James's unit. Roman felt a glow of happiness at being treated like a regular guy. "Come on then, Tinkerbell."

"Yeah, yeah."

Matt made it to the top and the two of them stood and took in the view.

The ridge line of mountain 497 on the geological survey map had Roman's favorite views of the entire Mad Creek basin. It wasn't the tallest point, but it was in a great location, and a fire that had burned here years back—the charcoal odor was still strong—had removed impediments to the view. Now only bright green brush and baby pines covered the ridgeline, and a natural trail went along the hill's bony spine for a mile so you could see different parts of the valley.

The sky this morning was completely clear, the sun a blinding orb, and the valley was green, only spotted here and there with the reds and golds of changing leaves.

"Holy shit," Matt breathed, looking around. "You weren't kidding when you said this was a good overview of the area. He pointed to the distant town. "There's Mad Creek."

"Yes."

"Man, it was an interminable drive up here from Fresno. But still, you can't appreciate how there's *nothing* else around until you get a view like this." He turned, looking over the entire vista.

"There are houses. And cabins."

"Yeah, but nothing even a little bit like another town."

That was true, Roman thought. And that was just the way they liked it.

He took off his backpack and opened it. "I divided the area up with a grid." He'd brought the large survey maps from the office, the ones he'd used when he'd set up his drug patrols last spring. He spread them out in front of Matt and used rocks to pin down the corners so the breeze wouldn't take them.

"We're here." Roman pointed to the mountain on the map.

He described the area to Matt, comparing their view with the map, and telling Matt what he knew about each section on the grid—and what he didn't know. He pointed out Broad Eagle Drive, where the shooting at Tim's place had taken place. He showed Matt where the major streams and rivers were, and what was private land and state protected forest. He talked, and Matt asked a lot of smart questions. He had a good brain. But after a while, Matt's eyes started glazing over, and Roman decided he'd said enough for the first day.

There was so much more he wanted to share. He felt an urge to tell Matt about where the bears liked to play in the streams and the boundaries of their territory by urine-scent and claw marks. He wanted to tell Matt about the families of foxes and how much they'd spread even since he'd moved here. He wanted to talk about the meadows where the hawks found the best rabbits and mice, and where he had too, when he had been without a job and had fed himself by hunting. But none of that was related to the drug search, and maybe not something a human would care about anyway. So he didn't tell Matt any of it.

Matt ruffled a hand through his hair when Roman fell silent. He looked at the map and at the view, lost in his own head for a time.

"You've done a hell of a lot of work on this. Damn overachiever." Matt's tone was teasing, but there was another thread in it, like he found it strange.

"It's my job to protect the town and the forest and land around it."

Matt cocked an eyebrow. "Most sheriff's deputies would do that by parking on Main Street near the diner. This is... military. It's so detailed."

"That is my background."

"I know. Don't get me wrong. I'm impressed." Matt huffed, looking back over the view. "It's a hell of a lot of territory, though."

"It is a lot of land to guard with just a few men," Roman agreed adamantly. "I used to have patrols but Lance—Sheriff Beaufort—he needed me to do other things too."

Matt waved his hand. "Well, no way could one person— or two, or ten—know what's going on in all of that. Not even if we patrolled constantly. Fortunately, that's not what I'm supposed to do here."

"It's not?"

"Consider me an advance scout. If there is something going on out there, sooner or later there'll be some sign of it—a forest clearing, smoke, debris floating downstream. And even illegal pot growers have to eat and gas up their cars. If there is suspicious activity, I call Dixon and the DEA will deal with it."

Roman said nothing. He didn't like the idea of depending on anyone else to defend his town for him. Besides, as Lance said, more DEA in town meant more chance of their secret being discovered.

"Do you have a pretty good idea who lives in town? On sight?" Matt asked.

"Oh, yes." That was an understatement. Roman knew every single pack member and human in Mad Creek almost as well as Lance did himself—by sight and smell.

"So you'd know if new people showed up?"

"Yes."

Matt nodded. "I almost think it's more valuable to be in town than out here. This is just... huge. It's easier to notice someone suspicious in town. It's like the difference between tracking wildlife in the woods and waiting at the watering hole. Am I right?"

It made sense, but Roman knew Lance wouldn't like that idea at all. The last thing Lance wanted was for Matt to be sitting in town with an eagle eye on all the comings and goings.

"I have another idea." Roman drew Matt's attention back to the map.

"These areas are large, that's true. But not many roads access them. Most are like the one we drove here on—unused dirt roads and fire roads." He pointed to some thin lines on the map. "If someone wants to start an operation in these woods, they have to come in through one of these roads, and they'll need a good-sized vehicle to move their gear. So we rig fishing line across the roads. If it gets broken, we know there's been a vehicle there. That will give us a smaller area to search. If the line isn't broken, we know that whole area hasn't been touched."

"That's good." Matt scratched his chin. "I like it. It'd be even better if we could rig cameras or something to the trip lines."

"I asked Lance about that before. It's too expensive. Plus, we'd need a lot of battery packs. There's no power in most of these areas. It's hard to hide all of that too."

"Right," Matt agreed. "So just the line for now." He hesitated. "This is excellent work, Roman. I appreciate your sharing it with me. You've given me a good head start."

Roman cocked his head and studied Matt. Was he truly pleased or annoyed that Roman was trying to tell him what to do? But Matt's face, clean-shaven for the first time since Roman had met him, was relaxed and open. His eyes were warm. Very warm.

Matt cleared his throat and looked away. There was more color in his face than usual. He was squatting down by the map on the ground, like Roman was, elbows resting on his knees. And he was close. Roman felt a flush of embarrassment as he realized he'd gotten too far into Matt's space when he'd laid out the maps, closer than a human would get. Their sides were nearly touching. Personal space was a concept it had taken his dog a long time to comprehend and sometimes he forgot.

Matt looked out over the view, saying nothing, but the tip of his tongue ran along his bottom lip. The wind gusted, and Roman caught a waft of Matt's scent—heady and rich with the sweat of the climb and... there was that smell again, the one he'd smelled in the bathroom in Fresno, the musky tangerine smell. Why was that smell so yummy? It was awesome!

The closest thing to it that Roman could remember was a scent from his days in the Army, one found in the crotches of the soldiers—sometimes subtle and sometimes strong. But he'd been trained in no uncertain terms not to sniff there. It wasn't a urine scent. This was more elusive, muskier, richer.

It had to do with sex, Roman realized. Huh. So why did he smell it so clearly on Matt sometimes?

It was strange how the smell wrapped around Roman's brain and dug in like demonic Velcro. It made him want to move even closer to Matt. He had the urge to give him a pack rub along the arm or lean in and smell his neck and anyplace else he could reach. It made him want to lean against Matt so that Matt would touch his head and back.

But those were all dog behaviors. And Matt wasn't his owner, friend, or even pack. He had no reason to touch Roman and vice versa. Roman was supposed to be his watchdog, Lance had said so.

Roman got to his feet. "If we hike along the ridge, there's another good view of the east valley at the end."

Matt stood up and nodded, not meeting Roman's eyes. "Right. Let's do it."


\*               \*               \*

By Friday night, Matt Barclay was happy to have 'such a great head start' on his job, as he'd told Roman. Lance was happy because Roman had kept Matt out of town every day that week. And Roman was happy the week was over and everyone was pleased with him. Now he only had another three-hundred-sixty days of Matt's assignment to go.

He ate dinner alone in his small cabin, warming up a can of beef chili, then putting it over a potato he'd cooked in the microwave, the way Lily had shown him. He sat at the kitchen table, and it was so quiet he could hear himself chew. He whined happily a few times into the silence, thinking about things Matt had said. Matt had a really good sense of humor for a human, even though Roman didn't always get it. He liked the way Matt teased him or said things as if they were buddies, equals. Like the men in the Army.

Roman read for a while after dinner, a fifth grade book about children stuck in a museum overnight that Lily had given him. She held classes on Wednesday nights for all the newly quickened. He marked a few words to ask her about. He hoped to be reading high school level by the end of the year and then get his G.E.D. But that night, his attention kept wandering. Finally he put the book down and went to bed.

His body was tired from the long day in the woods, and his mind was exhausted and strained from trying so hard to act human in front of Matt. But still, sleep wouldn't come. His mind remained half awake, running images of Matt.

The part of Roman that was Sheriff Lance Beaufort's deputy was cautious about Matt Barclay, viewing him as a potentially dangerous outsider.

But Roman, the dog, liked Matt a lot. He liked Matt's lively facial expressions. He liked Matt's brown eyes, which were usually warm and sparkly. He liked the way Matt moved, the way he smelled. Matt had good energy, strong energy. He seemed like a good man. He was a sad one too, now and then, some private sorrow Roman could sense but not ask about. Even so, Matt was a happy human being to be around, and that made Roman feel happy too.

Maybe, Roman thought, even if Matt found out about the quickened, he wouldn't tell anyone. Maybe he'd protect their secret. But Roman knew he couldn't count on that. It was too dangerous.

It was in this half-asleep state that Roman's mind ran again over the mystery of that smell Matt sometimes had—the musky tangerine one, the one that made Roman's insides itch. They itched now at the memory of it. They itched *a lot.*

Roman finally sat up in bed, frustrated at being unable to go to sleep. That's when he discovered he had a problem. Frantic with fear, he didn't think about the time or anything else. He got his department-issued cell phone and called Lance.

Lance answered, alarm in his voice. "Roman? It's almost midnight. What's wrong?"

"I think I need a doctor."

"What's the matter?"

"My... my penis is all swollen up and hard. Could it be a spider bite or... or..." Roman swallowed, pressing down the panic. "I don't know. Cancer?" He knew cancer killed a lot of humans and involved lumps and tumors.

There was silence from the other end of the line. A long silence.

"Lance?"

"Yeah, uh, Roman...." Lance sounded strained. "You've never had this happen before? I mean, since you've been human?"

"No."

"Ah." Lance covered up the phone with his hand and said something. Roman didn't understand his words, but he thought he heard Tim giggling on the other end. Lance came back. "Sorry about that."

Roman felt a tinge of annoyance creep in among the fear. "Do I need a doctor, sir?"

Lance cleared his throat. "Okay. So. From what I've heard from others in the pack who are newly quickened, there's, um, sort of a slow boot up of various functions. Human functions. It can take years sometimes."

Roman nodded, even though Lance couldn't see him. He was aware that he was becoming more human by the month, or maybe just learning how to truly *be* in his own body. Hair had only recently started growing under his arms, for example, even when he was shaped like a man. He'd been worried about it, that his dog was somehow 'leaking out', until he remembered that James had had hair there too.

"And one of those functions... Okay. Let me ask you this. Are you, er, intact?" Lance muttered something like *I can't believe I'm having this conversation.*

"I don't know that word, sir."

"Your testicles, Roman. Your balls! Do you still have them? Sometimes pets have them cut off, you know."

"I still have mine, sir." Roman thought about the other military dogs he'd seen. All of them had their balls, for crap's sake. Maybe being an army dog wasn't like being a pet. And thank God for that. Roman really liked his balls!

"Good. Wonderful." Lance's voice was dry. He took a deep breath. "Okay. So probably your human sexuality is kicking in. It's fine, Roman. It's perfectly normal. Didn't you ever get, um, excited, maybe by a female heat scent when you were a dog?"

Now Roman was embarrassed. "I think so, sir. A few times. But I couldn't *see* it!" Roman looked down at himself. He didn't like sleeping in clothes, so there was nothing to keep his penis from being terribly obvious. It sure *looked* swollen and red and hard, like there was something wrong with it. He touched it experimentally with the fingers of the hand not holding the phone, squeezed it to see if it hurt. It did ache a little, but it also felt *amazing*. The fear inside him loosened its grip and slunk away abashed.

Oh. Of course. The male member had to get hard to penetrate. He'd seen animals mating in the woods, he'd just never looked that closely at the details.

"Sorry I called you, Sheriff," Roman mumbled, now mortified that he'd been so stupid.

"No, that's...." Lance huffed. "Fine. Just... take care of it."

"Take care of it?"

"Oh my God," Lance said. There was a muttered *I can't* and then Tim came on the line.

"Hi, Roman?"

"Yes, Tim?"

There was laughter in Tim's voice, but his words were gentle. "Okay, buddy. Here's what you do. Do you have any lotion or Vaseline, anything like that?"

"I have gun oil."

Tim snorted. "No, definitely not gun oil. God. Okay, never mind. You don't need it. Just wrap your hand around your—"

In the background, Lance said, "You are *not* having phone sex with Roman."

"I'm just giving him starting instructions! Hold your horses."

By now, Roman had his hand wrapped around the swollen monstrosity, and it did feel quite pleasurable. He experimentally squeezed it and gasped in a breath. *Oh my God!*

"Okay, so Roman, basically what you want is to move your hand up and down. And as you… um, feel so inclined, you can go faster. At the end, you'll be going very fast, okay? And when you orgasm, semen will come out. That's perfectly normal. In fact, that's the end goal. After that, it will go down. Got it?"

"Yes. I have to go now," Roman said gruffly, already lost in how his hand felt moving up and down.

"I think that's wise. Have fun, buddy!" Chuckling, Tim hung up.

Roman tossed the phone over his head. It landed somewhere—he didn't really care where. He shoved the blankets onto the floor and sat on the bed with his back propped against the wall, legs spread.

Holy shit, did that feel amazing! His left hand couldn't stay away either, so he alternated the up-down tugs with both hands, and then reached down with one hand to feel his testicles too. They were hotter than usual and the skin had gotten tight. It felt good to touch there, but not as good as his swollen shaft, which was now hard as a rock inside while the skin over it slipped up and down in a delicious way. His thumb rubbed the head on a stroke and hot lightning shot up his back.

"Oh. Oh, shit," Roman muttered, pressing his back into the wall and spreading his legs farther.

A waft of musky air rose from his groin and hit his nostrils. The smell reminded him of Matt, that intriguing scent Matt had sometimes and—

The moment he thought that, *smelled* that, his chest gave off a heavy grunt and the pleasure pulsed and peaked. White stuff shot out of his penis and stuck his chest and his chin, three, four times. All Roman could do was squeeze and squirm and try to hang on to the incredible feelings.

When it was over, he slumped down on the bed, trying to catch his breath. His heart pounded loud in his ears.

That? That had been the best thing ever. Better than sardines! It was practically worth becoming a man all by itself.

And hands? Roman looked at his hands, which had some splatters of *semen* on them, according to Tim. Roman had already thought hands were the best thing in the world, but now? Dear God, how did humans get so fortunate to be one of the only animals with these marvelously dexterous appendages? No wonder they ruled the planet.

Though he wasn't sure at the moment why humans ever left the bedroom. He had a feeling this could seriously cut into his work and study hours if he let it. Was his human sexuality a brief thing? Or would he live with this forever now, like the hair under his arms?

*Dear God, let it be forever.*

It was the last thought he had before he fell asleep.

# 4

## Don't Make Me Blush

### *Dogma #3*

"You're the best dog in the world," James said, as he lay dying.

Roman licked his face and pawed his chest, but the smell of blood was iron-sharp, so sharp it hurt. Too much. Too much blood.

*You shouldn't have risked it. Why did you?*

James and Roman had been in Afghanistan for two years. They often traveled in jeeps and trucks at the front of long convoys. The jeep would stop and Roman and James would get out. Roman went ahead to sniff at the road, see if the tricky, explosive things were hidden there. The explosive things could have different smells, ones with names like *C-4*, *Tovex*, or *potassium chlorate*, but Roman had been taught to recognize them all.

He and James swept open land, too, big hot fields where the sun beat down like a clenched fist and the grass was

77

exhausted and sparse. Roman would run and smell and James would follow. If Roman found something, James would mark it for men to come and dig it up.

There were other dogs in Afghanistan, always traveling with their handlers the way Roman traveled with James. He and James were never apart. Never. When James went to the bathroom or shower, Roman sat right outside and waited. Roman knew that he was different than the other working dogs they met. *More intelligent*. He knew, for example, that when he found the explosive things in the ground, he saved lives. He'd seen men with legs blown off. Anyone who walked over ground Roman had checked was safe. He made sure of it! He and James together made sure. They were the smartest and the fastest and the best!

"I swear that dog knows everything we're saying," Wako, one of James's friends, liked to say.

Sometimes in the evenings, James played cards with Wako and some of the other guys. Roman would sit on the floor pressed against James's leg. At least he would when the other soldiers weren't calling him over for pets.

"'Course he knows what we're saying," James would drawl. "Roman's IQ is a damn sight higher than yours."

78

"Fucker. Ro, come 'ere!" Wako liked to pet Roman a lot. Roman could sense it eased something tense and anxious and bleeding inside him, so he gave himself over to it, even though sometimes he was tired, and he just wanted to lie down next to James and rest.

*James.*

Why had he done it? That day it had happened—that day had been wrong from the start. Roman sensed it when he woke up, and he tried to warn James. They shouldn't go to work today. But James had dragged him out anyway.

"What's the matter with you?" he'd scolded lightly. "Come on, Ro. Time to rock 'n roll, buddy."

Roman had gone along, because James said so, and he knew best.

The convoy of vehicles they were traveling in that awful day had been attacked. Mortars and gunfire rained down on them from both sides of the road. The glass on their Jeep shattered, flying everywhere. There was the *thwump, thwump* of bullets hitting metal. James pushed Roman down and laid on top of him.

Someone outside screamed, and Roman's head burned like fire. He struggled and whined under James's chest.

James sat up a little and looked at him. "Jesus Christ! Roman's been hit!"

"What?" The officer in the front of the vehicle looked up over the console.

James touched Roman's head by his ear and it hurt. When he drew his hand back, it was covered with blood. "Fuck, I gotta get him to a doctor!"

His voice was shaky, shakier than Roman had ever heard it. He felt weak and scared, and the noise outside, the noise he'd been trained to accept, was suddenly too loud and too threatening. He buried his nose under James's knees, tried to crawl into the space below.

"Fuck, I gotta—"

"You will not get out of this car, Sergeant. We're under fire!"

"There's a medic van at the back of the line. And it looks like our guys have taken out the hostiles on this side. I can make it."

"Goddamn it, just wait for the all clear. "

"He was shot in the fucking *head*. I gotta go!"

The door opened and James pulled Roman from the jeep. He pushed him up until Roman was draped over his shoulders. "I've got you," James said, "I've got you."

He ducked and ran. He ran close to the line of trucks, using them as a shield. The convoy had been ambushed on a curve in the road, and the medic's van—it had a white and red cross—was at the end of the line. Roman could see it, but it seemed so far away. Gunfire and explosions sounded from the other side of the vehicles as James ran. They were halfway down the line now, and James's breath was harsh as he ran doubled-over.

Then the world went white. The explosion threw Roman off James. He flew through the air and landed-rolled a dozen feet away. The bottom of his feet stung with cuts and the wound on his head raged. The world was weirdly silent as he looked around. He could see bursts of lights and the tanks firing into a low mound of hills where black smoke rose up. He could see men shouting in the distance, lost in the battle. But none of these sounds reached his ears. It was like he was under water.

*James.*

He looked around and saw him. James was on the ground, blood and torn canvas where his legs should be. So much blood. Roman crawled his way to James through the silence and the gore.

"You're the best dog in the world, you know that?" James's words were far away, but Roman understood him. Those beloved hands rubbed Roman's neck. Tears made channels in the dirt and blood on James's face. "You're gonna be okay. You're gonna be okay."

Roman licked the salt away. *I love you. I love you. I love you. Please don't leave me. Please don't leave me!*

Roman said it over and over in his head, even after James's eyes went blank and he wasn't there anymore. He chanted it in his mind until the medics found him and dragged him away.

*           *           *

On Matt's second Friday in Mad Creek, he got into the sheriff's office early. He and Roman were headed right back out again, but before they could leave, the front door opened. Sheriff Beaufort walked in followed by a young man with shoulder-length brown hair and long, asymmetrical bangs. The stranger wore a light jacket and tight skinny jeans. Matt couldn't help but notice that his legs went on forever. He silently chided himself for gawking and forced his gaze up to the guy's face.

"Tim!" Leesa came running out of the break room in the back. She must have heard the door, though how she knew it was 'Tim', Matt didn't know, since neither the stranger nor Lance had yet said a word. Leesa threw herself at Tim and he hugged her back, one hand squeezing the back of her neck.

"Hey, Leesa."

"Oh my gosh! What are you doing in town so early?"

Tim rolled his eyes. "The farmer's market organizers are meeting this morning. A few prime booths opened up, so there'll be a scramble for the spots. You can't believe how vicious

83

farmer's market sellers can be! Oh, hello." Tim said the last to Matt. Despite the faked surprise of his greeting, the direct look in his eyes told Matt this Tim knew all about him. "We haven't met yet. You must be Matt Barclay, from the DEA."

Tim walked over to where Matt and Roman were still standing by their office, waiting for an escape route to clear. Tim's tone was friendly, but he gave Matt a warning glare. Who the fuck was this guy?

Tim held out his hand. "I'm Tim Weston, Lance's partner."

"Good to meet you." Matt shook Tim's hand, which was heavily callused for a guy who was otherwise on the twinky-adorable side.

*Partner?* Matt dismissed his first association with that word. Beaufort couldn't be gay. Did he have a side business then? Did it have to do with a farmer's market? Of course, they wouldn't be selling drugs at a place like that, though given that it was Mad Creek, Matt wasn't ready to rule anything out completely.

His confusion must have showed on his face, because Tim, still shaking his hand up and down, repeated himself firmly. "You know—Lance's partner. It's like a girlfriend only with bonus accessories."

"Oh. Good." Matt nodded maniacally, trying not to sound shocked. Sheriff Beaufort *was* gay? Holy shit!

"Hey there, Roman." Tim let go of Matt's hand in order to give the big guy a rub on his head, like noogies only nicer. Roman seemed to like the gesture, if his immediate smile was any indication. What was it with this town and weird greetings?

"You have a problem with that?" Beaufort asked pointedly. He stepped up behind Tim and put a possessive hand on his shoulder.

"Me?" Matt asked. "No. Huh-uh. Absolutely not."

"Good." Lance glared at him one more time, then gave Tim a peck on the lips. "See you tonight. Feel free to throw my weight around in that meeting."

"You know I'd never do that." Tim grabbed Lance's shirt and pulled him back for a real kiss—Matt had a feeling it was for his benefit. As if he'd ever try to steal Lance-hardass-Beaufort.

85

When the kiss broke, Tim and Lance looked into each other's eyes meaningfully. It was downright embarrassing.

"Okay! Well, we were on our way out, so...." Matt said desperately. He'd never wanted to see the inside of Roman's truck so badly.

"Have a good day, you two." Tim smiled. "By the way, Matt, I'd love to have you over to our place for dinner soon. You and your girlfriend, Luci!"

"How did you know about—?"

"Bye!" Tim was out the door.

Beaufort gave Matt a look that meant something like *I can't believe he asked you to dinner*, or *You'd better not mess with him*, or maybe even *That's how a real man is 'out', maestro.*

Okay, probably not the latter, because Beaufort had no idea Matt was closeted. But that's what it felt like. Because yeah, that had been as fuck-you-this-is-who-I-am as Matt had ever seen. And goddamn, but he envied that. Beaufort went into his office and Leesa went back into the kitchen.

"Let's head out," said Roman, walking toward the front door. "Busy day."

"Sure," Matt replied distractedly.

His respect for Sheriff Beaufort just went up by a few dozen degrees. On the other hand, *Lance Beaufort gets laid regularly by* that *and is still so intense? God help us if he ever has to go celibate.*

Right?

\*              \*              \*

At the trailhead, Matt got out of Roman's truck and stretched. They'd been out every day this week setting lines on various dirt roads and checking out trails. Matt felt like he was starting to know the area. And he liked it.

The Sierra Nevada mountains were so different than the hot and dry Sacramento Valley where he'd spent the last few years, and from places like Texas and San Diego, where his dad had been stationed while Matt was growing up. It felt good here. It was fresh and open with rolling expanses of green pines and the red-gold-browns of autumn leaves. It was like a secret pocket in the universe where Walmart was only an evil legend, and you could look out over a landscape in which man was not the dominant species.

Matt had always felt most comfortable out of doors, in nature. Maybe that was because no one had expectations of you there. In the woods, there were no military bases or schools where everyone watched you because you were the general's kid, no impossible role models to emulate, no one to disappoint. Biking or hiking or skiing, Matt could excel for his *own* sake, push to the rhythm of his own body and not beyond. He had no one to please or impress but himself.

Of course, lately, he'd had Roman Charsguard along too. But Roman was easy to be with. He always seemed simply happy to be outdoors, and after that first time when Matt had fallen behind, he let Matt set the pace. Today they were hiking into an area on the far northern bounds of what Roman considered 'Mad Creek territory'. The trailhead had been a fifty-minute drive from the office and Matt had consumed his entire thermos of coffee. Roman, as usual, had sipped *broth* from his travel mug.

Apparently the sheriff's mother made big batches of the stuff for the station, and everyone loved it. Matt hadn't yet figured out if it was a Paleo thing or what.

Anyway, the coffee needed to come out. Matt stepped into the woods to relieve his bladder while Roman started setting up lines. When Matt returned, he stretched to loosen up his muscles and watched Roman work.

They were parked at the end of yet another dirt road that petered out into unpassable brush. They'd parked back from the end so that Roman could set up the line where a car would likely go if any ventured this way. He used clear fishing line and liked to set them up four feet high to avoid being triggered by most animals. He used trees where they were conveniently placed for stretching the line across the road, and had heavy wooden stakes in the back of the truck for where they weren't.

The mountain scenery around them was stunning, but the built guy with the serious face, golden brown eyes, and dark buzz cut wasn't bad either. Matt indulged himself by looking longer than he should have. Roman was all muscle, and he could be damned intimidating when he wanted to be. But there was a sweetness to his face at times like this, when he was focused on what he was doing. The tip of his tongue stuck out as he concentrated on tying a knot in the slippery line using those big fingers. Jesus. Roman was a dork—but an incredibly hot one.

Today they were hiking in eight miles to an area where there was a bare patch they'd found in satellite images provided by the DEA. It was likely the bare patch was from a forest fire, but they'd have to look at it from the ground to be sure, Roman insisted. By golly.

Matt was in the weird position of doing his job well and having it all go far easier than it really ought, yet still feeling anxious about it. He and Roman had been out hiking every day. Matt *loved* it. So much in fact, he was considering applying to the Forest Service if his job with the DEA ended up as a desk job. The General would have a fit, of course. He hadn't approved when Matt had left the Marines and joined the DEA, but at least they were 'real' law enforcement.

Matt felt guilty about how much fun he was having, in fact. But the head of Operation Green Ghost, Dixon, was thrilled with the progress he'd made. In the last group video call, he'd had Matt explain what they were doing in Mad Creek—with the lines, the survey map gridding and numbering, and satellite images—and advised other agents to do the same in their territories. Matt was the golden boy of the hour.

Even so, he knew damned well he was being misdirected, that all this fieldwork was keeping him out of town. He wasn't an idiot. The question was: why? And should he be concerned about it or not?

"All set," Roman said. "Want to get moving?"

"Yeah." Matt shook his head. "Sorry, I'm a bit distracted this morning."

"Because of Tim?"

"What?"

"You were surprised when you met Tim." Roman sounded a little defensive.

"No! I mean, yes, I'm surprised Beaufort is gay. But... hey, more power to him."

Roman nodded, as if satisfied. "Tim is good for Lance. Everyone says Lance is much happier and less intense since they moved in together."

91

"Beaufort used to be *more* intense?"

Roman smiled. "Oh, yes. If you think he's bad, you should meet his mother."

"Yeah, think I'll take a pass on that one." Matt chuckled. He slung on his backpack and they set off.

Roman was a quiet hiker, focused on the woods. But today, Matt was in the mood to talk.

"I was thinking about how much more active this job was than I anticipated. It's been great." Matt stretched out his left arm. It had been feeling better lately, good enough that he'd stopped wearing the sling, though he still couldn't lift much without getting twinges.

"I like this better than being in the office," Roman agreed. "It was fun at first, having a desk like a real hu—uh, deputy. But I don't like being inside all day."

They were on a fire road, and it was wide enough that they walked abreast. Roman smiled at Matt, a genuine smile. Matt could count on one hand the number of times he'd seen Roman smile. He looked ten years younger when his face lit up like that, almost childlike. Which was a little pervy.

"Sheriff Beaufort doesn't mind you spending so much time on this?" Matt asked.

Roman's smile vanished. "No. This is my job."

The drug hunt was? That must be what Roman meant.

"You didn't like your job before this one?" Roman asked.

Matt shrugged. "SWAT was cool and prestigious, but it was always either boring as hell or full-on dangerous. And I had to leave it because of this." Matt lifted his arm a bit. "After that I was on desk duty in Sacramento. That sucked, and, you know, not in a good way." He waggled his eyebrows. *Stop. Do not flirt with Roman.*

"I've always liked my job," said Roman earnestly. "The only thing that made me really unhappy was when I didn't have a job at all."

"After the military?"

Roman nodded, his lips pressed thin. It wasn't the first time Matt noticed there was something Roman didn't like to talk about in his past. But today, Matt pressed on. "What did you do in the military?"

Roman hesitated before answering. "All kinds of things, but mostly bomb-sniffing."

"Yeah? You mean like K-9?"

"Yes. K-9."

Matt was impressed. And he could see Roman in that job too. He had a natural earthiness and kindness that probably made him great with animals. "That's fantastic. I knew a couple of guys who really wanted to do K-9, but they didn't get in. That program is really selective."

"About their dogs?" Roman asked, a frown of confusion on his brow.

Matt laughed. "Well, I meant about K-9 officers. But I bet they're pretty picky about their dogs too."

"Oh." Roman blushed. It was a full-bore, bright red flush that crept from the collar of his T-shirt and spread up his face and into his hairline. His ears turned a hearty pink, especially the one with the scars.

Matt figured Roman must have felt stupid about his remark, but it was no big deal. Being a guy, though, he couldn't help but pick on him. "Hey, it's nice to see your cardiovascular system is in good shape. In case you were wondering." He chuckled.

"What do you mean?" Roman stopped on the trail.

Matt waved his hand at Roman's face, smiling. "You're blushing, Roman. Big-time."

"I don't blush."

"Uh, yeah. You do and you are."

Roman dug into his pocket for his phone, fumbling a bit in his haste as if he was worried he'd grown a second nose. He turned it on. It appeared he had a mirror app, which Matt found rather funny. He had the idea Roman was the type more worried about having something green in his teeth than how hot he looked.

Roman peered at himself closely. "I am! I'm blushing!"

"Yes. Yes, you are."

Roman pushed his sunglasses up to the top of his head and turned his chin this way and that, looking at his reflection. He visibly relaxed, like it wasn't as bad as he was expecting or something. Then he grinned. "First time. It must be another gradual thing, like sex."

"Huh?"

Roman looked up and met Matt's gaze. He froze. He looked stricken and his blush, which had been starting to fade, deepened exponentially. His mouth worked slightly, but nothing came out.

Matt couldn't figure it out—sex? Gradual? What did he mean? But at the mere word 'sex' coming out of Roman's mouth, his lizard brain licked its chops and certain areas below the belt started to perk up.

They stared at each other. Matt hadn't noticed any flirting or anything but obliviousness in Roman since that strange incident in the men's room, much to his disappointment. But suddenly, the air between then felt charged and there was something in Roman's eyes—heat… and panic.

"I… just recently started to…. That is…." Roman stumbled.

Oh. *Oh.* "You mean, you had a bit of a dry spell after the military?" Matt guessed. He'd heard other vets talk about it.

PTSD could do a real whack job on the libido. Some guys couldn't even get it up, which was a hell of a sacrifice to make for your country, in Matt's humble opinion.

Roman looked relieved. He nodded.

"Yeah? That sucks. Were you hurt? Shot?"

Roman touched his damaged ear. His voice was strained. "I had a minor gunshot wound. But that's not it. I was... changed. After. It was difficult."

That was the broadest hint yet that something very bad had happened during Roman's time in the military. Matt felt for the guy. The more time he spent with Roman, the more Matt saw his strength like a hard veneer over a core of vulnerability, sadness, and something Matt's brain wanted to label 'innocence', though it couldn't be, surely. Matt wanted to hug the guy, but instead he just put a hand on Roman's shoulder—Roman's very large shoulder.

"Hey, it's okay. I have some friends who got real messed up over there. I feel you."

Instead of shrugging him off, like a normal guy would do, Roman stepped closer. His shoulder bent toward Matt as if encouraging him to move his hand.

Matt wasn't sure what to do for a moment. Then, thinking about Tim rubbing Roman's head this morning—okay, this was maybe a little awkward—Matt rubbed his hand on Roman's shoulder soothingly. Roman turned his face away and sighed. It was a relieved sigh. Matt, wondering what the hell he was doing, rubbed Roman's shoulder some more. He could barely fit his palm over the round cap of it, and its muscles were dense and hard. His hand slipped down to Roman's arm before he could think better of it, rubbing there. The large bicep flexed under his thumb. Roman gave a contented hum.

But Matt... Matt was getting turned on. He'd wanted to touch Roman for two weeks by then, longer if you counted the months he'd thought about Roman after that Coarsegold raid. And with those muscles under his fingers, it was oh so tempting to keep going. This was either going to become sexual in about two heartbeats or end up being the weirdest bro bonding experience ever. He couldn't believe that even then, he had no idea if this was a come on, or if Roman would punch him if Matt tried to kiss him. He liked Roman, but he didn't understand the guy—at all.

Matt swallowed. "So—"

"Look," Roman said quietly.

Matt looked up the trail. A red fox stood there, frozen in midstride, staring at them as if it had been minding its own business and crossing the trail when they'd appeared like ogres and thieves, beamed there by black magic.

"Wow. It's beautiful," Matt whispered.

Suddenly Roman moved. He hollered a big "Whoo!", and he took off running toward the fox. The animal did a double-take, cartoon-like, and flew off into the brush. Roman dove after it, disappearing from sight.

Matt followed, laughing. Roman being playful was quite a sight. Matt heard crashing in the woods, followed by the slow return of a sheepish-looking Roman. "Lost him."

"I see that." Matt snorted. "Slippery devil, was he?"

"Yes." Roman put his hands on his hips and smiled. "I feel better."

"Good." A warm feeling glowed in Matt's chest like a fucking beacon. Friendship, maybe? At least that. He pushed down the longing for more.

Roman drew a deep breath and rubbed his hands together. "We should hurry. We have a long way to go to get to that clearing, and it's slow moving on two feet."

"Whatever you say, Roman." Matt shook his head, but he was smiling.

# 5

## Pod People Unite

The clearing from the satellite image turned out to be a natural clearing. Roman said there'd been a fire there long ago, but Matt couldn't see it. They went out to trail check again on Saturday. It seemed like hardly anyone at the sheriff's office knew the meaning of the word 'weekend'. But Sunday, Matt took the day off. And he found himself not really knowing what to do with his time.

"Let's drive to Yosemite," Luci suggested at breakfast. "It's a two-hour drive from here, but it'll be worth it."

That didn't sound like fun to Matt. "I dunno. I've been out in the woods all week."

"Okay, so let's go see a movie. I need to get out. If I spend one more day studying, my head will explode."

Luci had dressed up, Matt noticed. Around the cabin she wore old jeans and T-shirts, but that morning she'd showered, she wore her black hair clean and long, and had on new jeans and a lacy long-sleeved top. She was practically drumming her fingers on the kitchen countertop.

"We can do a movie. Sorry I've been working so much."

Luci waved this away. "That's what you're here for, *cariño*. I'm glad it's going well. Besides, I found a coffee shop in town. I go there when I have to be around people."

That reminded Matt about Tim's mention of Luci. "You must have met some people in town. Someone mentioned you to me."

"Oh, yeah!" Luci smiled. "They're really friendly at the coffee shop. And the grocery store. And the used book store. And the post office—my God, don't get the guy at the post office talking! Ay yai yai."

"So have you noticed anything weird about the place?"

Luci pursed her lips. "Well. Now that you mention it… the people are a little different."

"Like how?"

"This lady I met in the coffee shop? Lily? She sat down with me and we talked for, like, two hours! She was so friendly.

Almost too pushy, you know? But I liked her. She was really pretty for her age. She's fifty-six, but you'd swear she was no more than thirty-five. She was telling me about this skin care thing she does—"

Matt felt uneasy. Two hours was a long time. "You didn't talk about us, did you?"

Luci looked guilty. "Well. I might have told her a little."

"Luci!"

"Only that my family thinks we're engaged, but we're not really."

"You told her you're my beard?" Matt felt his chest grow tight.

"No!" Luci rolled her eyes, but she reassured him, putting her hand on his arm. "I would never tell anyone you're gay, Mattie. That's your business. I just said we were only friends and that both our families put pressure on us so we pretend we're together. That's all."

Matt sighed with relief. Then he wondered what he was so worried about. Beaufort was gay, so it wasn't like he'd lose his job, and no one in the town knew his father. Hiding was getting to be too deep a habit.

"We mostly talked about *my* parents, to be honest," Luci went on. "Lily is right. I need to just tell them the truth, that my education comes first, and I'm in no hurry to get married."

"So besides this woman Lily, have you noticed anything else strange in town?"

"It all seems a little strange to me, but not in a bad way. You know I've never lived in a small town. I'm a city girl. So what do I know?" Luci's eyes narrowed as she studied him. "You think there's something going on in the town? Like what? Alien pod people? Cannibals? Satanists?"

"Not sure," Matt said honestly.

She patted his arm. "It's a nice place. I like it. So are we doing that movie or what?"

Mad Creek had a small movie theater, one of the old-timey ones with a marquis on Main Street. They were showing a double feature of "Old Yeller" and another dog movie, "Eight Below". Luci was totally up for it, and Matt didn't want to drive all the way to Oakhurst or Fresno to find something more current, so they went.

When they walked up to the small theater about a half hour before showtime, and stood in line to get tickets, Matt found himself the center of attention. Everyone stared at them. There was a good-looking family of five, all with black hair and blue eyes, that were in front of them in line. They got their tickets and then stood outside the theater, staring at Matt and Luci. And the guy at the ticket window, an older man with droopy eyes, seemed so nervous, he could barely count out their change.

"What the hell did you do, Barclay?" Luci asked Matt in a whisper.

"Nothing!"

"It's like everyone is scared of you or something."

"I didn't do anything!" Matt insisted.

He collected his tickets, and he and Luci headed for the front doors of the theater. The girl who took their tickets—a teenaged girl with a huge head of red hair—watched them warily, like they might bite. And inside the theater, when Matt

105

and Luci took a seat in the third row, a couple that was sitting behind them got up and moved.

What the ever loving hell?

Luci looked at him with mocking wide eyes. "Oh, Mattie! You must have done something baaaadd."

"How could I do anything? I'm out on the trails with Roman all the time!"

"Maybe you remind everyone of that axe murderer who used to live in town."

"What axe murderer?"

She shrugged. "I don't know, but the way they're looking at you, there has to be one."

Five minutes before the first movie was to start, someone came plowing down their aisle. It was Sheriff Beaufort. He was dressed in jeans and a long-sleeved denim shirt, and his face was flushed like he'd been running. Behind him came his partner, Tim.

"Hey! Barclay! What a coincidence." Beaufort plopped down in the seat immediately on Matt's right.

"Excuse me." Tim brushed past their knees to sit on the other side of Beaufort.

Matt looked around. Although the theater had good attendance for a showing of older movies, there were plenty of empty seats. So why did Beaufort have to sit right next to him?

Also: everyone was still staring at him.

*What the fuck?*

Matt turned back to look at Beaufort in time to see him wipe some sweat from his brow. Call him paranoid, but he was 95 percent certain Beaufort and his boyfriend had had no plans to come to the movie today—until someone called him.

"Big fan of dog movies, are you?" Matt asked dryly.

"Oh, you have no idea." This was Tim, who leaned forward to look past Beaufort at them. His eyes settled on Luci. "Hi. I'm Tim. You must be Luci. This is Lance. He's the sheriff."

Luci smiled with pleasure. She leaned over Matt to shake Tim's hand, then Beaufort's. "Hello! So nice to meet you. How did you know my name? Has Matt been talking about me?" She batted her eyes.

Tim tilted his head. "Actually, it was Lance's mother, Lily. She knows everyone in town."

"Oh God," Matt muttered, sinking lower in his seat. Beaufort's mother was the one Luci had spilled her guts to. Great.

"Lily! Right. She's very... friendly," Luci said carefully.

Tim smirked. "I think the word you're looking for is 'nosy'. She is, but she means well."

"Can we not talk about my mother?" Beaufort asked Tim with an edge to his voice. "It's my day off. I'd like to let my ulcer rest today."

"Sure, babe." Tim pecked Beaufort's lips, then did it again.

Luci grinned like the sun had broken out on a cloudy day. She raised her eyebrows at Matt. *You didn't tell me about* that? *Seriously?* "Well. I'm going to go visit the little girl's room before it starts."

"It's starting any second!" Matt said.

"So I've got to hurry!" Luci got up and went out. She was entirely too happy to have their little party invaded as far as Matt was concerned.

A moment later, the theater darkened and previews started. A heavy body fell into Luci's seat—heavier than it should be. Matt turned his head to find Roman Charsguard sitting next to him.

"Hello, Matt," Roman said in his polite-and-serious voice.

Matt groaned internally. Unbelievable! Was the entire sheriff's department tailing him? "Hi, Roman. Had a last minute yen for a dog movie, did you?"

The sarcasm went right over Roman's head. "I've seen 'Old Yeller' before, but not the other one," he said seriously. "Have you seen them?"

Matt sighed. "No. Not that I remember."

"Older Yeller is really sad. You'll probably cry." Roman's voice held not the slightest trace of humor. "Would you like some popcorn?" He held out a bucket.

"No th—"

Beaufort reached over Matt to grab the bucket. "Thanks for getting popcorn." He grabbed a huge handful and passed it to Tim.

"No problem. Thanks for leaving a ticket for me at the window."

Matt gave Beaufort a glare. Beaufort ignored it. "Shhh! The movie's starting."

Then, Beaufort compounded the weirdness. Because, you know, this wasn't already strange enough. He stood up, faced the people sitting behind them, and loudly said. "We're just going to *quietly* enjoy the films. *Quietly.* Without comments, talking, or noises of any kind." Then he sat back down.

Matt put his hands over his face and shook his head. It felt like he'd entered some reality show, the kind where some poor sucker was punked within an inch of his life.

Luci came back and stood in the aisle. She blinked at Roman. "Hello."

"Hello, ma'am." Roman stood up as if to let her pass.

Luci looked at Matt.

"Luci, this is Roman. Roman, this is Luci."

"Oh. Did you want to sit next to Matt?" Roman sounded embarrassed, that weird little tremor he got in his voice when he thought he'd said or done something stupid.

Matt didn't want to know what it meant that he recognized that sound and wanted to react to it immediately to make Roman feel better. "It's fine," Matt said.

Luci winked at Matt. "Yes, it's fine. You sit right there, Roman. And I'll sit next to you. Okay?"

Roman sat back down. So Matt would be sharing an armrest with Roman for the next four hours. And the other one with *Beaufort*. And he'd so been looking forward to zoning out without sexual frustration or feeling unwanted for a few precious hours.

It wasn't that he minded sitting next to Roman in a darkened movie theater. He wasn't above fantasizing any more than the next guy. But this was about Beaufort keeping him on a leash. And Matt felt... annoyed. The longer he sat there, the more pissed he became. There was no doubt in his mind that he was being played. Beaufort was hiding something from him. In fact, the whole damned town was.

And Matt swore to himself, right then and there, that he was going to find out what it was.

*       *       *

On Monday morning, Matt didn't go right into the office. He knew if he did, Roman would be there, waiting to hustle him out on their rounds. But that day, he was determined to get a better look around town.

He parked on a side street where he hoped his Cherokee would go unnoticed for a while, He walked to Main Street and took a left, away from the sheriff's office. He saw a few people on the street. A couple of them greeted him in a friendly way, but at least three people seemed to recognize him and scurried away, like rats from a cat.

What the fuck had Beaufort told the town about him? And why? Was it possible Beaufort was running some kind of illegal scam and everyone in town was in on it? That seemed so unlikely. Even if Beaufort had a secret drug operation or something, why would he tell so many people? It just didn't make sense.

What else could the town be trying to hide? Murder? Some kind of cult thing? The lost treasure of the Sierra Madres?

Of course, it was possible he was being paranoid, and they weren't hiding anything. But Matt couldn't square that with the way Beaufort had overreacted to his assignment to the town, or the way everyone looked at him like he was a guillotine blade waiting to drop.

Shaking his head at his own unproductive reasoning, Matt turned a corner onto a side street and nearly ran into a young man. It took a few blinks for Matt's brain to register what was going on. The man was on all fours sniffing at a fire hydrant. Matt watched him, mouth open, as the man stood up, unzipped his pair of older cargo pants, and started peeing where he'd just been sniffing. The golden arc sparkled prettily in the morning light.

"Hey! What the—! You can't do that!" Matt immediately went into 'cop' mode, though he wasn't, technically, a cop.

The young man turned his head to look at Matt and grinned. "Hello!"

"What are you doing? Stop it!"

The young man had curly brown hair that was pronounced at his ears, like some little Victorian girl or something. His eyes were big and brown. He didn't look drunk or mentally disabled, but he had to be.

"Can't stop it," the guy said apologetically. The pee flowed on.

Matt folded his arms across his chest and glowered.

Without seeming the least bit embarrassed, or worried, the guy finished peeing and zipped himself up. "Okay, bye!" He trotted down the sidewalk, heading away from Main Street. And trot it was—not a jog, but a shuffling gait with his elbows bent, his bare feet scraping along the pavement, and his hands flopping around. It was totally bizarre.

Matt started to call out to the guy to stop, or halt in the name of the law, or something. But then changed his mind. He kept his mouth shut and followed.

The young man trotted fast enough that Matt had to break into a slow jog to keep up. They went down one block of small residential homes then another. The guy had just turned into a house with a white picket fence when suddenly he freaked out. He ran to a big tree that was in the yard and started *barking* at it. There was no other word for it. He sounded so much like a real dog, he could have made a fortune in voice-over. The guy's slender hands scrabbled on the bark of the tree looking up at—an orange cat. It was up in the branches, its back raised in an aggressive arch.

"*Hiss!*" went the cat.

"*Ruff ruff ruff!*" went the guy who was pawing at the tree. His brown curls bounced in time with his moving head.

Matt shut his eyes hard, pinched himself, and then opened them. No, he wasn't dreaming. There really was a guy barking at a cat in a tree. He pulled out his phone and started recording a video. He'd told himself he was going to start logging everything the least bit strange. And this was way more than 'the least bit'.

The door of the house opened, and an older woman hurried out. She had the vibe of a grandmother, with her modest floral print dress, and the white streaks in her black hair. Her face was stricken with fear. She glanced at Matt, who was still holding up his phone recording, and then ran over to the young man.

"Ruben!" She said loudly. She tugged on his arm. "Ruben, stop! I mean now!"

Her voice was commanding, and the young man stopped barking at the cat in the tree. He looked at the woman. "Oh, hello, Ester."

"Come inside, dear. I have your breakfast ready." Her voice was steely.

"Oh, goodie, goodie!" The young man clapped his hands.

"Ma'am!" Matt called to the woman as she led the young man toward the house. She glanced at him, frowning. "I need to speak with you a moment."

The older lady, Ester, nodded, but she saw Ruben safely into the house first. "Your breakfast is in the kitchen. And stay in the house, Ruben!"

"Okay!"

She shut the door and walked over to Matt. Her face was pale and worried. So worried, in fact, it seemed extreme for the circumstances. "Yes?" she asked Matt nervously.

"Is that young man a relative of yours?"

"Not exactly," she hedged. "But I am looking after him for the time being. He doesn't have anyone else."

"I caught him… relieving himself near Main Street. On a fire hydrant."

"Oh dear." Ester's hand flew to her mouth. "I'm so sorry."

"What, exactly, is wrong with the boy? Ruben, is it?"

"He…" Her eyes shifted back and forth as if she was looking for an answer on the inside of her eyelids. "He has the flu!"

"The flu?"

Ester nodded vigorously. "Yes. The flu. He's been sick as a cat!"

Matt scratched his forehead, fighting not to call the woman a liar to her face. "I'm, um, going to have to report this to Sheriff Beaufort."

"Me too," the woman agreed heartily.

Matt did a double-take, but Ester didn't seem to be threatening him. Was every person in this town on speaking terms with the sheriff?

"You'd better keep a close eye on him until he's better," Matt said lamely.

"I will. Thank you, Mr. Barclay." Ester turned and went into her house.

It took several minutes for Matt to realize he'd never said his name.

Inside the sheriff's office, Matt went right to Beaufort's door and knocked. Beaufort opened it, his face grim. "Come in, Barclay."

Matt went in and shut the door. "Sheriff, I saw something this morning."

"I heard. Look—"

"No, *you* look. I saw a man sniff at a fire hydrant, pee on it, then chase a cat up a tree!" Matt said it with an edge, as if it was proof of something. But as the words reached his own ears, he realized how lame they sounded.

Beaufort merely grunted. "Ruben. Poor kid. He's new in town. A little slow, from what I've heard. And he has the flu."

"Having the flu does not make a person act like a dog!" Matt couldn't restrain a disbelieving laugh. Did everyone think he was stupid?

"Who said anything about dogs?" Beaufort asked sharply.

"What?"

"Other animals sniff and… chase things. Foxes, for example. Bears. Pretty much any animal."

"What does that have to do with anything!" Matt was not following this conversation. He gritted his teeth, trying to stay polite.

"I'm just saying, there's no reason to bring dogs into this," Beaufort insisted. "Flu causes fever. And fever causes

119

hallucinations. Am I right? And that's all there is to it. End of story. But thanks for bringing it to my attention. I'll make sure Ester has all the help she needs caring for Ruben." Beaufort put his hand on Matt's shoulder and led him to the door. "Have a good day."

The door opened, Matt got a shove that had him stumbling a step forward, and then the door closed with Matt was on the lobby side of it. He stared at the door, angry and not at all sure he had a good reason to be.

Maybe Ruben *was* slow. Maybe he even had a fever. But that didn't explain everything else. Like... the broth and the weird greetings and the theater. Like why everyone in town knew who he was and was afraid of him.

Roman came up behind him, put a hand on his shoulder and *rubbed*, lightly, his fingers strong and kind. Fuck, Matt shouldn't like the rubbing. But he did.

"Ready to go? I got us egg sandwiches."

"I don't want to go out today," Matt said stubbornly. "I need to spend some time at my desk getting caught up on reports."

"We have to," Roman insisted worriedly. He passed Matt a fax. The cover letter was addressed to him. The next page was another satellite image, this one of an area of forest where there was some cleared land with visible tree stumps and something bright that created a light flare. It had to be something metal—like a car or a trailer.

Under the image were the GPS coordinates and a few simple handwritten lines: *Forest service says this is public land. Shouldn't be anything here. Check it out first opp. Dixon*

"You shouldn't be looking at my faxes," Matt said without much bite.

"Sorry. I looked at it before I saw your name."

Matt sighed. So much for desk time today. "Where is this? Have you looked it up yet?"

Roman nodded. "Far north of our territory. An hour drive and maybe a five-mile hike in."

Matt nodded. Suddenly, the idea of getting away from Beaufort and Mad Creek for the day didn't sound so bad. But first, there was one thing he had to do.

"I'll hit the restroom and we can go," he told Roman.

"Okay. I'll fill our thermoses and meet you at the truck."

"No broth for me!" Matt reminded him dryly.

But Roman didn't seem to catch the sarcasm. "Coffee, black. I remember."

In the restroom, Matt went into a stall and pulled out his phone. He reviewed the footage he'd taken. Unfortunately, he hadn't thought to record the fire hydrant part, but Ruben barking at the cat was there, in all its stone cold oddity.

He hesitated, thumb hovering over the 'send' button. He'd emailed Dean Dixon from home on Sunday, after the theater incident. He was no longer sure he trusted the email at the sheriff's office.

*There's something going on in Mad Creek,* Matt had written. *I'm not sure it's anything illegal or drug-related, but there's definitely something weird here.*

*Keep digging,* Dixon replied. *Beaufort's been sheriff there for ten years, and his father before him. If he's up to no good in that town, we have to help those people.*

Matt imagined Ruben's face, so friendly and oblivious, and Ester's pale worry. Would Dixon even care about something like this? Would he just chalk it up to mental illness? And why did it feel like sending this video to Dixon wouldn't be 'helping these people' at all? That he'd be the worst kind of slimy snitch?

Matt hesitated, then canceled forwarding the video. He'd save it until he had more to go on. He flushed the toilet and went to find Roman.

# 6

## Bursting Through

### *Dogma #4*

They shipped Roman back to the K-9 facility in San Antonio in a huge plane. He was in a crate strapped to the wall along with half a dozen other dogs. One of the dogs trembled so hard his crate rattled.

That wasn't Roman, not on the outside. He had a bandage around his head, but he'd heard the doctor say he'd been lucky. Part of his right ear and a chunk of skin and fur had been blown off, but the bullet had grazed his skull rather than penetrating it. He'd been stitched up and declared good for travel.

Nevertheless, he was broken. He lay on the pad in his cage, tucked his head under his paws, and he slept and slept. The bullet might not have penetrated, but there was a giant hole in him where James had been. And there was something else too. Something itched and buzzed under his skin, in his muscles, in his bones, and pounded painfully in his skull. He constantly felt the urge to stretch, *stretch*, longer and longer, draw himself out as long as he could, even when it hurt his wound. But he couldn't stretch in the cage.

He wished he were dead with James. They had never been apart, not since that first day James walked into Roman's kennel. They should have gone home in the same box.

In San Antonio, he was put in a single kennel like the one he'd been in when he was a pup. He curled up in the corner and slept—or he woke and paced and stretched for hours, his butt in the air and his front legs splayed forward, hard. He could understand every word they said about him.

"Nice looking dog. Why's he keep stretching like that?"

"I dunno. PTSD. His handler was killed, and he's lost a lot of heart."

"Is he gonna be put down?"

"What? No fuckin' way. We don't put down military dogs. He's a fuckin' hero, man. No, if he can't hack it anymore, he'll get adopted out. But hopefully he can come back up to speed. Gonna give him a bit of rest time, then see how he does with a new handler. Isn't that right, Roman?"

The man banged lightly on the cage with his hand and made a noise with his lips, wanting Roman to come over there. Roman ignored him, his limbs compelling him into more frantic pacing. The men weren't James. Roman didn't care about them. He wasn't sure what to think about what the man said.

A new handler? Did he want that? Going back to Afghanistan, searching the roads and the endless dirt for bombs?

*No, not without James.*

But James would want him to, wouldn't he? Roman could find bombs in Afghanistan. He could help James's friends. He could help the Army. He knew he should like the idea, or at least be ready and willing. But he wasn't. God, he wasn't. He hurt everywhere and he longed for James so much he could hardly breathe. The idea of starting over with someone new.... *No.*

Roman had been in the kennel for a few weeks, and he'd been looked over by three different vets. None of them knew what was wrong with him, but Roman got sicker and sicker. Then one night, his sickness finally came to a head. It was a dark night. In the distance, there were bright white lights that lit up the compound, but in Roman's kennel, it was dark, so he didn't realize what was happening to him.

126

He woke from his sleep feeling worse than ever. His muscles were on fire, he had cramps and nausea, and everything itched. He panted with the pain and got up off the floor with difficulty. It hurt to move, but he had to, so he began pacing, running fast, banging into first one of the chain link walls of his kennel and then running as fast as he could and hitting the other. The dog next to him started barking and then all of the dogs barked.

*Bang,* went Roman, *bang, bang.*

It felt good to hit the smooth metal links with his body. It reached some itch deep inside him and gave him relief. *Bang, bang, bang.*

Roman's bones felt like they were breaking, but in a good way, like a sore tooth coming out. *Bang, bang.* His paws felt funny and awkward as he ran, getting larger and larger, more and more swollen. *Bang, bang.* His legs felt too long to run on all fours, and he had to bend his knees to keep going. *Bang, bang.*

*Good boy*, James said. *You're the best dog in the world.* And he'd meant it too. James thought he was the best dog. *Bang, bang.* The dogs barked and then grew silent. It was a silence tense with fear.

127

Roman ran until his body felt so strange and awkward and large he couldn't run anymore. He fell onto the floor on his belly, panting. His blood rushed in his ears like a raging flood.

His belly. The pad of the kennel was cool against his bare skin. His arms and legs were stretched out on either side of him, long and straight in a way he'd never lain before. He raised his head and looked around. The dog in the kennel to his left, a Doberman, was cowering in the corner. He looked away from Roman, trembling with stark fear.

Roman tried looking down at himself, but he was still on his belly and it was so dark.

He crawled forward toward a patch of light shining into the front of his cage. His paws felt strange on the texture of the cement kennel pad, hypersensitive. And when he reached the edge of the light, he paused and then, slowly, moved his front leg into the light.

But it wasn't his leg. It's was a man's arm and hand.

Roman stared and stared, unable to believe what he was seeing. And then he rolled the rest of himself into the light too.

Roman had changed into a man.

128

*          *          *

Colin "Kingpin" Clery rolled into Mad Creek, already impressed. It was such a long fucking drive to get there and, man, talk about a small shit town in the middle of nowhere. It would be a pain in the ass to haul gear and merchandise back and forth from L.A. But then, it would be a pain in the ass for anyone to *find* them, too. And that was the point.

The map Rufie had shown him! All those glorious acres of *nothing*, just trees and rocks and hills. They'd be a needle in a haystack here. Or a heroin needle in a poppy field, maybe.

"See, Colin," said Rufie as they pulled slowly away from the first of the town's two traffic lights. "It's perfect, just like I said. Right? Right?"

"We'll have to wait and see, won't we?" Colin replied testily. Rufie was way too full of himself over this whole deal.

It was Rufie who, during his last stint in the hole, had heard about Mad Creek. A guy he'd had for a cell mate was talking about this little town tucked far away from everything in

129

the California mountains, how he and a buddy had scouted it out before getting busted at a marijuana farm in Coarsegold. The guy bragged that when he got out, he was going to set up shop there.

But Rufie got out before his cell mate. And Colin—Colin considered himself open to new business opportunities.

He'd moved to L.A. ten years before from Columbus, Ohio, sure he was going to be a movie star. He had visions of being an old-time villain, like James Cagney. He'd be a good one too, not one of those stupid-ass German ones like in the *Die Hard* movies, or that lisping dickhead in that *Kingsmen* flick. Colin would be an all-American motherfucking bad guy.

But the movie industry hadn't been interested in Colin. Assholes, all of them. Eventually he'd realized being a real-life villain was way more profitable anyway. He'd been making a fortune selling drugs for the past five years. He was sick of the city. And he was bored with the losers and addicts and wasted ex-somebodies he dealt with in L.A. day in and day out.

Now a marijuana farm... that was interesting. The sales of pot were booming, and it was even legal in California now with a medical prescription. Word was, it would soon be legal without a prescription, and when that happened, the industry would explode. It'd be like Starbucks, with a pot store on every corner. *Legal*—completely unlike the hard core stuff he'd dealt in L.A.

No, pot was the future. Low risk and huge reward. He envisioned it like the start of Vegas, baby. And he was getting in on the ground floor. Only he had to start out on the down low. The current regulations for *growing* the shit involved state licensing, a clean criminal record, approval from the local authorities, and so much red tape your balls would end up plastered to your throat. Fuck that. Colin had never let the law stop him from building a business before, and he wasn't about to let it stop him now. No, he'd start his own way, like he'd always done, and make it all nice and legal once the law caught up and his operation was too big to fail.

They drove into Mad Creek about 2 p.m., and Colin was fucking starving. He spotted a diner. It was across the street from the sheriff's office, conveniently enough. "Let's stop there," he pointed. "We can check the place out while we eat."

"Yeah, dude. I need a burger," Rufie agreed.

The main drag in town was right out of some fifties Americana movie. It had slanted parking spots, and Rufie pulled into one not far from the diner. Colin checked his hair in the

131

mirror. It was thinning and receding—fuck you very much, Mom—but still copper red. He fluffed it with his fingertips, pretending he was just itching his scalp. He wiped his nose, which had looked a bit squashed ever since a junkie had busted it. Good enough. His aviator sunglasses had green lenses. Yeah, he looked cool.

He put up the visor and opened the passenger side door of the Buick. Rufie was waiting for him outside the door. He looked around and whispered.

"Just be cool, arright? 'Member I told you what Rico said about that military guy, Roman, who gave them a hard time when they were just driving around. So we need to not be obvious. Cool?"

Colin felt a spark of irritation. "It was one guy. Jesus, Rufie. Don't be such a pussy. And you're the one who looks like an ex-con. Put your hood down and brush your hair, for God's sake. This is business."

Rufie shoved down his hoodie and started fingering through his dark hair. "Sorry. Habit."

"Well this ain't L.A, and we don't have anyone looking for us here, so don't act all paranoid. None of your nervous crap, no playing drums with your silverware, no bouncing your legs. Got it?"

"Sure, Colin. I got it."

Colin left Rufie to his pathetic grooming. The guy was a total doormat, which was exactly why Colin liked him. When you had a lot of ideas, you didn't need people who had any of their own. And Rufie knew pot. He'd been growing it in one form or another since he was a kid. He had a walk-in closet in his apartment that looked like a fucking jungle. Colin needed Rufie, 'cause a plant had never been invented that Colin couldn't kill. Still. Rufie could be annoying as fuck.

Colin pulled open the diner door and a bell chimed overhead. A blonde waitress in an old-fashioned fifties-style blue uniform looked up from where she was pouring coffee at a table and smiled at him.

"Hey there!" she said, all sugar and cream. "Just take a seat anywhere you can find a spot!"

Colin gave her his killer smile. She looked a little too goody-goody for his taste, but pickings would be slim in this rat trap. "Why, thank you, doll," he said, slipping into a booth.

The diner, holy shit. It had tables and booths with shiny red leather and Formica table tops with glittered swirlies in it, a jukebox in the corner, a curved counter, and old-fashioned stools. It didn't feel Disney-fied either. No, this retro shit was the real deal, so old it was in again. In fact, this whole town felt old-timey. That was fine with Colin. The more *Leave it to Beaver* they were, the less they'd be prepared to deal with someone like him.

Who knows? Colin might be here for years if his first few seasons went well, and he made a shit-ton of money. If they did legalize marijuana, Colin could buy land legitimately, and become a regular founding father. He had money to buy land right now, if he wanted to. But he wouldn't. If he purchased something on the books, that would put him in the system, make him a known target. And that wouldn't work at all. No. He'd rented a cabin where they could sleep, but the farm would be someplace else, someplace secret. No one would know where the gold mine was. That was the smart way to do it.

Colin smiled to himself as he studied the laminated menu. Yeah, this felt right. He was gonna like it here. And if that Roman guy cropped up, no problem. He or Big T would deal with him. No way one guy with a Neighborhood Watch hard-on was gonna stand in his way.

In fact, he decided smugly, it would take a small army.

     \*           \*           \*

Matt was gone for the day, and Roman was at his desk on his computer, watching videos and sweating. When Lance came in without knocking, Roman jerked back from the keyboard, caught in the act.

Lance, of course, read the situation in an instant. "What you got there, Roman?" He smirked and came around the side of the desk. "Don't tell me you've discovered porn?"

Roman wanted to hide what was on his computer screen, but it was too late. Lance peered at it and then looked at Roman, his eyebrows raised high in surprise. "A... bulldog skateboarding?"

Roman looked away, deeply embarrassed. "It's..." He stopped. "That is, Matt..."

"Go on."

"Yesterday when we were hiking, Matt saw a trail and said he wanted to try it with his mountain bike. He invited me along. I wanted to say no. But then I thought about how you want me to watch him all the time. So...."

"When is this supposed to happen?"

"Sunday. *Oh God.*" Roman covered up his face with his hands.

"Look at me, Roman."

Roman obeyed, though he didn't want to. He could feel how warm his cheeks were. Blushing, he decided, was not something he liked very much, as human traits went. And it certainly wasn't nearly as fun as masturbating.

Not that he could fool Lance about his feelings anyway, blush or no blush.

"You know," Lance said slowly, "You don't have to watch Barclay off hours. I don't expect you to do it on your one day off work. You need a break too, Roman."

"I don't mind." In fact, he'd been happy that Matt had asked if he wanted to mountain bike on their day off. Like... like they were friends. That is, he'd been happy until he realized that he had no *clue* how to ride a bike. Or even if he could. "But it sounds like he's really good at it. He even has two bikes, a new one and an older one, and I can ride one of them, he said. But... dogs and wheels...." He shuddered. "What if I make a fool of myself?"

It was ridiculous. He'd run obstacle courses in the military, been in hundreds of cars and planes, but the idea of having to balance himself on two wheels scared the living shit out of him.

Lance turned his face away, and his shoulders shook gently. He was laughing, Roman knew. He didn't take offense. He just wished Lance would get on with it, and tell him what to do.

Lance turned back, wiping tears from his eyes. "Roman, you're priceless."

"Sir—" Roman huffed.

Lance held up his hands in surrender. "No. No. I get it. Riding a bike for the first time can be a little intimidating, especially when you're used to four legs."

"Is it even possible?"

"Of course it is. Haven't you seen Fred Beagle riding around town on his bike? Daisy rides one too."

"But they were *born* quickened."

"Doesn't matter. I tell you what. Tim has an old bike in the garage. Let me call him and see if he would mind showing you how to use it. Maybe you could come over tonight so you can practice before Sunday."

"Thank you, sir." Roman felt hugely relieved. Something warm turned over in his chest. Lance and Tim were so good to him. He would do anything for them. Anything at all.

"And, uh, the reason I came in here was because Tim wants to invite Matt and Luci, and you too, over to our place for dinner Sunday night. Would you like to come?"

"Yes." Roman loved Tim's cooking. It was way yummier than the microwaved potato and soup and other simple dishes Roman knew how to make.

"Good." Lance slapped Roman's back and went to the door. He turned and looked at Roman warily. "You and Matt...." He scratched at an ear uneasily. "I know it's likely you'll become friends, spending so much time together. Just remember, Roman. He's not one of us. You can't let him see your true nature. The town comes first. Got it?"

"Of course, sir."

Lance nodded. "Good." He left.

Roman meant what he'd said, but, for the first time, it didn't sit well with him. It left a bad taste in his mouth, like a lie. But it had to be true, didn't it? The town did come first.

Roman didn't understand why that made him feel so sad.

# 7

## Blowing It At The Top

Early Sunday morning, Roman watched out the window as Matt pulled up in his Jeep Cherokee and got out. It was the first time Matt had come to Roman's cabin, and he was so nervous. He looked around one more time, but everything was even neater than usual. He'd swept the floor the previous night and that morning too, and he'd polished the small pine table where he ate his meals until it reeked so badly of medicine and lemons that he couldn't even eat his cereal there.

He tugged up the tight biking shorts he was wearing. Tim had loaned them to Roman. He said they were good to wear because they had a big pad and without it your balls would hurt. The shorts were a little small. They also felt weird—they went to mid-thigh, were black, and clung like a second skin. His penis and bits were all caged up in there like they were being punished in solitary confinement. He'd never worn anything like them, and he thought he looked stupid. At least, he did until he opened the door.

140

Matt stared, his mouth open like he was saying 'ah' at the doctor's office. Roman wondered if there was something wrong with his legs and looked down. They were very muscular. The muscles above his knees were cut like diamonds. And they were also pretty hairy, with soft, curly tan hair. But they looked human enough to Roman.

"Uh..." Matt swallowed. "Wow. You're in great shape."

Roman fidgeted with the door handle, uncomfortable.

"You must work out your legs a lot. Those quads are..." Matt looked up at Roman's face and suddenly blushed. "I mean..." He coughed. "You'll have to tell me about your workout routine. It looks killer."

"Workout routine?"

"Yeah. How much do you squat? Or deadlift?"

For a moment, Roman panicked, having no idea what Matt was talking about. Then something clicked into place. James took Roman with him to the gym on base where James would grunt and groan and sweat and lift big heavy weights on a bar. The soldiers liked to brag about how much weight they lifted. That must be what Matt was talking about.

"I just walk and run a lot," Roman said.

"Man, you must have good genes." Matt took another look at Roman's legs and then looked away.

Roman felt a little warm and his stomach went wobbly. He clutched the doorknob harder. "Come inside. I mean… if you want to."

"For a second, sure." Matt smiled.

Roman stood away from the door. Matt walked in and looked around. The cabin where Roman lived was one of twenty the town owned. It'd been built on town land by volunteers from the pack. Roman had helped build another one this past summer. They were always in need of places for the newly quickened to stay since most of them had no money and no job.

Roman's cabin was so tiny, it only fit one person, so he didn't have to share. It was also farther out of town than most of the pack cared to be. It was a single room with a futon against one wall that made into his bed, an old plaid couch in the middle, an older TV, a coffee table, his small kitchen table where he ate and studied, and a wall of kitchen cupboards, oven, sink, and fridge. He loved it fiercely because it was his. Now that he worked full-time for the town, he didn't even feel guilty about living there without paying rent.

"Geez, Roman, you're so neat and uncluttered. I'm afraid you wouldn't be impressed with my place. I've got so much stuff." Matt went over to the pictures on the wall.

Roman joined him, his chest growing tight. He wanted Matt to look at the pictures, but suddenly they felt so, so private.

"Who's that?" Matt pointed to the picture of James and Roman. It had been taken by a military photographer, and it was Roman's most prized possession. After he'd gotten to Mad Creek and learned to write, he'd written a letter to James's sister. Lily had helped him find her address and get the words just right. He'd written that he'd been a friend of James, and told her how brave and wonderful a man James had been. James's sister had replied with a very nice letter and that photograph.

In the picture, James was squatting down, one knee on the ground, and he had his arm over Roman's shoulder. Roman's tongue hung way out and he looked full of joy. That was before he'd ever become a man.

"That's Sergeant James Pattson." Roman hesitated. "He was my best friend."

Matt turned to look at Roman's face. His smiled faded. "Was?"

"He was killed by a land mine."

"I'm sorry." Matt's voice was quiet. He kept staring at the picture. "My older brother, Mitch, was KIA in Iraq. I was fifteen at the time. Man, that fucked my dad up. Me too. I mean... trying to live up to his memory, you know? So yeah, I get it."

"Do you have a mother?"

Matt huffed and gave Roman an amused look. "Yeah. It's sort of mandatory." He swallowed, his sparkle fading. "She died of breast cancer when I was a kid."

There was an acid thread of pain in Matt's voice that worried Roman's dog, made him sit up and take notice. But Matt changed the subject and the tone vanished. "Hey, do you have any pictures of you with your dog? You were in K-9 too, right?"

"I don't have any pictures like that."

"Was your dog like this one? A German shepherd? He's a beaut." Matt nodded at the photo.

Roman felt out of his depths, like the floor had gone liquid. Lying was so foreign to him. "Y-yes. My dog was just like that one. Can we go now? I have water if you need to fill a water bottle."

"No, I'm all set." Matt pulled away from the picture with a regretful look. Something eased in Roman's chest now that they were off the subject. "I've got both bikes in the back of my Cherokee, so you want to take that?"

"Okay."

"Great. Let's go."

There was unmistakable unease in the air as Roman led them out of his cabin. But he didn't have any idea what it meant.

*      *      *

Despite practicing at Tim and Lance's place, Roman was still nervous about riding a bike. When they set out from the trailhead, being on two wheels felt all wrong. Roman was wobbly and hesitant. Matt rode in front, but he glanced back often. A little way up the trail, he stopped, and Roman awkwardly came to a halt behind him, relieved to put his two feet on the ground.

"You okay?" Matt asked.

"Yes. I don't have much experience on a bicycle."

Matt looked confused. "Oh. Hell, Roman, you should have told me. We don't have to ride today."

"No. I want to try it." And Roman realized that he did. Matt had been looking forward to this, and Roman wanted him to have fun.

"If you're sure. Let's head to that first ridge and see how it goes. We can always turn around."

They continued up the trail. It was a lot harder than when Roman had practiced in Tim's driveway because they were going uphill and there were roots and small rocks. It was difficult to go fast enough to stay upright.

Roman decided that he did not like biking at all. Figuring out how to manage on two legs was hard enough. But then he heard James's voice in his head. *Come on, Roman. You can do it*! He'd done harder things than this in his training, like climbing up a slippery wet roof with a steep slant. It was about confidence and speed. He pedaled harder, using his quad muscles and picking up speed despite going uphill. That made it much easier not to wobble.

He kept up with Matt, sometimes right on his back tire, because he needed to go fast in order to go at all. Before he knew it, they reached the ridge.

Matt got off the bike and stretched. He grinned at Roman. "That was a nice little workout." He had sweat on his face and neck. Roman found the glistening skin there fascinating. He wondered what it would taste like if he licked it. But dogs did that, not humans.

"Yes, it was hard but good." Roman's heart pounded, *thump thump*, from the climb.

"The best things always are." There was a funny, flirty tone in Matt's voice. Roman blinked at him. Matt cleared his throat and looked away. "You up for some more?" He nodded at the spine of the ridge they were standing on. "It'll be easier going now."

Roman considered it. The ridge had mild, rolling ups and downs, and it went for miles. They'd hiked up there last week, and Matt had fallen in love with it. Roman couldn't blame him. The ridge they stood on was low compared to the mountains around them, so the view was like being in a bowl full of hills. The sky was completely clear and blue, and the day was cool and breezy. The changing leaves were at their peak and the shirring, glimmering blanket of gold and orange had to be the most beautiful thing in the world—Roman was pretty sure. You couldn't even see Mad Creek from there since it was hidden by another ridge. It was like they were all alone on earth—just them, the forest, and all the life Roman could sense in it.

"I want to go on."

"*There's* the hard-ass I know and love. Come on." Matt mounted his bike and went first. Roman followed.

It was much easier now, especially with Matt's words of praise glowing in his chest. Roman liked to be a hard-ass. And he liked the dips in the trail. They went so fast downhill, their speed made them fly up the short inclines. The wind buffeted his face and hands and he found himself smiling. It was a little like being in a car, but he felt as close to the land as he did while hiking.

148

After a few miles, he decided riding a bike wasn't so bad after all. A few miles later, he was filled with joy.

Maybe it wouldn't have been so much fun by himself, but he liked riding behind Matt, seeing his tight form in black biking shorts and an oversized red T-shirt that clung to him in the wind. Matt was his friend. He was pack.

*No. He's not pack.* Lance's voice spoke in Roman's head, warning him.

But Roman's heart insisted Matt *was*. He'd been spending so much time with Matt, and Matt was easy to be with. Even when Roman made mistakes, scratched his ears or said something humans would find peculiar, Matt just shook his head fondly or laughed like Roman was being funny on purpose. Matt laughed at almost everything. His spirit was filled with light even when he was feeling sad. He had a good heart.

They rode for about an hour on the ridge until it came to an end, and the only way to go farther was a steep drop down. Matt got off the bike and stretched again.

"Hey, I brought some brunch."

"Brunch? Isn't that something fancy people do?"

149

Matt smiled. "Hey, we're fancy. Besides, it's Sunday, isn't it?"

His bike had bags on the back. He unzipped them and pulled out a piece of material that was silver on one side and white on the other. It was very small, but it unfolded to blanket size. Matt put it on the ground and held the corners down with rocks so it wouldn't fly away. Then he brought out a small bottle of champagne and several plastic containers.

"Have a seat." Matt patted the blanket next to him.

Roman lowered Matt's spare bike carefully to the ground and sat down. The containers held little salmon sandwiches in triangles with the crust cut off, grapes and strawberries, and rolled up taco-like things. Roman was really surprised.

"You went to a lot of trouble, but it's just me," he protested, even though his stomach growled. His inner dog was always hungry.

Matt smiled, a warmer smile than usual. The breeze ruffled his dark hair. He shrugged. "I had a lot of egg sandwiches to make up for."

"But those were from the diner. I didn't make them."

"This wasn't that hard. Luci made the taquitos and the rest was no big deal."

"Okay."

The mention of Luci made Roman frown. She'd seemed nice when Roman had met her at the movies. But she was a pretty girl, and the idea that she lived with Matt, and got to spend all that time with him at home, maybe even sleep in bed with him... it made Roman feel bad. He ate a salmon sandwich as delicately as he could manage and tried to figure out why he felt that way.

When he'd been with James, they were together 24/7. No one had been closer to either of them than they'd been to each other. Roman felt a tug inside himself to Matt, to *be* like that with Matt. And it was confusing, because he knew that wasn't how it was. Matt was not James, and Roman wasn't a dog any longer. He had responsibilities of his own now, even if most of those currently revolved around Matt.

The mental complexity of it bothered him, fuzzed his brain. His dog wanted to simplify all of it, wanted Matt to be pack and to be his friend all the time, and for that to be the end of

151

it. It wasn't. Matt went home at night and Roman wasn't allowed there. Besides, Lance wanted something else entirely.

"What do you think?" Matt waggled the small bottle of champagne. "It's not enough to get us drunk, but think you can steer that bike downhill with a little bit of this in you?"

"Yes. Does it have bubbles? I had one once with bubbles. I really liked it." It had been at a pack New Year's Eve party. Roman remembered it well.

"Yes, it has *bubbles*, tough guy," Matt said with a smirk. He unwrapped the foil around the top and pointed the bottle away, popping it. Spray flew out and hit the rocks and a gust of wind blew it right into Matt's face. He sputtered in shock.

Something about it was *so, so* funny. Roman felt a pain in his stomach that worked its way up his throat and burst out of his mouth. He thought it was a bark but, no, it was a *laugh*. A big one. The sound coming out of his own mouth was so surprising it made him laugh harder.

Matt grinned at him, wiping his face with his sleeve. "It gets shaken up in the paniers."

The word *paniers* was hilarious too! The laughter erupted from Roman's chest in an almost painful way. Fortunately, it was more *ha ha ha* than howl. He pulled up his knees and put his forehead against them until he could get it under control. *Laughter.* Real human laughter. Another first. God, what a wonderful feeling!

When he finally caught his breath and raised his head, Matt was watching him with a warm, happy expression. "Found that amusing, did you?"

"Yes." Roman's breath was still shaky and a smile stretched his lips.

"Uh-huh. Remind me to watch out for banana peels around you. Wouldn't want you to hyperventilate." Whatever his words meant, their *sound* was light and friendly, so that was all right.

Matt took a drink from the bottle and handed it to Roman. Roman decided it must be okay, even though Leesa got really mad if he drank from bottles at work. The tip smelled and tasted of Matt, sweaty and clean at the same time. The champagne was sour in a good way and the bubbles fizzed in his mouth.

Roman handed Matt the bottle, took a taquito, and bit into it. It was crispy and cheesy and very yummy. This? The champagne and the food and the day and the view and the laughing... this was very good. This was perfect. And Roman knew enough to appreciate a perfect moment when he had it.

They ate the meal, passing the bottle back and forth between them. Roman liked the taste of Matt on the neck of the bottle even more than the champagne, and he tried to discreetly lick to get more of it. Inside the biking shorts, he started to feel tingly and the material got tighter.

He looked up to find Matt watching him, his brown eyes darkened. Roman passed him the bottle and turned away on the blanket. He brought his knees to his chest to hide what was going on down there. *This isn't the time for that!* He was going to break these shorts, and then he'd really look stupid. He ate some grapes.

"Roman?" Matt's voice sounded funny.

"Yes?" Roman didn't turn around.

Matt cleared his throat. "There's something I wanted... that is..."

Roman waited.

Matt huffed. "Okay. So, obviously Sheriff Beaufort is still not happy about having me in town."

Roman didn't think that was what Matt *meant* to say, but he answered. "He likes you okay as a man." He shifted back around so he could see Matt's face.

Matt batted his eyes in confusion. "Right. Well, that's good. But—" He rubbed his jaw with his hand, uncomfortable. "Look, I'm not an idiot. Clearly the sheriff has told the whole town something about me. Everyone acts like I've got leprosy. And you've been doing your damndest to keep me *out* of town."

"Our work is in the woods," Roman said earnestly, though he could feel his face grow warm.

Matt held up a hand. "I know. I'm not saying... look, you've been tremendously helpful. And I do believe you're as interested in stopping any possible drug farms as I am—"

"I am."

"Right. So. I'm not trying to come down on you or anything. I just... there's something going on in town. And I wondered if you would tell me what it is."

Roman didn't know what to say. His mouth would not form the lie he needed. He stared into Matt's eyes, not wanting to show fear or appear to back down submissively.

"Roman?"

"Lance Beaufort is a good man," Roman said. "He's a very good man."

Matt nodded. "Okay. He seems to be. But—"

"Mad Creek... it's a different kind of place." Roman expelled an anxious sigh that was almost a whine. "The people there... there are a lot of vulnerable people there. People who need protection. Lance only wants to keep them safe. And so do I. We're like a big family."

Matt shook his head, confusion all over his face. "Safe from what?"

"From..." Ideas tripped through Roman's head, but none of them felt like the right thing to say. Either they were too close to the truth or they made no sense. He felt helpless. He closed his eyes. "Trust me. There are things that—if people outside knew, it would hurt my town and all the people in it. But it's nothing to do with drugs or your job. And it's nothing bad. Please believe me." He put his heart into his words. He didn't want to be at odds with Matt. He wanted to be Matt's friend. He wished so hard that he could just trust him and tell the truth.

Matt looked at Roman for a long time, as if making a decision. "All right, Roman," he finally said. "But I hope someday you can talk to me."

"Me too." Roman wondered if that would ever be possible.

They went back to eating. Roman sensed that Matt was still frustrated, but that he was letting it go for the time being. But for how long? Would there come a time when he'd find himself on opposite sides of the battlefield from Matt? He hoped that day wouldn't come.

Soon every container was empty and the bottle was too. Matt leaned back on the blanket with his arms propped behind him, face to the sun. His eyes appeared to be closed behind his sunglasses, so Roman let himself stare. Matt was very fit. He was a healthy-looking animal. And his face made Roman feel happy inside. Strange. When he'd made that bad mistake in Coarsegold, lost his mind and thought Matt was James during that firefight, maybe he hadn't been so wrong after all. Matt wasn't James, but something about him *was*. Roman liked him almost as much.

Matt opened his eyes and caught him. Roman looked away quickly.

"Roman?" Matt said, his voice soft.

"Yes, Matt?"

"There's something else I wanted to ask you."

Roman waited. When Matt didn't speak again, he wondered if he was supposed to say it was okay. "You can ask."

Matt cleared his throat and took a heavy breath. "I wondered... that is.... Dumb question but... are you straight?"

Roman looked out over the view at an eagle soaring nearby, but he was very aware of Matt in his peripheral vision. He sensed in Matt's body language and tone that the question was important, but he didn't understand why. Hell, he didn't understand the question.

*Was he straight?* What did Matt mean by that? Was he asking if Roman was a liar? Or a thief? There was some phrase Lance used sometimes—something about being 'on the level'. Was that what Matt meant?

As usual, when Roman was unsure of what was going on in human communication, he faked it. "Sure," he said, casually.

"Sure... you are straight?"

"I'm straight." Roman looked right at Matt and nodded confidently.

"Right. Of course. Yeah, dumb question."

Something changed in the air between them. Matt went back to basking in the sun, but there was tension in his body and something sad or even angry crackled in the air. Roman wished he could fix it, but he didn't know how.

"Well, we should head back," Matt said after a minute. "I promised Luci I wouldn't be too late. We were invited to dinner at Beaufort's place tonight."

"Okay." Roman got up and helped put things away. In just a few minutes, everything was stored back in Matt's paniers.

"Beat you to the bottom," Matt said, but his tone didn't make it sound fun the way it should have.

Roman tried to play along anyway. "Never." He hopped on his bike and took off fast.

He stayed in the lead because it was easier going downhill. The wind still whipped his arms and face, but the day felt ruined. And when Matt dropped Roman off at his cabin, he didn't think either of them was sorry it was over.

# 8

## Roman Learns About The Rainbow

Roman went into the office on Monday morning at 5 a.m. He wanted to catch Lance before Matt got in. Lance came in at 6, hung up his coat, and hesitated as he saw Roman hovering around his office door.

"Is there something you want to talk to me about, Roman?"

"Yes, sir."

Lance nodded. "Well, let me get some coffee first."

They went together into the break room. Lance poured himself a big cup of coffee, while Roman warmed up some beef broth from the fridge in the microwave. Roman didn't like the taste of coffee or how it made him feel all jittery. He had a feeling it was one human habit he'd never pick up. Most quickened preferred the yummy taste of bone broth when they wanted something warm to drink.

They went together into Lance's office and Lance shut the door.

"I didn't have a chance to talk to you alone at dinner last night," Lance said. "How did your bike ride go?"

"The bike riding wasn't so bad."

"Good." Lance narrowed his eyes, sipped at his coffee, and waited for Roman to speak.

The previous night at Lance and Tim's place, the dinner had been awkward. Matt and Luci had shown up wearing blue jeans and smelling like crisp fall air. They brought a bottle of wine, and Luci had made a delicious salsa and fresh corn chips to share.

Luci and Tim had gotten along right away. Luci had been friendly to all of them, and she loved Renfield, aka Renny, Tim and Lance's Bernese Mountain Dog mix. But Matt had not been himself. He'd looked everywhere but at Roman. He'd talked a lot with Lance and Tim, and only a little to Roman. He'd petted Renny. He did look at Roman and smile a few times, but the smile did not reach his eyes, which were sad. He hadn't been the same Matt he'd been all week, or even that morning when they'd started biking. Roman didn't understand.

Maybe Matt only liked Roman when no one else was around. Maybe Tim and Lance were better to talk to. Lance had been quickened since birth, so he was much better at acting human. And Tim was full human. Tim could be shy, but at least he knew what people meant when they said things. When they asked you questions.

Or maybe Matt hadn't been that way because Lance and Tim were better company. Maybe it was because Roman had done something wrong.

He didn't like how it felt to be with Matt when he acted that way. It felt like someone was stepping on his chest with big, ugly boots. So as soon as dinner was over, Roman had made an excuse and left for home.

Now he stood in front of Lance's desk. He put his cup of broth down, stepped to the side with one leg, and put his hands behind his back in parade rest. He lifted his chin. The position made him feel a little more secure. He hated to have to ask Lance about human things, because he wanted to be strong and independent. But sometimes there was nowhere else he could turn.

"It's about Matt."

Lance perked up. If he were in his dog form, his ears would have tilted forward. "What about Matt?"

"He has some behavior I don't understand. And I... I fear I have said or done something wrong, and he doesn't like me anymore."

"Go on." Lance half sat on his desk with one hip, but his eyes were bright. "Tell me what happened."

"On the bike ride, we took a rest and ate some food he brought." Roman swallowed at the memory, the way the neck of the bottle had tasted of champagne and of Matt. "He knows that you're trying to hide something from him, and that I'm keeping him out of town. He asked about it, but he wasn't angry."

Lance pursed his lips. "I suppose it's pretty obvious."

"He...." Roman hesitated. "I told him it had nothing to do with drugs. Or anything bad. I think he believed me."

Lance sighed, blowing out a deep breath. "I knew this situation would be trouble."

"I don't think Matt means any harm."

"He doesn't have to *mean* harm to destroy this town. What else did he say? Did he ask questions?"

Roman hesitated. "Yes. He asked me if I was straight. I wasn't sure what he meant so I said yes, I was straight. But I think that was the wrong answer. He would hardly even look at me last night at your place. I'm sorry if I did something wrong."

Lance gaped at Roman for a moment, then buried his face in his hands. "Shit. Tim was right!"

"About what?" Roman's heart ached a little more.

Lance groaned. "Oh my God. As if this whole thing isn't already stupid enough." He looked up at Roman. "After Matt left, Tim said he was gay and that he had an unrequited crush on you. I told him he was crazy. After all, Matt has Luci. But Tim insists they're just friends."

"I don't understand."

Lance's eyes darted to the wall over Roman's shoulder. He fidgeted. "Look, human men are either 'gay' or 'straight'. Well, there are other options, but let's not get into that right now. Anyway, the word 'straight' means a man who likes women. So most men are straight. But some human men like other men instead and that's, um, called being gay. They like men, you know, for sex. Sexually. Mating." Red dots of color appeared on Lance's cheeks. "You know. Like... like Tim and I are a couple."

"You're mates. Yes, sir. I know that."

"Which means we... you know... have sex." Lance looked panicked. "Only in human form, though! Me. Not him. I mean, he only has a human form. But—" He cleared his throat. "—to be clear, it's proper etiquette... if you want to.... I mean, most humans would not have sex with dogs. In dog form."

Roman was disciplined enough not to roll his eyes. "Yes, sir. I believe dogs feel pretty much the same way."

None of this was a surprise. Any dog with a nose that had been within ten feet of Lance or Tim knew they were sex partners.

"Well... um. Good. Anyway—" He cleared his throat again. His face was now a bright crimson. But he plowed ahead. "So Tim and I's, um, relationship, was only possible because Tim is a human male who likes *men*. Well, obviously, because I'm a man. That means Tim is gay. Got it?"

Roman thought he understood. He was still a little confused, because he'd heard the word 'gay' in the Army and it had always been used as an insult. But he decided not to worry about that for now.

"What about you, sir? Does that mean you're gay also?"

Lance braced his hands on his desk, his knuckles white. "Humans would say I'm gay, yes, because I'm mated with a man. But for me, it wasn't that I liked men before, it's just... once I met Tim, and, um, bonded with him, I fell in love with him and... and... it didn't matter to me if he was male or female. So..."

Roman frowned in confusion.

"Yes, I'm gay," Lance finished lamely.

"So... when Matt asked me..."

Lance dug the heels of his hands into his eyes. "Oh, God. Okay, so when Matt asked you if you were 'straight', he was fishing."

"Fishing?"

"He *likes* you, Roman! And he wanted to know if there was a chance you liked him too. But you told him you were straight, which means you don't like men... I mean, in a sexual way. So that means you wouldn't like him... for sex. And probably he was disappointed. Probably he does have a little crush on you, like Tim said, and he got his feelings bruised a bit."

"Oh."

"Don't worry about it, Ro. He'll be fine. Just act natural around him and continue to do your job, and he should get over it quickly. Okay?" Lance blew out a sigh, as if relieved the conversation was over.

Roman didn't feel relieved. He blinked, trying to sort through it in his mind. Matt liked him like that? Like the men and women he'd seen kissing on TV? The way Lance liked Tim and Tim liked Lance? Like *a mate*?

Suddenly he understood that smell he sometimes smelled on Matt, the lovely musky tangerine smell. He'd first smelled it on Matt in the bathroom in Fresno, when he'd done up Matt's pants for him. And there had been... swelling, under the fabric. Oh. *Oh.*

Matt had been aroused then. Well, for goodness sake, Roman's hands had been right there. Had Matt thought he was going to touch him... like that? The way Roman had learned to touch himself? And Matt had been aroused with Roman several other times too, when Roman had forgotten about personal boundaries and had gotten too close.

Roman felt hollow, like his insides had been scooped out and just a dull ache was left, and, weirdly, that ache went right down to his groin. His groin did not feel empty but rather, very full. This was obviously another level of human sexuality he hadn't given much thought before. It had been all around him. He'd just... missed its relevance to him personally, the way you can fail to notice the blue sky. The idea that *he* might... that he himself might have a mate like that....

"So a man can... can mount another man, even though men don't go into heat?" Roman clarified slowly.

169

Lance blew out a huff of a breath and stared at the wall. "Humans don't have heat cycles like that, Roman. They just have sex when they feel like it. Or every day. Sometimes more than— okay, you know what? I think Lily has a book on the subject because, seriously, I can't. I'll call her up and ask her to bring it by and leave it with Leesa. Okay?"

"Okay." Roman had a lot more questions, but it was clear he was making Lance anxious, so he decided not to ask. "Thank you."

"So, um, yeah. Like I said. Just act natural with Matt, like before, and he'll come around. It's fine, Roman. You did nothing wrong. Your job is to watch Matt, not be his best friend or... or anything else. Right? You'll tell me if he asks any more questions about Mad Creek?"

"Yes, sir."

"All right then. Let me know how it goes today."

Lance looked anxious for Roman to leave, so he took his broth and went to the office he shared with Matt. He sat at his desk.

He thought about what Lance had said, and what Tim thought too—that Matt liked him *like that*. A spark of hope and excitement warmed him from the inside.

Then he thought of Lance's parting words. *Your job is to watch Matt, not be his best friend or anything else.*

Roman felt something he'd never thought he'd feel in a million years. Right then he did not like being a deputy of Mad Creek.

# 9

## The Trap Is Sprung

### *Dogma #5*

Roman was terrified as daylight crept into his kennel. He practiced trying to balance himself on two feet and straighten his spine. He felt so tall it was scary. And he practiced using his voice time and again. It was so strange, hearing his own mouth and breath form the words he was used to hearing from James. He had to try *a lot* before it sounded anything like James's easy words.

He had to practice, because he instinctively knew, in the deepest part of him capable of fear, that he was in a terrible spot. He couldn't let the people here know what had happened to him. He just couldn't. Dogs didn't change into men. It was unnatural and maybe very bad. The Doberman in the next kennel was terrified of him. Probably men would be too. Roman was confused about everything, but not about that.

So he practiced talking, and then he practiced walking on two legs in his new towering, gangly form. He fell and got up again. And he fell and got up again and again.

In this body, his senses were dulled. Sight, smell, hearing—they all felt muffled. But he could think. His brain was a freight train, the thoughts coming so fast they tumbled into one another and vanished unless he grasped them tight. And his *hands*. His hands were *amazing*. He could close his fingers around the chain link and climb. But unfortunately, there was a cover on top of his kennel so he couldn't get out that way. He couldn't open up the door from this side either.

He tried things he'd seen James do—rub his hands together, point, makes signs he didn't know the meaning of. He could hardly believe the hands were his, but boy, did they work well.

After dawn, the man in camo came to bring his breakfast. Roman sat on his haunches, exposed and unable to do anything but wait.

The man saw him and froze. "What the hell? What are you doing here?"

Roman rose slowly to his flat feet, steadying himself with one hand on the chain link wall. "Let me out, please," he said, his voice hollow.

"What the hell are you doing in my kennel, soldier? Fucking *naked*? And where's Roman?" The man was angry. He put his hand on his walkie-talkie.

"I heard barking. Came to see the dog. He got past me and the door shut." The words were rough, but he thought they were right.

"He got out?" The man unlocked the door and opened it wide. "Do you know how valuable these dogs are? How did you get this door open? And where the fuck are your clothes? You'd better not be perving on my dogs, or I'll bust your ass back to Tulsa!"

Roman pushed past the man with all his strength and ran.

He managed to hide in the crawl space under a barracks until they stopped looking for him. When the sun got high, and the soldiers were all on exercises or in the mess hall, he crawled out and let himself into the barracks. It took several panicked minutes to get in, his hand was awkward on the door handle. But he got inside and he pawed through one of the trunks that held clothes. He dressed himself, which was way harder than it looked, and then cowered in the empty barracks bathroom, crawling up onto a toilet and closing the door.

What was he going to do?

He could try to go back to being a dog. There was an itchy feeling in his body that made him think he might be able to shift back. He was afraid, though, afraid of the pain he'd had before. And some instinct inside him urged strongly that it was not a process that *should* be reversed. That felt wrong.

Even if he could go back to being a dog, what then? He would wait in his kennel until they assigned him to another handler. There would be obstacle courses, and loud noises, and fiery hoops. There would be days of work in the rain and mud and other days in the heat. And then there would be another big plane, and he would go back to Afghanistan, and he would sniff for bombs. He would see men blow up and there would be gunfire, always. And his new handler might die too.

He shivered and cringed, sitting on the toilet with his booted feet on the rim and his face in his knees.

He couldn't go through that again. He didn't want to. If James were here, Roman would do it again for him. He'd be that brave, put up with the noise and the dust and the heat and the blood. But without James? He would rather lay down and die than do that all over again without Sergeant James Pattson.

There was a burst of artillery fire outside, and Roman startled and shook.

There was not a great deal of reasoning involved, in the end. Only gut instinct, only *can'ts* and *won'ts* that ran deep in his bones. He knew what had happened to him was very special. It wasn't right to go back to being a dog all the time, not before he'd even tried to be a man. And he wouldn't go back to war without James.

Roman did what he had to do. He uncurled himself, left the stall, left the barracks, and walked to the base's front gate. He watched for the guard in the little booth to be busy talking to the driver of a car and he walked out.

He didn't look back.

\*   \*   \*

By Monday morning, Matt had pulled himself together and was determined to act professionally. Not that he'd ever *not* acted like a professional, exactly. But he'd allowed his mind to go where it shouldn't have gone, and he'd paid the price. He'd been shot down big-time, and he'd never been too good at hiding it when his heart hurt.

*Just ask him, cariño,* Luci had said that Sunday morning before the bike ride. *Are you a man or a mouse? Better to know for sure so you can stop tormenting yourself.* Damn the woman and her stupid lawyer logic.

Of course, it had turned out that Roman Charsguard was straight. Fine. Good. He was the last man on earth Matt should mess around with anyway. For God's sake, he was Matt's work partner and not even the kind of partner that you could totally trust. He worked for Beaufort, not the DEA. Matt could have really gotten himself into a quagmire if he'd acted on his attraction.

So it was a good thing that Roman had shot him down. It was a good thing Matt had gotten that wake-up call before he did something stupid. It was a done deal.

But another voice in his head knew the truth—it sucked ass. Matt had been crushing on the guy hard. Roman was the guy who'd rescued Matt, the guy Matt had thought about for months, unable to forget those burning, sad eyes. He was Matt's ideal man with his powerful body, soft eyes, and that whole military vibe. They both loved the outdoors. Matt could do things with Roman that he hadn't been able to do with any other guy he'd hooked up with. He was gorgeous, sweet, honest to a fault, good-hearted, poignantly vulnerable, strong, and inexplicably naive at times in a way that brought out Matt's protective side.

And... it didn't matter. They were colleagues, nothing more.

It was with that anthem humming in his mind like a Gregorian chant that Matt went into the office on Monday. He found Roman at his desk. Roman blushed when Matt walked in and stood up, practically going to attention.

"Hey," Matt said casually. He sat down and got on his computer without further conversation.

"We should... go out and check lines today," Roman said hesitantly, as if afraid Matt would protest. "It's been a while since we've checked the early ones."

"Sure," Matt said without looking up. "And I'd like to cover that northwestern part of the grid this week—sections A1 through 10. Assuming nothing comes in from the satellite that's more important."

"Okay." Roman sounded relieved.

"Give me ten," said Matt, tapping away.

Roman mumbled something about egg sandwiches and left the office.

When he shut the door, Matt sighed in relief. He could do this. From now on, it was strictly business. He had to find his SWAT persona again—tough, determined, kick ass, impersonal. He had a job to do. In fact, he had more than one. He had his DEA job and he also had to figure out what Sheriff Beaufort was hiding. Now that he'd put to rest this romantic foolishness, maybe he could actually be effective.

*       *       *

The fishing line Roman had put up was broken. It'd been strung across the end of a fire road on the side of Mountain 882.

Roman called it Hawk's Point, but that name wasn't on the map. At the end of the fire road, there was a little-used trail that ran into dense woodlands. They'd hiked it one day a few weeks ago. Matt recalled dense woods, a long, slow uphill, and an eventual lookout to a lake where hawks soared overhead. But he wasn't positive he was remembering it right. The trails were all starting to blur together now.

"It could have been anything." Matt watched Roman as he squatted on the road, looking over the broken ends of line. "A bear. Hikers."

"No, there was a vehicle." Roman's nostrils flared as he sniffed. He pointed to some faint movement of stones on the gravel road. "Two men. They smell of the city. One smells... sick." His nose wrinkled, his eyes lost in thought.

*Ooo-kay.* Matt thought Roman was playing up the whole Indian tracker thing. He couldn't help but voice his skepticism. "Are you seriously telling me you can smell that two guys were here?"

Roman looked up, his brown eyes startled. "It's... I have a very sensitive nose."

"If you say so." Matt shrugged. He could see the tire marks, though, now that Roman had pointed them out, and those were convincing enough. "Well, the truck's gone, so they're not here now. Maybe we should hike in a ways. See if they did anything."

"Yes." Roman stood up. His posture was stiff, his face tense and unhappy. "I should call Lance and let him know there are strangers around." His fingers went to the phone in his pocket.

"Why don't we check it out first? Then we can both make a full report to our superiors."

Roman put his phone back in his pocket reluctantly. He nodded.

They walked up the trail. Roman appeared to be tracking. He looked around at the brush and trail constantly, and he appeared to be sniffing too. He was dark and intent, and Matt just let him be. He wasn't sure he believed Roman could smell anything. But he'd heard of some guys in the Marines who were gifted trackers by sight, so he didn't comment.

The trail was level for about half a mile, then started gaining altitude quickly. Matt kept scanning the forest around them for any signs of vandalism. They only went up the steep grade for about five minutes when Roman called out from behind him.

"Stop."

Matt looked back at Roman.

He shook his head. "They turned around here and went back to their vehicle. Probably they didn't like the trail."

"Are you sure?"

"Yes." Roman said firmly. "Very sure. There's no point going farther."

Matt slowly walked back to Roman. "What do you suggest?"

"Let's go back to the truck and get the map. We can check the lines at all the points close to here."

"That's good," Matt agreed. "Maybe we'll even run into them. Assuming the line here was broken recently, that is."

"It was broken on Saturday."

Matt looked at Roman doubtfully.

"I think," Roman added with a blush. "Because it rained last Thursday night. There would be less evidence if they'd been here before that."

"Okay, so since Thursday night. You're probably right that it was over the weekend." Matt ran a hand through his short hair. "Could be hikers or hunters."

Roman tilted his head in that quizzical way of his. "Hikers have plenty of good trails that are marked. And hunters are permitted only on state game lands."

"If they're hunting *legally*."

Roman started to say something, then shook his head. "Let's check the other lines."

They spent all day checking lines in a circumference out from that one broken line. They found two more lines that had been snapped and evidence that a vehicle had been both places. Roman seemed convinced it was the same vehicle, and the same two men, but Matt didn't see how he could possibly know that. Still, there was no doubt someone had been driving around scouting out-of-the-way areas. There weren't many legal reasons for someone to do that.

Matt had to agree that hikers were unlikely. They chose trails that hardly deserved the name and didn't go far down any of them, if Roman were to be believed. And if they were illegal hunters, the Forest Service would want to know about it.

Or they could be looking for a place to start a meth lab or a marijuana farm.

It was 6 p.m. when they returned to Roman's truck from the last trail they'd checked. The sky was orange on the horizon.

"I'll call the Forest Service and my boss," Matt said. "See if they know of anyone who's been in this area."

"It's not them," Roman said positively.

"Doesn't hurt to check."

"That's true."

It was the most they'd said to one another in hours. Once Matt had stopped trying so hard to ignore Roman—*not ignore, just treat him as he should be treated, which is to say, like a guy I'm not interested in, at all*—he'd realized Roman was acting funny toward him as well. He'd catch Roman looking at him with a sad or confused look, or purposefully not looking at him, even turning his back to him when they stopped for water or to check the map.

Maybe Roman had figured it out. Maybe he'd realized a regular guy did not ask another guy if he was straight and then act pissy at the answer. Matt could admit he hadn't played it nearly as cool as he should have. He'd just... he'd been really disappointed.

Whatever. It didn't matter now. It was better this way. It would be easier on Matt if they didn't try to be friends. He didn't want Roman's pity.

# 10

## Back In A Cage

After they got back to town, Roman went straight into Lance's office and shut the door behind him. He told Lance about what they'd found, about the broken lines, the vehicle, and the two strange men he'd smelled on the trails.

Lance, looking grim, grabbed his jacket, and he and Roman went over to the diner. When they walked in, Lance's eyes went suspiciously to everybody in the room. But they were all people they knew, pack members or harmless humans who lived in the area. There was one young couple with a baby who were strangers. The mom looked tired and smelled of breast milk. Lance looked at Roman and Roman shook his head. *It's not them.*

Lance sat on a stool at the counter and ordered pie for both of them, coffee for himself, and broth for Roman.

"Tell Daisy who we're looking for," Lance prompted Roman.

Roman described the smell of the two men. He also showed Daisy a few long red hairs he'd found in branches along the trail. He'd seen shoe prints too. One of the men wore fancy hiking boots and the other a cheap pair of tennis shoes that had soles worn smooth.

Daisy listened to him and looked at the hair samples. She nodded. "I've seen these two. They were in the diner Friday. Both had hamburger and fries and one had a Coke and the other a vanilla shake."

"Why didn't you call me?" Lance asked with a huff.

Daisy's nose twitched. "Now, Sheriff, you know I can't be bothering you every time a new face walks in the door! And they seemed nice enough. The red-haired man was very pleasant." She smiled at the memory.

Lance's hand clenched on his fork, and Roman knew what he was thinking. Daisy would happily wag her tail at a bank robber and lick an armed psychopath in the face.

"What did the other one look like, the one that doesn't have red hair?" Roman asked. "He smelled sick to me."

"That's the little guy with dark brown hair. He did have a sort chemical smell." Daisy wrinkled her nose. "He was very nervous and jumpy."

"Did they say anything about what they were doing here? How long they were staying?" Lance asked.

"No, Sheriff." Daisy's eyes were wide.

"Okay. If you see them again, you text me immediately. Got it?"

Daisy nodded, worried. "What have they done, Lance? Are they dangerous?" She frowned, glancing at her other customers.

"I'm not sure yet. But we need to watch them."

This seemed to reassure Daisy. She went off to work other tables.

Roman took a bite of pie. It had been a long day, and he was really hungry! He ate it in three big bites, and just as he finished, Daisy dropped off a plate with a double cheeseburger on it without being asked. She gave him a sunny smile and a little wink.

For the first time, Roman found himself wondering about her smile and wink. Why was Daisy so nice to him? Was she flirting with him? Did she like him *that way*, the way Matt did? Or was she just being friendly?

How did people ever figure it out without smells... heat smells... to make it clear who was and wasn't receptive and when? What if you were wrong? How did you ever find out? Did you just say 'Hey, would you like to be mounted?' Or was that considered insulting?

It seemed so overwhelming. Roman felt lost.

He hadn't enjoyed being with Matt today. Matt had put a wall between them, even though Roman couldn't see it. And though he wanted to break through it, he didn't know how or if he should try. And he also kept thinking about what Lance had said.

Matt was his job. Not his friend. And not... not anything more either.

Roman ate his burger gratefully while Lance chatted with someone on the phone. His eyes rolled in ecstasy. Cheeseburgers were amazing! There was yummy beef, and cheese, and bread too! All at the same time! Humans definitely had the best ideas ever.

"So..." Lance punched off his cell phone with an annoyed jab of his thumb. "The motel hasn't seen anyone like that. It's been a slow week, Bert says. Let's go see Minnie."

"All right." Roman gulped down the rest of his burger. For once, Lance didn't admonish him with: *Chew, Roman. Humans take their time and chew.* So Roman knew he was really distracted.

They said good-bye to Daisy and left the diner. The bell on the door tinkled, a sound Roman normally loved, but today it sounded tinny.

They walked a few doors down Main Street to the Mad Creek real estate office, which was run by Minnie. The pictures in the window were of sad-looking, run-down properties and dried-up lots. Minnie herself had wild curly brown hair and was enormous for a woman. She was a second generation Newfoundland by descent. Her movements were ponderous, but her mind was sharp as glass. When they walked in, she was talking to a gray-haired couple in nice clothes.

"—well, you're right, there are some attractive properties in the Squirrel Flats area, but of course, most of them have been restored since the last big flood. Insurance is quite pricey there, I'm afraid. Due to the gas leak issues."

The man and woman exchanged a troubled glance. "What about northeast of town, by that pretty mountain? What was the name of that mountain, dear?" the woman asked her husband.

"I believe it was Mount Francis."

"That's right. We're both retired and we love to be active, so ideally we'd like to find a place close to hiking trails. That mountain looks like a popular place to hike."

"Oh, yes! There's a very popular trail up Mount Francis," Minnie agreed, her eyes huge. "I hear it's a wonderful view from the top. As for *living* near the mountain, I do have two properties in that area, but I couldn't show them to you today." Minnie looked around conspiratorially and leaned closer to stage whisper. "The exterminators are in."

"Exterminators?" The woman's face fell.

Minnie nodded. "Rats. It's just the perfect little microclimate there with the snowmelt that comes off Mount

191

Francis in the spring. But people who live there say they hardly even notice the vermin, other than the teensy-weensy little turds they leave in the cupboards."

The woman took a step back, looking horrified, and the man cleared his throat. "I think we'll, um, just take one of the magazines and get back to you." He grabbed a property magazine and he and his wife scuttled out the door.

Minnie turned to Lance and Roman with a big smile. "Lance! And Roman! What a pleasure." She greeted them with a rub along Lance's chest and Roman's arm, a happy wiggle in her steps. Roman liked her smell. Minnie smelled like dirt and flowers, and it wasn't a fake scent either. He liked her a lot. She'd found Roman his little cabin, as if she'd known just what he needed. He'd be forever grateful.

"I see you're doing a fine job as usual, Minnie," Lance said.

Minnie waved her hand like it was no big deal. "I feel like a rat myself, turning humans away, but I have a hard enough time finding places for the quickened these days. Did you hear Dr. Jason Kunik is moving back to town?"

"No!"

Minnie nodded sagely. "Yup. He called me to find a rental close to town. Someplace he can have an office and a lab set up. Sounds like he's planning to carry on with his research here! Wouldn't that be something if he can figure out how this whole quickened business really works? Why dogs get the spark and, you know, how we actually change? I'm sure it'll be fascinating!"

"That would be interesting," Lance said, but Roman thought he didn't seem to really like the idea. "Anyway, Roman and I are looking for two guys we think are staying in the area." Lance described their quarry to Minnie.

Minnie shook her head regretfully. "No, I haven't seen anyone like that, not looking for property to buy or rent. But you know, Sheriff, I don't control all the rentals around here, only about half of them. If someone wants to sublet their place out, I likely won't hear about it. And then there are vacation cabin rentals that are managed by other companies. And the campgrounds. I don't do anything with those."

"That's all right, Minnie. I was just checking to see if they'd come to you. I'll keep looking."

"I'll call you if I see them!" Minnie assured Lance.

"Thanks."

Roman started to follow Lance out the door.

"Just a minute, you!" Minnie barked out.

Roman paused.

Minnie, beaming, came up to him, her body vibrated with energy. She lightly bonked her head against the side of his. She was one of the few women tall enough to do that. "How are you doing, Roman? I bet Lance is working you to death! Haven't seen you at a Howl at the Moon night lately."

Roman couldn't help but return the smile and give her a gentle head butt of his own. "Nah. Lance and Tim like to go, so I'm on duty that night."

"Well, that's not fair! Not every time! You need to let Roman attend Howl night, Sheriff."

Lance stood at the doorway, looking awkward. "I offer every month, but he'd rather—"

"Oh, pooh! Promise me you'll come next month, Roman. There's a quickened I want you to meet. Her name is Penny, and she's just the sweetest little thing! She's only been quick about six months, and I thought you two might hit it off."

Roman looked down at his feet, feeling like a searchlight was shining on him. It was not a good feeling. "Okay," he mumbled.

"Okay. Bye, you two! See you soon!"

They left and crossed the street to return to the sheriff's office. Lance had his head turned away, but his shoulders shook.

"What's the matter?" Roman asked.

Lance guffawed. "Penny! Oh my God, Roman. She is cute. She'd come about to here on you." He karate-chopped Roman at his diaphragm.

Roman glowered, but he refrained from telling his boss to shut up.

"She's a poodle. A little ditzy but, wow, so enthusiastic. I can totally see it!" Lance seemed to think this was hilarious.

"I'm not interested in a poodle." Roman glowered harder.

195

"I don't know, buddy. Minnie's a very determined matchmaker."

Lance was teasing him, Roman knew. But he didn't find it funny. As usual, he just didn't get humor. What was funny about the mismatch of Roman mating with a little poodle?

That thought reminded him that he *did* get Matt's humor. And even when he didn't understand the joke, the laughter in Matt's face and voice always made Roman smile anyway. Except Matt hadn't laughed around him that day.

"Okay, so here's what we're going to do," Lance said, as they drew close to the sheriff's office. He turned to look at Roman, growing serious again. "I'm gonna keep an eye out for these guys in town. But meanwhile... Roman, are you listening to me?"

Roman had been noticing that Matt's Cherokee was gone, so he must have gone home. He looked Lance in the eyes. "Yes."

"Okay, so I'm gonna keep a lookout for these guys in town, and we're going to let Matt hunt for them out in the woods. You'll be with him, of course, but I want him to feel like this is his show. If he's got a real suspect to track, maybe he'll forget

196

about Mad Creek for a while. After all, this is supposed to be his job, so let's let him do it."

"I understand."

Lance nodded. "Good. So tomorrow, keep him on their trail. I've got a few other places I want to poke around, but it's getting late. Feel free to take off if you want."

Lance went into the station. Roman looked at the sky. It was fully dark by then, but the moon was still low. Main Street was starting to wind down for the night. The few stores in town were closed and only the diner and the movie theater were still glowing like stubborn pulse points. On weeknights, pack members tended to go home and cuddle up with their friends and loved ones. Those that had them, that was.

Roman sat in his truck for a while, thinking about those broken lines and the smells he'd come across today. Matt thought they might be poachers—men hunting illegally. Roman wasn't sure that was the case. Even if it was, he didn't like it. Sure, he'd hunted himself illegally when he'd needed meat for food. But he took his quarry as quickly as possible and turned away from hunts when he sensed babies or a healthy will to live in the animal. And when he took one down, he killed it swiftly and ate it all.

He didn't much like the idea of men with guns in his woods. He'd once watched men from the brush as they photographed themselves with a dead buck, cut off the head, and left the heavy carcass for scavengers. The animals never had a chance against a bullet, and the hunters never got close enough to their prey to see if they were good animals to harvest or not.

Roman growled lightly, hands tight on the steering wheel.

But… if Roman had to guess, he didn't think these men were hunters. They didn't smell of stiff canvas and lures and rifles. They smelled of the city and smoke and… chemicals. Lance said if they were real drug growers, they could distract Matt's attention from the town. But Roman didn't like that idea. What if the strangers hurt Matt? Or what if they got past him and endangered the townspeople?

He started the engine and pulled out onto Main Street. Halfway through town was a side road where he normally turned left to wind his way up the mountain to his cabin. He'd just reached the turn-off when it occurred to him: There was another turn off farther down Main Street that went south. And down that way was a road to a small lake with a few rental cabins dotted around its edge. It was one of the places Roman had routinely patrolled last spring, but he hadn't been by there in a long time now.

It wasn't that far from town. What if the two men were camping out there? Or staying in a cabin? He'd be able to recognize their vehicle by smell.

He had nothing to go home to, and he'd already eaten his dinner. He might as well go check.

*        *        *

When Roman reached the little lake, he didn't see any campers around its edge. But two of the rental cabins were occupied. Their lights shone yellow in the night and reflected off the black water. The smaller of the two—not much bigger than Roman's place—had an old VW beetle with yellow paint in the driveway. Roman parked on the road and snuck up to the house. He sniffed around the car and in the front of the cabin.

The car belonged to a young couple—man and woman. They were hikers. He could smell the forest dirt they'd carried on their boots and the pungency of their sweat from a long day on the trail. From inside the cabin came the faint sounds of a movie they were watching on a laptop computer. Their smell was nothing like that of the two men he was looking for.

He cut around the lake to approach the second cabin. It was the biggest one on the lake and it was fancy. It had a high wooden deck and, on the first floor, double glass doors that faced the lake. By the doors was an outdoor shower for swimmers. There was a dock and a rowboat that hadn't been taken out in a long time.

There were two vehicles in the driveway—a huge, white, expensive-looking SUV that said "Cadillac" on the back and a gray truck with a trailer. It looked like a small moving truck, but there were no markings on it.

Roman glanced up at the windows. Most of the lights on the upper floor were turned on and there was a blueish flicker that was probably a TV. He didn't see any movement.

He slunk down and approached the Cadillac. He smelled at the seam of the passenger door and then, not smelling enough, risked reaching up to touch the handle. No alarm sounded. He tried the door and found it unlocked. He opened it a crack, which turned on the interior light.

That sickly chemical smell leaked out along with a stronger scent of the other man—the redhead. His smell was spicy, like anger or spite, and he wore a bottled scent that tickled Roman's nose in an unpleasant way.

He shut the door as quietly as he could. The light went out.

He squatted there in the dark beside the car, thinking about what to do next. He should call Lance. Maybe he'd decide to move on the men tonight. Or maybe he'd wait and see what Matt did. But Roman wanted to check the cabin's windows first. He wanted to see the two men Daisy described for himself, so he'd recognize them by sight. Maybe he could also check to see what was in that moving truck.

A faint noise registered on his left. Roman turned, but it was too late. A large form loomed in the darkness and a gun pressed against his temple.

"Don't move, don't even breathe, or you're a dead man." The man's voice was deep and cold, and Roman sensed how easily he would pull the trigger. He wouldn't care at all, not this man. He was big too. Even bigger and taller than Roman.

Roman didn't move.

"That's right," the man said. "Now—slowly—hands out in front of you, palms together. *Do it.*"

The voice of command and the press of the gun together were too much. It brought back the sound of artillery fire rattling in Roman's brain. He slowly moved his arms off his knees and out in front of him, palms together. The man snapped on tight plastic restraints.

"Now your feet. Put them out in front of you, ankles together."

Those, too, were snapped together by a plastic device.

The man put away the gun then and patted Roman down. He was so close, Roman could see his flabby, pitted face, receding gray hair, and smell the beer on his breath. It felt to Roman like the man was dead inside. There was a blankness to him that made Roman shiver.

The man found Roman's holstered gun and took it without a word. Then he hoisted Roman up with a grunt and slung him over his shoulder. "You were in the wrong place, wrong time, guy," the man said flatly. But he didn't sound sorry.

Inside the cabin, the man headed down some carpeted stairs, Roman still slung over his shoulder. He opened a door and threw Roman bodily into a small bathroom with no windows. Without having the use of his legs or arms to catch himself, Roman fell face-first and his forehead cracked on the side of the tub. The man closed the door and wedged something under it so it couldn't open.

Roman shifted his hips on the floor until he could lay down. Blood ran into his eyes from his forehead. He didn't think he was badly hurt. Head wounds bled a lot. But he *was* in trouble.

He should have texted or radioed Lance before he'd driven up to the lake, so Lance would know where he was going. Or, if not then, he should have done it the moment he was sure that SUV belonged to those two men. But he hadn't. He'd made a mistake. And now no one knew where he was.

*My truck is out there.*

If the men were not stupid, though, they would move the truck, drive it someplace out of sight. Roman didn't think they were stupid. No, he was the stupid one. He'd screwed up again. And now he was helpless, as helpless as he'd been in the kennel.

Trapped.

# 11

## Desperation

### *Dogma #6*

A week after he'd escaped from the military base, Roman was dropped off in Las Cruces, New Mexico by a trucker. The trucker's name was Sam, and he had picked up Roman on the road near Fort Stockton, fed him a meal at a roadhouse, and let him sleep in the bed behind the driver and passenger seats.

Sam had a son in the military, he'd explained. He'd asked Roman about his military service, but Roman had difficulty with speech, so he said only a few words at a time. Sam seemed to accept that something was wrong with Roman, and he stopped prying. This left Roman with a lot of time to stare out the window and feel afraid.

He had nowhere to go. There was no one who knew he even existed. He was terrible at being a human. In the week since he'd shifted, he'd learned a lot, but only by doing everything wrong. It turned out you couldn't just run into a restaurant and take food off the counter. You had to 'wait to be seated' and

205

'place an order'. After you ate, you had to pay for it. Since Roman had no money, he'd spent several hours washing dishes in a diner. But he was so bad at it—he hadn't yet learned how to coordinate his hands very well—they finally just threw him out.

He'd walked and walked, falling down a lot as he stumbled on his over-long feet. He'd slept under bridges in the cold and wet. He'd drank water from a stream on all fours. The water was bad and it made his stomach explode. You had to find a place to hide when you pooped too. People got very mad if you did it where they could see.

By the end of his first week of being human, Roman was shaken, exhausted, and lost.

Sam left Roman at a truck stop, and, while he'd been kind, he didn't seem sorry to say good-bye. Roman couldn't blame him. He was a freak, and he made so many mistakes.

Roman walked slowly into downtown Las Cruces.

James had taught him about bravery and perseverance and figuring things out. But Roman could not gather together any threads in his mind that made sense. He could go back to being a dog, but he didn't want to go back to war, and he was afraid if he was just an ordinary dog, he'd be put in a cage or even killed. If he stayed a man, he needed money to eat, to live. But how did a man go about finding a job? And what could he do with his poor speech, lack of coordination, and the way he startled at any loud sound? The skills he had—attack, corner, sniff out bombs and drugs—they were not skills he could use as a man.

He would watch, he decided. Watch and learn and practice and hopefully, one day, he would be able to do a job and earn money.

In Las Cruces, he learned where and when to find the best food in trash bins. One very cold night, another homeless man was at the trash bins too, and he took Roman's sleeve and led him down block after block to a church. There, they spent the night on cots in a warm room. In the morning, Roman stayed.

The military fatigues he'd stolen were dirty and they smelled very bad, but a kind man at the church gave him clean clothes and put him to work lifting boxes. Roman learned how to wash dishes the correct way too. And the cooks gave him heavy pots to lift at mealtime. It was better than sleeping under bridges, but Roman was alone. He was not like anyone else, and no one understood him. They talked to him in loud, slow voices like he was damaged in the head. And at night... at night, he dreamed about blood and explosions and the way James looked at the end. *You're the best dog in the whole world.*

Roman missed James so much his entire body hurt with longing. He missed his smell and his voice and his calm leadership. If this was going to be Roman's life now, he wasn't sure he wanted it.

Then one day, something extraordinary happened. An old man came into the shelter for a meal and a bed. Roman knew right away—the man was like him. He smelled of dog and human all mixed together, and he looked right at Roman and his nose wrinkled—he could smell Roman too. The old man, who was short and had a head full of thick, white hair, came right up to Roman and sniffed at his chest, then walked around him, rubbing his arm against Roman to leave a scent.

"You're like me," Roman said, getting very excited.

"I'm the first one you've met?" the man asked. His face was sad.

Roman nodded.

"Come with me." The man led Roman outside the church. They found a place away from the door to talk in private.

"My name is Granger. How long have you been human?" The man peered up at him curiously.

"Not long. A few full moons. My name is Roman."

Granger patted Roman's shoulder. "Big and strong. What breed are you?"

It was an odd question, and Roman had to search in his memory for the answer. "German shepherd."

"Ah! A service dog?"

"I was in the Army. You?"

"Aw, I'm just an old mutt who got lucky. I had the best human. We loved to travel together. Went all over having adventures. Then my arthritis kicked in, and she got sick. She passed in her sleep." Granger's face went slack and grim. "That was two years ago. I've been walking ever since, Roman. It's a hard life."

"Yes." Roman thought it was a very hard life.

"But listen." Granger's face brightened. "I talked to a quickened in New Orleans who told me about a place. There's a town in California called Mad Creek. There are a lot of us there. They can help us find jobs and a home and all sorts of things. I'm going there if you want to tag along."

"Yes," Roman said with no hesitation at all.

Granger's eyes got damp and his smile wobbled. "Would you? It would be nice not to be alone."

"It will be cold tonight. We can leave in the morning," Roman said.

And so they did.

\*               \*               \*

The head wound Roman got when he was thrown into the bathroom must have been worse than he thought, because he slept. When he woke up, he was tied to a chair. He was wearing only his boxer shorts and undershirt. The room he was in looked like a small bedroom with white walls, green carpet, and a window with an old pair of wooden blinds drawn closed. Other than the chair, all the furniture had been removed and a heavy plastic tarp lay beneath the chair. That was not a good sign. Roman swallowed down fear.

The door opened and a man with shoulder-length red hair stood in the doorway. He studied Roman, a dark look in his eyes. "Good. I thought T might have been too rough with you. Have a nice nap, did you?"

He stepped into the room and the big man who'd captured Roman came in behind him. The man stood by the door, hands clasped in front of him, his cold eyes on Roman.

Roman couldn't stop the growl that arose in his throat at the sight of the big man. His dog *hated* that man and wanted nothing more than to threaten and warn him to stay back by snapping and growling. He pulled against the ropes, but he was tied tight to the chair's back and legs.

"Going a bit beastie, are we?" The red-haired man tutted and shook his head. "You might as well play nice. You aren't going anywhere."

The red-haired man was not old and not especially ugly, but his brown eyes were mean. Roman sniffed and smelled the stinky cologne he wore. It was the scent from the trail and the Cadillac. His lips pulled back from his teeth.

"I have your wallet and your car keys." The man stood in front of Roman, just far enough away that Roman couldn't have reached him, even if he crashed the chair and somehow got a hand free of the ropes. His eyes bored into Roman's and there was an evil little smile on his lips. "Your ID says you're Roman Charsguard."

Roman saw no reason to lie. "Yes. *Deputy* Roman Charsguard." He spat out the words out.

The red-haired man laughed. "T, *this* is Roman," he said to the big man. "How fuckin' lucky, are we? We didn't even have to look for him. He came right to us. That guy was right. He is a nosy fucker."

Roman didn't understand. His eyes shifted to the big man, who neither moved nor cracked a smile.

"Are you going to kill me?" Roman asked, though he could guess the answer. There was a plastic tarp on the floor, after all. A year before, he wouldn't have minded so much. But now? Now, he would miss his pack, his life in Mad Creek. He'd miss hiking with Matt, very much. And he'd be sorry to have failed those who needed him.

Roman fisted his hands behind his back. If only he could take out one or more of them, he wouldn't have died for nothing.

Red-hair looked at T, not answering right away. His mouth was pursed, his eyes amused, but it wasn't a good sort of humor. "Will we kill you? Good question. The thing is, T over here is a professional killer. He doesn't kill for free. Know what I mean? So I'd have to pay him a big, fat bonus to get his hands dirty. I'm not sure you're worth it. Besides, I think you might be useful. I strongly recommend you don't prove me wrong."

He stepped closer to Roman and leaned over, peering into his face. "What I want, *friend*, is for you to tell me all about Mad Creek. I want to know every person in law enforcement here. I want to know what they're like, how many kids they have, the names of their wives, what kind of beer they like to drink, and if they pick their nose, teeth, or butt crack. You feel me? And I want to know what the fuck you were doing out there by my car. I ain't done nothing yet. What made you show up here?"

"I won't tell you anything."

"Oh, yeah. You will." The man leaned back, smirking. "Let me tell you my torture philosophy, Roman. See, I am a lazy guy. It takes a lot of arm muscle to use a whip. But fortunately, your body will do all the work for me. All it takes is time. I leave you in this room, no food, no water, no way to sleep, tied to that chair.... Within forty-eight hours, you'll be begging to talk. Guaranteed."

"I won't."

"Keep telling yourself that, asshole."

Red-hair turned for the door. The man he called T stepped aside to let him pass. But at the last minute, the red-haired guy stopped and took the gun from T's body holster. He turned back to Roman. "You know," he shrugged, "you convinced me. Maybe you are a hard case. This will help."

He took two strides to Roman, put the barrel of the gun's silencer below his right shoulder, and pulled the trigger.

The sound was a soft 'thwunk', but there was nothing soft about the explosion that ripped through Roman's body. A scream-howl tore out of his throat as the two men turned and left the room.

Oh God, his shoulder was on fire! Pain shot back to his spine and down into his stomach. He retched and the burger he'd had at Daisy's threatened to come back up. Dark spots floated on the edge of his vision.

He ground his teeth and shook his head, trying to clear it. Pain. So much pain. Men could die of pain, he knew that. Shock, it was called. It happened on the battlefield all the time. He had to try to calm down.

He closed his eyes and stopped thrashing. He took deep breaths, even though it was agonizing to expand his chest. Lance. Leesa. Charlie. Tim. Daisy. Lily. *Matt.* His mind brought up their faces, each one so dear to him. He thought of the way Lance rubbed his head or arm in greeting. He thought of the time Leesa had jumped on his back, laughing. He pictured the smile in Matt's eyes when they reached a summit, his easy teasing. He wanted to see Matt smile at him again. He wanted to laugh with Matt again like he had when Matt sprayed the champagne.

Roman took deep breaths through his nose. Bones were broken in his shoulder; he could feel it. The blood ran thick and hot down the front of his shirt, making it sticky. He tilted his body in the chair so it was almost up on two legs, trying to get the blood to run around his torso and onto the ropes that held his hands. Would that even help? Maybe it would make his skin slick enough to create some give.

His ears picked up a low conversation taking place outside. They were discussing where to dump his body. He wasn't surprised they planned to kill him. The question was: would they get anything out of him first?

Roman could not risk telling them anything. And he might. What if he went out of his head, like wounded men he'd seen in the Army, and didn't know what he was saying? And what would happen once he died? Would his body shift back? What if he gave away their secret?

He felt a little less like he was about to pass out. The breathing had helped. Trying to *think* had helped. He had to escape, that was all there was to it. What would James do? Or Matt, for that matter? He'd been in SWAT. Matt would be brave. God, he wanted to see Matt.

There was blood on his hands now, slick and hot. It would dry quickly, though. Roman worked at the ropes. He slid his wrists back and forth a little, but it caused his shoulder to scream in agony, and he couldn't get the fat part of his palm loose. The harder he tried, the more fresh blood streamed down and the weaker he felt. He got nowhere.

He stopped, panting hard from the stress and waited for the pain to subside. Blood stained the white of his boxers and matted the hair on his thigh. It pooled on the plastic tarp and made the room smell of death. If only his hands were smaller....

Roman took a shaky, fearful breath at the thought. *If he were smaller.*

He could shift. He was pretty sure he'd be able to slip the ropes in dog form, or at least get his hands and feet free. But the idea of shifting with the bullet wound in his shoulder was horrifying. Shifting was already painful enough, bones breaking and reforming, muscles strained and stretched. He could seriously damage his body—both bodies—shifting form with a wound like this. And what if the men came into the room while he was in the middle of it? They'd certainly know about the quickened then.

He wished so hard that someone was there to tell him what to do—to give him an order. He would die if they told him to, or shift and risk it all if they said that was the right thing. If someone told him to do it, it wouldn't be his fault if he was caught. But there was no one. No James or Lance or even Matt. He had to make this decision himself.

If he stayed like this, they would definitely kill him. And they might get his secrets from him before he died—or from his body after death. If he shifted, he at least had a chance to get away.

There was a window to his left, hidden behind the old blinds. If he shifted and got out of his ropes, maybe he could escape out the window?

The pain from fighting with his ropes had faded a little. His shoulder was throbbing, but the pain was manageable if he didn't move at all.

He didn't know who to pray to, so he thought of James. *You can do it, Roman. I know you can!* This time, it wouldn't be a can of sardines that was his reward if he succeeded. He could maybe save his friends. And Matt—he might spend the day with Matt again, in the woods, with Matt's easy presence and humor. He wanted that more than anything.

Roman started to shift. The pain was white lightning. His shattered bones ground against muscle. He couldn't bear it—but he did. He gritted his teeth and fixed his tongue against the roof of his mouth to keep in the scream.

*                    *                    *

Roman became conscious slowly, floating on a black and red sea of agony. He blinked open his eyes. He was on the plastic sheeting on the floor. Red blood, most of it dried, was all around him like he'd fallen asleep in a butcher shop. He blinked and tried to focus on the white wall. His throat was dry to cracking, and his lips, his lips... weren't there. Instead he found sharp canine teeth and a long snout.

*Thank God. Thank God.* The shift had worked.

The memory of his mission came rushing back to him on a wave of fear and adrenaline. He wasn't out of trouble yet. Cautiously, he tried to raise himself up to sit on his haunches. Everything in his body hurt, including his stomach, lungs, and head, but his right shoulder—that was a no-go. He whined in pain and shifted his weight to his left haunch and paw. He panted and blinked, his left paw trembling on the floor.

He was still in the white room. The chair lay on its side with the ropes around and over it. He was still alone. No one had come in. Perhaps they were upstairs watching TV. Perhaps Red-hair was letting him stew in his pain, like he'd promised, 'softening him up'.

*Good so far. Must get out.*

He managed to get to all four feet and limp heavily over to the window, but he was shaky and so very weak. He got his good front paw up on the windowsill and nudged aside the blinds with his nose. His paws left red on the paint as he looked the situation over.

His reflection in the glass was frightening. There was blood all over his fur and his tongue hung out limp and pale. The window was a double-paned slider, and it didn't budge under the pressure of his nose. Aluminum latches locked the window at two places. They'd be a simple matter for his hands to pull them open. He couldn't manage it as a dog.

He slid back to the floor and hung his head, panting into the plastic sheeting on the floor. Could he shift again? He was pretty sure he couldn't. Even if he could bear the pain, he'd probably lose consciousness quickly and the shift would fail.

He heard footsteps outside the door, shuffling on the carpet. With nowhere else to hide, Roman limped over to the wall behind the door.

The door opened. The big man walked in. His hand still on the doorknob, he blinked at the chair and ropes. "What the *fucking hell*?"

Fury trickled through Roman's veins like venom. Summoning every last bit of strength, he launched himself around to door and straight at the man's throat. His jaws closed around it with a satisfying force.

The man thrashed and went down, Roman on top of him. Roman knew if he kept pressure on the man's throat, he would pass out. He'd rather not kill the man. He'd been trained to do it in the Army, on dummies, but he'd never had to do it for real. But it took time for a man to pass out from lack of oxygen, and Roman's strength was waning fast. He felt the man's hand moving at his side, felt him draw his gun.

Roman had no choice. He couldn't allow himself to be shot and risk giving away the town's secrets. He bit down hard and shook his head. The heavy taste of blood filled his mouth.

The man's hand, still holding the gun, shuddered and skittered but didn't point at Roman. He went slack. His eyes were stunned and already lit by the fires of hell as Roman left him on the floor and limped out the door.

The hallway was quiet. From upstairs came the sound of the TV. Roman moved slowly, favoring his hurt shoulder as much as he could. The hall opened into an empty room with linoleum floor, a bar counter, and big double doors out to the lake. One of the doors was slid open to a screen, letting in the night air.

Roman limped to the screen door, trailing blood. The flimsy thing opened under the pressure of his nose, then paw. Without a look back, he slipped out into the night.

He was bleeding so much, a blind grandmother would be able to follow his trail. So he dragged himself to the lake and walked through the water, going in up to his shoulder in hopes the cold water might help stop the bleeding. He traveled around the lake a short distance to hide his trail, trying to think.

He was too weak to shift back, so his truck was useless. There was no point trying to make it home on foot. There was no one there to help him and he'd die. Town was too far away, and

Lance and Tim lived up a long steep climb on the opposite side of that.

Matt. Matt's cabin wasn't too far from here. A mile? Two? Two maybe, if he cut through the woods. Matt didn't know he was a dog, but Roman didn't care. Matt would help.

Roman left the lake and slunk into the woods.

# 12

## Stranger At The Door

Matt was asleep when someone turned on the light. He startled awake, saw Luci standing in her red flannel pajamas in the doorway of his room, and flopped back down, covering his head with a pillow.

"Eeehh." He moaned in protest and headed back to sleep.

"Matt! Get up! There's something at the door!" Luci sounded frightened.

Reluctantly, Matt uncovered his head. "Whaddya mean?"

"Something's scratching at the door and… and… making sounds! Matt!"

"Prob'ly raccoon," Matt muttered, shutting his eyes.

"It's not a raccoon! Matt, it's hurt. I can hear it. Matt!"

The idea of whatever it was being hurt was enough to rouse Matt. If a wounded animal had wandered onto the cabin's property, he supposed he should look into it. He didn't want it to suffer.

"Fine," he complained, sitting up and shaking his head to wake up.

He stood up and shuffled toward the door. He liked to sleep in his boxers and a T-shirt. The nights were chilly in the mountains.

"Put on shoes and jeans," Luci scolded. "It might try to bite you."

Matt glared at her. "Great. You know, you could look into this yourself."

"Seriously? I live with a marine. Why would I do it myself?"

She had a point, even if Matt was an ex-marine. She had a point about the clothes too. He didn't want to end up in the ER with a bite wound on his tender bits. He pulled on some jeans, added a sweatshirt from a drawer, and stuffed his feet into his running shoes. She watched him from the doorway. As soon as she saw he was dressed, she slipped away down the hall. He followed.

In the cabin's living room, the depth of the night felt strange. The lamp light Luci had turned on was too yellow and too insubstantial against the gloom. Luci paused by the front door and held up her finger to her lips. *Listen.*

Matt listened. He didn't hear anything.

Luci spoke up. "Hello? Is something out there?"

Immediately there was a response—a scratching at the bottom of the door, a pained whine, then a barely there bark. It sounded like a dog.

The cabin door didn't have a window. Matt peeked out the one in the living room, but saw no car or other signs that people were around. Of course, that didn't mean they weren't. He couldn't see much of the front stoop from here.

The whine came again. It was a heartbreaking sound. *Fuck it.*

Matt cracked open the front door, still on its safety chain, and looked out. The sight that greeted him slammed him in the gut. He forgot all about taking precautions. He ripped the safety chain off and opened the door wide.

On the doorstep was a large German shepherd. It lay on its side on the rough boards of the porch. It was badly wounded and looked half dead. Its fur was matted with blood from its head and throat down its chest to its paws. Golden eyes stared at him pleadingly as it panted. He dropped to his knees.

"Oh, no! Oh, poor baby!" Luci cried out behind him.

Matt tried to find the source of the bleeding. At first he thought the dog's throat had been cut. But no, the wound was in his shoulder. "Someone shot him," Matt said, horrified and very angry.

"Why would someone do that?" Luci was in tears.

"I don't know. We need to get him to a vet. Go get a blanket. I'll take him in the car."

"I'll change too," Luci agreed fervently.

"There's no time! I can drive him myself."

"No, Mattie! Someone should be in the back with him! What if he's dying? Poor thing!"

Matt grunted. "Hurry then. I'll get the blanket and put him in the car."

227

As quickly as he could, Matt grabbed his wallet and keys and an old comforter from the closet. It would be ruined, but he didn't care. He took it out to the porch where the dog hadn't moved.

"I'm trying to help you, okay?" Matt lowered the comforter onto the dog and tried to get his arms under him to pick him up without hurting him too badly.

The dog gave a yelp of pain as Matt's arm slid under his chest, but made no more sounds as Matt carefully raised him up and cradled the dog and blanket against his body. He looked down into the dog's eyes. They were fixed on him and in pain, but they were trusting. They were fathomless, eternal eyes. The dog licked Matt's chin and Matt's heart clenched.

"You know I'm trying to help, don't you? Gonna get you to the vet. Hang on."

He reached his Cherokee and opened up the back door with one hand. He hesitated to lay the dog in the backseat, to let him go. The dog lay heavily against him as if Matt's presence offered comfort. Matt put his foot up on the footwell, helping to secure the dog's weight on his knee. The dog gazed up at him. Where the hell was Luci?

228

The German shepherd was larger than Matt had thought and quite heavy. He'd been healthy recently, in his prime, but now his body was limp other than the trembles that ran through him every few minutes.

Matt had grown up with dogs. The General loved them. Matt couldn't remember a time when he'd seen his father sit in his chair and there hadn't been a dog at his feet. His dad liked big dogs, like this one. They'd had a German shepherd when Matt was small, and then a Doberman and, later, a black retriever that had retired from K-9 and was adopted by the General. They had all been great dogs, and Matt loved each one of them. They might have been his father's dogs, technically, but when his father wasn't around, they slept on Matt's bed and were his very best friends.

Dogs were so accepting and loyal. It made Matt sick that anyone could abuse one like this.

*Only a coward hurts an animal, a child, or a woman, Matthew. Don't ever be that kind of coward.*

"Ready!" Luci ran out of the cabin. The door slammed shut behind her. "I'm here! Let's go!"

It was the momentum Matt needed. He carefully lay the dog on the backseat. Luci scrambled in the door on the other side.

"Can you hang on to him while I drive? Made sure he doesn't fall off the seat?"

"I will! I will! Just go!"

All the way into town, Luci talked to the dog—silly, loving nonsense. And every mile or so, Matt had to ask, "Is he still breathing?"

"He is, *cariño*. He's alive."

*        *        *

Roman opened his eyes to a very bright light. He felt fuzzy and floaty. He closed his eyes again.

"He's awake!" That was Tim's voice.

Roman peeled his eyes back open. Tim's anxious face hovered over him and then Lance's.

"Let me see him." That was Matt's voice. Tim stepped back and Matt was there. He had a soft smile. "Hey, there, pup."

Next to Matt, Lance rolled his eyes. His dark brow furrowed and his jaw clenched as he looked at Roman. "What happened?"

"I told you," said Matt. "He just appeared on my porch."

Roman knew Lance had been asking him, but he couldn't exactly answer. Funny Lance. His eyes started to drift closed.

"The surgery went well, so he's in no immediate danger, but he'll need three to four weeks of complete rest." That sounded like Bill McGurver. "Excuse me, please."

The doctor pushed in, and Matt and Lance stepped back. Roman opened his eyes to see Bill checking the pulse in his left front paw. He had an IV line inserted, Roman noticed, the hair there shaved away.

Bill saw him looking at it. He petted Roman's neck reassuringly. "That's just fluid we're giving you right now, but you had to have a blood transfusion earlier. You almost died. It's a good thing Matt and Luci got you here when they did."

"If Luci hadn't woken me up, I might have slept through his scratch on the door," Matt admitted with a vocal shudder from somewhere behind Bill.

Bill nodded. "Both of you saved his life."

"Who shot him? That's what I want to know." Lance sounded furious.

"We didn't see or hear a car," Matt said. "I think he must have come through the woods. Or possibly someone dumped him out on the road near us."

"Can't Charlie track his scent? Find out where it happened?" Tim asked.

"Charlie?" Matt sounded confused.

"Charlie, um, works with sniffer dogs sometimes," said Lance. "Good idea, babe. I'll call him now. Excuse me."

There was the sound of a door as Lance stepped out. Roman was taking all of this in with a sense of unreality, lying on an exam table in Bill McGurver's clinic. His body was so heavy there was no way he wanted to move it, and his chest and shoulder dully throbbed despite all the meds. Bill's hand was still on his neck. He licked Bill's wrist.

Bill smiled at him a little and winked. "You're welcome," he said quietly. He stepped away, and Matt and Tim immediately refilled the space, hovering over Roman. Tim held his paw, stroking it with his thumb while Matt stroked his head.

Roman closed his eyes, overwhelmed with gratitude. It filled his heart so full it was a tight, heavy bubble. He was lucky to have such good friends. So lucky.

"As I said," Bill went on. "He'll need complete bed rest for three to four weeks. And by that I mean, he's not to move other than to be helped to the bathroom a few times a day."

The door opened. "He'll stay with us," Lance said firmly as he came back in. He peered at Roman over Tim's shoulder.

"He should stay with me," Matt said, equally insistent. "We found him. He came to our door. I'm not abandoning him now."

"You're not abandoning him if he comes home with us. He'll be in good hands."

"But you work all hours, Sheriff Beaufort!" Matt insisted.

"So do you, Mr. Barclay!" Lance snapped back. "Anyway, Tim is home most of the time."

"Luci is home *all* the time!"

Roman huffed out a sigh and closed his eyes. They were so ridiculous.

"Oh, yes, thank you. I'm such a pathetic wallflower," Luci grumbled.

"Well you are studying at home! I mean—" Matt floundered.

"No, I want to take him too. No one will take better care of Paco than us," Luci said with passion.

Roman raised an eyelid to stare at her. *Paco*?

"No, no, no," Lance said. "Look, I appreciate that you are worried about Ro—the dog, but you can't—"

"Paco," Luci interrupted.

Lance sighed. "*Paco*. But believe me when I tell you, honestly, you don't know what he needs. He needs to be with his own people."

"What does that mean?" Luci sounded insulted.

"Yeah, what does that mean, Lance?" Tim asked, his voice ironic.

Lance growled in frustration. "Bill, tell them! The dog needs to be with us!"

"Well, I think—" Bill started.

"I think we should ask him. Paco. Let's ask Paco what he wants to do." Tim's face swam closer to Roman, a smile on his lips. "Am I right, buddy? You should decide where you want to recoup."

"Tim..." Lance began in a warning voice.

"Nope, this'll work. Watch." Tim pulled Lance's hand in to rest on the edge of the exam table and then Matt's so they were side by side only inches from Roman's paw.

"Okay, Paco. Where would you like to spend your recovery? At our house, where I'll take extra special care of you—"

"And me," said Lance.

"And Lance, when he's not out scouring every inch of bare earth for the people who did this. Or at Matt and Luci's?"

"I'll be with you all day, baby," Luci cooed. She reached in to pet Roman's head. He was starting to feel like a lucky Buddha statue or something with all the rubbing. Not that he really minded. The touches were almost as nice as the drugs.

Roman knew who he should pick, what Lance, his boss, would want him to do. But he was tired and floaty, and he just didn't care. He lifted his heavy paw and put it on Matt's hand.

"Ooo-kay then." Tim raised his eyebrows at Roman suggestively.

Roman closed his eyes so he wouldn't have to see Lance glaring at him. It was all right to be a coward when you had just gotten out of surgery for a bullet wound, he decided. That was the definition of the term 'free pass'.

"But—!" Lance complained.

"Nope, it's his call," said Tim. "It'll be fine, Lance. He's just going to rest and... and stay down. We can visit him often. Right, Luci?"

"Of course!"

"I'll be by to check on him every day, at least at first," said Bill.

Matt's hand was on Roman's jaw. He recognized the smell of him. He didn't open his eyes, but he licked it once. *Thank you.*

"I'll take care of him when I'm home," Matt said, his voice soft. "And he can sleep in my bed at night, in case he gets into distress. That way I can hear him."

"I think that's a super idea," Tim said, too enthusiastically. "Night is the most dangerous time when you're recovering from surgery."

"Right!" That was Bill, slightly amused. "Now can all of you people please go into the waiting room? I need to...

examine… Paco again before we can release him, and I think he'd appreciate a few minutes of quiet time."

They all filed out. Roman could sense he was alone with Bill, and he opened his eyes. They felt like they were made of lead—lead backed by sandpaper. He had to go to sleep.

Bill leaned over him and sighed. He gently rubbed Roman's back. "Okay, listen, Roman. I don't know what happened, but I know you shifted after you were shot. You're very, very lucky it didn't kill you."

Bill looked grave. Roman whined. He'd known that, but he hadn't had a choice.

"So we're not going to repeat that mistake, are we? You're not to shift for the foreseeable future, not until those bones in your shoulder are healed. Got it?"

Roman panted.

"I don't want you to even attempt it until I've said it's all right. And don't you go letting Lance browbeat you into it. Whatever you have to say, it's just going to have to wait."

As if on cue, Lance slipped in the door. Bill didn't look surprised. "Were you standing just outside? If you heard me tell Roman he's not to shift, I meant it. With luck and therapy, he'll be able to use his right arm again. But if he shifts again while he's torn up, he might as well just write it off." Bill huffed. "No pun intended."

Lance grumbled, but he didn't argue. He leaned in to look in Roman's eyes. Lance's blue eyes burned with anger. He spoke quietly.

"You do what Bill says, got that, Roman? You need to rest. Now if Charlie follows your scent from Matt's place, will he find who shot you?"

Roman pawed the air once with his left front paw. *Yes.* His trail would lead Charlie to the rental cabin on Piney Top Drive and his truck, if the criminals hadn't already moved it. He wanted to tell Lance the men were dangerous—very dangerous. He wanted to tell him the red-haired man had asked about the law enforcement in town. He wanted to tell him about the big man with the gun, the one he'd had to kill in order to escape and protect their secret. He wanted to say he was sorry. But he couldn't say anything.

239

Lance frowned, narrowing his eyes in thought. "Does it have anything to do with those two men we were looking for yesterday?"

Roman pawed the air again once, *Yes*. Then he whined. *Be careful.*

"Okay, look, I appreciate that this is important, Lance, but he seriously needs to sleep."

Lance nodded. "Okay, doc." Unexpectedly he leaned forward and kissed Roman's brow. "I'm glad you're going to be all right. We need you, Roman. Get better, and don't you worry about anything. I've got your back."

With a suspiciously wet sniff, Lance left the room.

Bill smiled down at him. "Sleep, Roman."

With a grateful sigh, Roman did.

# 13

## Going To Ground

Rufie flipped out when they found T's body. "That Roman guy fucking bit him in the throat! How'd he get out of those ropes? And how'd he get the jump on someone like T?" Rufie flapped his hands in the air, his eyes bulging.

Colin knelt by T's body, trying to get a look at the wound, but it was a bloody mess. A chunk of it had been ripped out by nails or teeth or something. "Well, he didn't have a fucking weapon on him, did he? We took his gun."

"So he just, what? Used his teeth? How come T didn't shoot him?"

"Maybe he did. For all we know Roman has a couple more bullets in him now. T's got a silencer, so we wouldn't have heard it upstairs. Just shut the fuck up for a minute, would you?"

Colin looked at all the blood. There were big pools of it around the chair—no doubt from the shot he'd put in the deputy's shoulder. And it seemed like there were gallons of it around T.

Colin followed a trail of blood down the hall to the sliding glass doors that went out to the deck. There was no sign of a body.

"Colin, we need to get out of here! We need to pack our shit and go!"

"Shut up! I'm thinking."

He tended to get calm in emergencies, slow and wary and dangerous. That's what a real villain did. He peered into the darkness outside. "First things first—you're going to go get the deputy's truck. T said it was parked down by one of the other cabins. I've got the keys."

"But what if he's down there waiting, Colin? Huh?" Rufie had timidity down to a fine art.

"Why the fuck would he do that? If he made it to his truck, he'd use the radio or maybe drive it off if he had an extra key stashed somewhere. So that's the first thing we need to check—*is his truck there*. Ergo, you go get the truck. If you don't see any sign of him, drive it back here and put it in the garage. I'll move the Caddy out of the way."

Rufie was still nervous. He glanced back down the hall toward T's body.

"Fuck sake, Rufie, the guy's got at least one bullet in him, probably more. Look at all this blood! I bet he's somewhere unconscious. Take T's gun and go get the fucking truck and hurry your ass up about it!" Colin took Roman's keys out of his pocket and tossed them to Rufie.

"Okay, okay." Rufie went down the hall to get T's gun and then silently went upstairs.

He drove the Sheriff's Department truck over, and they put it in the garage. The garage light was bright, and Colin was able to look the truck over real good. There was no blood in it. The deputy, Roman, had not been back to the truck since they'd caught him. Colin was sure of that at least.

He let out a sigh of relief, crawling back out of the truck's front seat. "Right. He didn't make it back to his truck to use the radio, so probably he's out there passed out or dead. That means no one else knows he was here."

"What if he went to one of the other cabins, huh? Asked to use a phone?"

"If he'd done that, dipshit, we'd be hip deep in cops by now, or at least an ambulance."

"I still think we should get out of here," Rufie grumbled, rubbing his arms with his hands like he was cold. "That guy, Roman, he's fucking insane. He got out of the ropes and past T and everything."

"You're such a pussy! I'm not running away unless there's a damned good reason to. Now go get some flashlights from the storage truck. We'll go out and see if we can find the fucker's body."

They didn't find a body, not around the house, not at the lake, and not in the woods. Colin thought he saw blood in the flashlight's beams. But there wasn't a solid trail, and he wasn't going to spend hours thrashing around with branches in the dark. Besides, the woods at night were stinking creepy.

"Okay, fuck this," Colin said. "Let's leave it 'til tomorrow."

"But we have to make sure he's dead!"

"No, we have to clean up the fucking house of all that blood and dump T's body. You want to keep crawling around here in the dark alone, be my guest."

Of course, Rufie didn't stay outside in the dark alone. They pulled up all the bloody plastic in the house, rolled T's body in a tarp, stashed it in the storage truck, and cleaned everything with bleach. Then they drove the deputy's truck down to the end of the hill and rolled it into a ditch. They stashed their storage truck off a fire road just in case anyone came to the cabin. The truck was full of shit for the farm, and it was incriminating as hell, even without T's body. By the time dawn came, there was nothing illegal on the rental property, and Colin's fear and adrenaline crashed. At this point, without Roman himself as an eyewitness, nobody could pin anything on him.

Now Rufie was asleep on the couch, fully clothed and snoring. Colin watched out the window as dawn lit up the mountain scenery. The fucking country, man. It was just plain wrong for anyplace to be so dark at night.

Colin's eyes scanned the brightening gloom, then he went to the front of the cabin to check that side. He didn't see anything—no body, no obvious signs of disturbance, no cops. He tensed at the front window, his ears perked for sirens. There were only two possibilities as he saw it: Either Roman had made it far enough to get picked up and rescued and he'd blabbed, in which case the cops should already be here. Or, he was lying out there dead or dying, in which case he wasn't saying shit to nobody.

But other than a flock of geese that landed on the pond, a fat raccoon that crossed the yard, and a rangy hound dog that was sniffing around, the dawn was quiet.

By then, Colin knew for certain he wasn't going to run. He wanted this. He needed this fresh start more than he'd even realized, and Mad Creek was the place to do it. Now that Deputy Roman Charsguard was out of the picture, problem solved, right? There might still be a few cops left in town, but they probably weren't anywhere near as persistent as Roman had been. Colin "Kingpin" Clery wasn't gonna run away from shadows. He would, however, call L.A. later in the day and replace T with two more wet men he could trust, real ballbreakers. And Rufie had been asking for some more labor for the farm too. Run away? No, Colin Fucking Clery was *expanding*.

Colin left Rufie asleep on the couch and went to his room to crash.

\*                    \*                    \*

Lance and Charlie stood in the woods near the small lake on Piney Top Drive. Lance watched the large cabin with binoculars while Charlie, now human again, thrummed with eager interest beside him.

It was the evening after Roman had been shot, and the lights were on in the cabin. Through the binoculars, Lance could see a skinny dark-haired man sitting at the kitchen table. He had a beer in one hand and a cigarette in the other. His head was back in a slouched pose. Food containers from *Lucky Dog Chinese* on Main Street littered the table. A red-haired man was pacing in the kitchen, talking animatedly on a cell phone.

"You're sure those two are the men we smelled on the trail today?" Lance asked quietly.

"Yes, boss!" Charlie said, annoyed. "Come on, there's only two of them. We can take 'em!"

Charlie was still caught up in a scent-lust, ready to attack his quarry. Lance made a downward motion with his free hand— *calm down*—and didn't bother to voice a reply.

Before dawn this morning, Charlie had tracked Roman's blood trail through the woods to the small lake, Lance following behind on foot. Lance had warned Charlie not to get close to any humans, but he'd been lost in the scent, and he'd left the woods and followed his nose to the large cabin, to a sliding glass back door. Lance had had to wait in the trees, gun drawn and cursing. Fortunately, either the men in the cabin had been asleep, or they hadn't been alarmed by the sight of a bloodhound, because Charlie ran back into the woods without incident.

That had been only this morning, unbelievably. It had been a very long day.

Lance knew Roman had been shot in that cabin—while in human form—and had escaped it as a wounded dog and made his way to Matt's place. Lance couldn't imagine the courage that took—the pain and terror of shifting when so badly wounded. Bill was right. It should have killed him.

But Roman's sheer bravery aside, Lance had been left with many questions. Why had Roman been shot? Who was in that cabin? Had they seen Roman shift? *Did they know about the quickened now?*

And soon as Matt had gotten into the office, Lance cornered him by the front door. "How's, um, Paco?"

"He's all right," Matt said, looking tired. "He's resting. Luci's going to be with him all day. She'll text me if anything changes."

Lance nodded. "I need you to take Charlie and me to the places where you and Roman found those broken fishing lines yesterday."

Matt's eyes narrowed in confusion, but he slowly nodded. "Sure. If you want. What about Roman? Is he coming?" Matt looked over Lance's shoulder as if hoping to see him.

"Roman called in sick," piped Charlie. He was lingering near Leesa's desk.

"He did?" asked Leesa worriedly. "Oh my gosh! What's the matter with him?"

Lance glared at Charlie. "*No*, Roman did not call in sick." He sighed and turned to Matt. "Roman had a family thing come up. He's going to be out of the office for a few weeks."

"Family? He told me he didn't have any family."

"Well, maybe it's distant family." Lance scratched his jaw awkwardly, hoping Matt would buy the lie. He clearly knew

249

more about Roman than Lance had hoped. "Anyway, he had plenty of vacation time accrued, so I guess it's his business how he wants to use it."

Matt didn't look happy. His brow furrowed.

"Can you show us right now?" Lance prompted.

Matt nodded, and the three of them left the station.

It had taken a while for Charlie to find the strangers' scents out in the woods. Another day had passed since Roman had smelled them, and there were Roman and Matt's scents to filter out too. Lance kept Matt busy chatting while Charlie sniffed around, but Matt still caught Charlie a few times—once sniffing the bark of a tree at its base and another time on all fours, sniffing at the road.

"Doesn't Charlie need a dog for that? I thought you said he had a sniffer dog?"

Lance had groaned inwardly. This whole situation was challenging enough without having to string Matt Barclay along at the same time.

He'd pretended to be embarrassed and spoke low. "It's a bit of an idiosyncrasy. Charlie says he can tell if it would be worthwhile to bring the dogs out or not."

Matt had said nothing, but his mouth had pursed suspiciously. As long as he had no proof, Lance figured, what could he really do about it?

Now it was nearing eleven that night, and he and Charlie were back watching the cabin from the woods. The men were still inside it.

"Definitely," Charlie said with furor. "The men in that cabin are the same ones that broke those lines Roman put up. There's no doubt. That's the vehicle they were using too." He pointed to the expensive white Cadillac SUV in the driveway.

"So somehow," Lance said, lowering the binoculars, "Roman figured out where they were staying and was here looking around last night. Only they caught him." *Shot him.* Anger burned in his chest and gut. He'd never been so angry in his life. How dare strangers come into *his* territory and try to murder *his* people!

251

"There's only two of them," Charlie repeated. "And we have guns! Maybe if I went up to the door like I was just checkin' out the neighborhood, and you went around the back—"

"No."

"But they shot Roman!" Charlie wasn't Roman's biggest fan, ordinarily. He was a bit jealous of him, truth be told. Roman was a newer deputy, but he was smarter and more capable, and Charlie knew it. But pack was pack and Lance understood Charlie's outrage.

"We don't have a body or any proof of what they did," Lance explained with a shake of his head. "All we have is Roman, and he can't testify until he can shift back, and that's gonna be weeks, Bill said."

"We could just, you know, kill 'em." They were bold words, but Charlie's voice was unsure.

"No, we're not going to do some gangland-style execution." Lance huffed. "Christ, Charlie, we're the law, not vigilantes. Besides, we don't know how much they know, or what they're up to. Not for sure. We don't even know exactly what happened. Roman can't talk."

Charlie rubbed his very large nose with one hand. "So whaddya wanna do, Boss?"

"We're going to keep an eye on them, that's what. Call in Jake, Bowser, and Gus. I want a man watching these guys 24/7."

"Me too! I want to watch them too."

"Yes, you too. We'll assign shifts. And when they drive, we'll need an unmarked car to follow them. That'll be you, Charlie. You can trade trucks with Tim for a few days. The sheriff's truck would be too obvious."

Lance suddenly felt very keenly the loss of Roman. Roman had become his go-to guy. He'd have been able to trust Roman completely to handle an operation like this one without any direction at all. But Roman was down, purposefully and almost fatally hurt by those men in that cabin. Lance bared his teeth and took one last look through the binoculars, memorizing the sight of the two men.

He was sure of one thing: They'd never get out of Sherriff Lance Beaufort's territory, not without paying for what they'd done.

## 14

### How Do You Mend A Broken Heart?

Roman only realized how badly he'd been hurt by how long it took him to recover. The first few days at Matt's cabin were a blur. His body hurt so much he escaped into sleep and the painkillers Bill McGurver had prescribed.

He was aware of Luci stroking his fur while he lay on the couch next to her. The trips out to go pee slowly got less painful. Bill visited and so did Lance and Tim. But the person he craved, the one whose touch seemed to provide a medicine of its own, was Matt. He came home every day before dark and he spent all evening and all night with Roman next to him or draped over him in one position or another.

Logically, Roman knew Matt wasn't James, but he was stuck in dog form, and he was hurting. His dog reverted to pure instinct, and his instinct was to want Matt. Matt was big and male and tough. He had a strength Roman could count on when weak, and a tenderness that seemed all the more special because of that strength. This was a side of Matt that Roman, the human, had never seen. The moment Matt walked through the door, he greeted Roman first, looking him over to see how he was doing, stroking his fur, kissing his head, and telling him how well he was doing. He held Roman's head on his lap while he watched TV. He took Roman outside for a pee and then lifted him up onto the bed to sleep.

At night, Roman slept on top of the covers with his back pressed close to Matt's body. In the hazy dreams of dog, man, and drugs, sometimes Roman thought he was in his human form in Matt's bed, that they were as comfortable and bound together as an old mated couple. And sometimes he dreamed of him and Matt out on the trails, and of guns and shouted warnings. And when he whined in his sleep, Matt would pet him until his dreams withdrew their fangs.

After the first few days, Roman was able to hobble around, despite his tightly bandaged shoulder. That meant he could sit on the floor next to the dining room table while Matt and Luci ate.

"You are so spoiling that dog," Luci told Matt in a teasing voice at the end of that first week. Matt guiltily drew back his fingers from having just fed Roman a bit of chicken.

"Yeah. My dad would have a fit. The General had very strict rules about dogs and table food." He smirked at Roman. "But we don't have to follow the General's rules here, do we, Paco?" He tore off another piece of chicken, and Roman took it carefully from his hand.

"You'll never get that dog out of your bed once he's well. You know that, right?" Luci said, without any rancor.

"It's not like I have anyone else who's clamoring to get in it. Besides, he needs some extra special TLC after what he's been through. Don't you, boy?"

Roman wasn't about to argue.

By week two of his recovery, Roman started refusing the pain meds. His body still hurt, but it wasn't the glass sharp, grating pain of damage, and Roman preferred a clear head. While Matt was gone during the day, he and Luci were cuddled inside, warm and dry from the fall rain.

And as his head cleared, Roman started to worry about what he was missing. What was going on with the men who had shot him? Had Charlie and Lance found them? Was Matt staying safe? Was Lance making sure no one else got hurt? Were the strangers still in town? What were they doing there? But there was nothing he could do to help until he could shift back. He had to get better.

When Matt was home, Roman spent less time worrying about the strangers, and more time contemplating his own future. It was so strange. The feeling of Matt scratching his ears or squeezing his paw while Roman snoozed was so familiar. It was like the entire last few years had been a dream, the dream of a sleeping dog—that he'd become a man, and moved to this odd little town in the mountains, and become a sheriff's deputy. With his head on Matt's lap and his eyes closed, he could almost believe he was still with James.

But that feeling faded, along with the satisfaction of being coddled as a dog. Because Matt wasn't James, and Roman was no longer a dog. Matt was Deputy Roman Charsguard's friend and coworker. He'd joked with Roman and made him smile. He'd treated Roman as an equal and, more than that, had liked him and wanted him as a sex partner. The longer Roman was with Matt, the more he wanted to be with him, not in his dog form, but as himself. He longed to have this—to be in Matt's home and in his bed—in his human form.

257

He'd bonded with Matt Barclay, he realized during one long and sleepless night. He loved Matt and didn't want to be separated from him once he'd gotten better.

And that was a serious problem.

\*           \*           \*

Matt studied the words on his monitor. He was alone in his office with the door closed, and he was trying to work on his weekly report. Every few minutes, as if he were one of those cartoon cat clocks, his eyes would shift over to Roman's desk. The chair was pushed in and the computer was dark and silent. Where the fuck was Roman?

Matt made himself focus on the task at hand.

He had an actual operation going in his territory. It had gotten very real lately. Nominally, he was in charge of said operation, though he had the gut feeling Sheriff Beaufort humored him about that. It wasn't that Beaufort wasn't cooperating. He was cooperating all too well. Half the time when Matt went to do something, he'd learn that Beaufort had already done it.

Matt shifted in his chair and typed some more.

*Suspects have cleared approximately three more acres of trees, giving them a total area of about five acres. The farm is set in about a quarter mile from the nearest dirt road. They used small bulldozers to knock down trees and rake up brush. They have camouflage tarps to hide the damage from overhead. So far no planting has taken place.*

*Six unique individuals have been seen and photographed with remote surveillance. Five are pending identification, but one has been verified as Rufus Weaser, an ex-con incarcerated for raising and selling marijuana and opium. I'm currently looking into Weaser's known associates.*

*Sending GPS coordinates of the farm for satellite imaging.*

*Regarding unusual activity in the town of Mad Creek, nothing new to report.*

Matt's fingers drummed on the desk as he looked at the last line. The weirdness in Mad Creek hadn't ceased. The other day he'd been driving back to the office late and had seen what looked like a fight going on in the town park. He'd stopped his car and run over there. It turned out it was just two guys wrestling around. For fun. Two full-grown, adult men, were wrestling and chasing each other in the park. When he'd asked them what the hell they were doing, they looked at him like *he* was the one who was crazy. But, as usual, there was nothing *actually* illegal going on, and he'd just sound bonkers if he reported it.

Besides, he had bigger fish to fry now. And his biggest worry was something that *wasn't* in town—Roman.

Matt uploaded the report to the secure portal. Dixon, at the Operation Green Ghost headquarters, was probably waiting for it before he went home for the day. Matt's was not the only active territory now. Hell, Samuelson over in Mariposa busted a twenty-acre farm the week before that had been hidden for several years. And a drug lord with a rap sheet a mile long had recently moved to Oakhurst. By comparison, the neophyte farm in Mad Creek was small potatoes. All Matt had to do was keep tabs on them without tipping them off, document and photograph what was going on, and give them enough rope to hang themselves when the DEA came in and busted them.

He was intent on the task, because he really wanted to bust these guys. And he could tell the sheriff did too. But it wasn't the only thing on his mind. What Matt really wanted to write in his report was this: "I'm very concerned about Deputy Roman Charsguard." But Matt had no proof whatsoever that there was any foul play involved. Beaufort kept insisting Roman was out of town and perfectly fine. Matt had driven out to Roman's cabin a few times. There was no truck in the driveway and no signs of a disturbance.

It'd been two weeks since Roman Charsguard had vanished. And, a bad omen for his budding investigative skills, he'd gotten exactly nowhere asking Sheriff Beaufort about it.

Matt shut off his machine and left the sheriff's station. He found himself smiling as he drove home. Paco would be waiting for him at the door. No one had ever been as happy to see Matt as that damned dog. And honestly, without a friend left in town except Luci, Matt felt the same way.

That evening, Luci made polenta and spicy beans, and they settled down to eat at the little kitchen table.

"I went to the market today to get groceries, you know?" Luci said, licking sauce off her spoon. "You should have seen it, Mattie. Everybody and his mother asked me about Paco."

"What?"

Luci nodded. "'How is Paco doing?', 'Is he walking?', 'Are you giving him chicken? Try fish because Paco will really like fish. Here, let me help you pick some out.' I swear, Matt. You would have laughed so hard."

"How do they know about Paco?"

Luci shrugged. "I guess I mentioned it to Lily Beaufort? Last week, you know? At the coffee shop? I swear, talk about a small town! And I thought *mi familia* was bad."

"Well, they can't have him," Matt said grouchily. Honestly, first Beaufort and Tim, and now the whole damn town, was way over involved with Paco.

The dog in question was sitting quietly by Matt's chair, watching him. Matt sighed. He was such a beautiful German shepherd. Stately. He had big ears and the tan of his face gave way to dramatic black on the top of his head and on his throat. Part of his right ear was missing—a wound Dr. McGurver said had happened long before he was shot. Matt liked the frayed and scarred ear. It gave Paco a rakish air. Also, it reminded Matt of Roman, truth be told. Paco's eyes were unnervingly wise and, sometimes, unbearably sad. He was also the best-trained dog Matt had ever seen. You could swear he understood every word you said.

Hell, Matt loved that dog. He was getting to be a total sap in his old age. How his brother, Mitch, would have teased him about it.

Luci held down a chunk of polenta and Paco gently took it from her fingers. "You know, Mattie, his owner may come for him eventually. I worry about you getting so attached."

"Yeah, like you aren't. McGurver said he doesn't belong to anyone in town. Maybe he was abandoned by someone vacationing in the area."

"Maybe," Luci agreed doubtfully.

"Anyway, they weren't there when Paco needed them, so they can't have him back now. Luci—I'm not sure polenta is good for dogs."

"It's corn! It's fine."

Matt gave Paco a baked kettle chip. "This is much yummier, isn't it, Paco? You like old Matt the most, don't you?"

Luci rolled her eyes. "Thank God I'm never having kids with you! So they still haven't found out who shot him?"

"No." Matt hated that. "We've been busy with this sting we're trying to set up. And Beaufort says he thinks it was probably poachers—illegal hunters who mistook him for a deer or a bear in the woods. Says they're probably long gone by now." Matt wasn't satisfied with that answer, but he couldn't exactly tell Beaufort how to run his office.

Matt pushed his plate aside and shifted back in his chair. Paco stared at him and Matt patted his leg. Immediately, Paco laid his chin there.

His father would be impressed. Paco never begged, but damn if he couldn't let you know exactly what he wanted with those big golden-brown eyes. He was a master of nonverbal manipulation.

Matt stroked his thumb across Paco's forehead. "When you were in town today, did you hear anything about Roman Charsguard?"

Luci clucked her tongue and looked pityingly at Matt. "No, *cariño*. I didn't ask the people I saw at the store, because I don't know who knows Roman. But Lily told me at the coffee shop on Wednesday that Roman is out of town visiting family. I think, maybe, he really is."

Paco stared up at Matt steadily. "I dunno, Luce. It's been almost two weeks. And I haven't heard a word from him."

"Why would he text you, though? I mean, you're a work colleague, and he's taking vacation time…. Honestly. You worry too much."

*But he would contact me*, Matt thought. Or… maybe Roman wouldn't. Not with the way it had been between them before Roman left.

*Yes. I'm straight.*

Matt felt his face heat up and his stomach clench around the recently eaten meal. He couldn't even think about that conversation without feeling sick and embarrassed—and so fucking disappointed.

Luci read his mind. "Oh, Mattie. You need to stop mooning over that guy."

"I am not mooning! I have never mooned in my life. My mind is a moon-free zone."

Luci muttered something in Spanish, which Matt decided he didn't want to translate. She got up and started clearing the table.

"Nope, you cooked. Paco and I have this," Matt said.

Luci smiled and dusted off her hands. "No argument from me, counselor."

She came over to their side of the table, and Matt thought she was going to hug him but, no, the hug, and kiss, went to Paco. Luci skipped happily out of the room. "I'm going to take a walk! Ciao."

Matt looked down at Paco, who watched Luci go, but didn't bother to get up. "That's right. You're a daddy's boy, aren't you? You want to wash or dry?"

Paco, predictably, did neither. But he did offer moral support, lying on the kitchen rug and watching Matt do it.

Matt was definitely going to keep Paco, he decided, as he scrubbed the frying pan. Not that it hadn't been a foregone conclusion since the night Matt had picked a bleeding Paco up in the blanket. The only question was how many rounds of boxing he'd have to win with Luci to keep custody when she went back to Berkley.

He finished the dishes and squatted down next to Paco, his finger toying idly with Paco's scarred ear. "I wonder what my friend Roman will make of you when he gets back." Not that it really mattered. Matt could run a reptile farm for all the difference it would make to Roman. Work colleagues. That was all.

"I should be looking for him," Matt whispered, more to himself than to the dog. "I should make sure he's okay."

If Roman wasn't back soon, he would. He made that promise to himself and to Roman. Hell, since Paco was lying there staring at him, he made it to Paco too.

# 15

## Back On Two Legs

Roman stood by the door of the cabin until Luci let him out. It had been three weeks since his surgery. He was doing so well she'd gotten used to letting him out alone. After all, they lived back from the road and Roman had always stayed close to the cabin.

Not today. Once Luci shut the door, Roman took off down the driveway. Bill had been to visit shortly before and had declared him almost as good as new. Roman moved on four legs with some stiffness in his right shoulder, but no sharp pain.

Bill's old red truck with the hard-top back was on the shoulder of the road at the end of the driveway. He got out when Roman approached.

"You sure you're ready to do this, Roman?" He hesitated with his hand on the liftgate.

Roman barked once and stared at the truck fixedly.

Bill opened the back. "Okay." He helped Roman up. "I kind of feel sorry for Matt and Luci, you know."

Yes. Roman knew, but it couldn't be helped. Bill closed up the back of the truck and drove down the hill toward town. Roman sat on the dog bed, anxiously looking out the window.

He was chomping at the bit. He needed to get back his body, his hands, his voice. He had things he needed to do and changes he was determined to make in his life. Oddly, being a dog again had made him appreciate the opportunity he had being human.

He wasn't going to waste it.

An hour later, Deputy Roman Charsguard walked into the Mad Creek Sheriff's Office. He was showered and dressed in jeans and a hooded sweatshirt Bill had let him borrow. His shoulder ached like hell, even though Bill had made him swallow some prescription strength aspirin. But he was human again, and Bill said he hadn't damaged anything too badly in the shift, so he was damned happy. He'd made it back to his life in one piece. He was walking on two feet again and could say what he wanted and could make it happen. He was a very lucky dog.

Leesa jumped out of her chair and almost climbed over her desk before remembering to walk around it like a human would. She plastered herself against him happily and rubbed her nose against his jaw. "Roman! You're home!"

Roman felt a balloon of happiness chased by a sharp stab of regret. The sheriff's office wasn't his home for much longer.

"It's nice to see you too, Leesa." His voice sounded rough. He wasn't used to speaking.

The door to the office he shared with Matt opened, and Matt looked shocked at the sight of him. Then he grinned. "Hey! You're back!"

"I am." Roman smiled back at him. He couldn't help it if his dog lit up his face, telegraphing his feelings.

Matt blinked and his smile wobbled a bit.

Lance's door opened. "Roman? You okay?"

"Yes, sir."

"Fantastic!" Lance strode over and clasped Roman's arms. Roman winced in pain. "Oh, sorry! God, I'm so sorry. Did Bill say you're all right?"

"I'm fine." Roman's eyes shifted to Matt who was watching them with a perplexed look. "Can I speak to you alone, sir?"

"Yeah, yeah. Come on." Lance herded Roman into his office and shut the door.

"How are you really?" Lance asked as soon as they were alone.

"My shoulder is stiff and sore, but it's not that bad."

"Can you use your arm?"

Roman demonstrated, curling his bicep and flexing his fist. He could move it fine that way, but putting his elbow out to the side, which rotated his shoulder, hurt. "Bill says there shouldn't be any permanent damage. He gave me some exercises I have to do."

"Lucky son of a bitch." Lance shook his head as if he could hardly believe it. "I'm glad to have you back, Roman. You have no idea." His eyes were warm as he rubbed Roman's unhurt shoulder. "I've come to depend on you a lot."

Roman's stomach, which was already in turmoil, churned harder. God, this was bad. This hurt a lot worse than his shoulder. He went to attention, stiffening his spine. "Actually, sir, I've... I've come to put in my resignation."

Roman hated saying those words on so many levels— letting Lance down, losing a job he loved, and leaving the town less well guarded. But he'd made up his mind.

Lance's face went slack with shock. "What? Why?"

Roman swallowed and looked down at the floor, unable to speak.

Lance sat on his desk, giving Roman some space, but he vibrated with tension. "I... understand, having been hurt, that you want to avoid risky assignments, especially after your experience in the military. But what if you stay in the office, do desk work? I don't want to lose you, Roman. Tell me what you need."

"It's not that, sir." Roman took a deep breath. "I... I want to be with Matt. He liked me before, and I... want to try that. To have a mate like you have with Tim. If Matt still wants that. So I have to excuse myself from any further duty guarding him or… or spying on him. I'm sorry."

The silence in the room was painful.

"Holy shit. I did not see that one coming." Lance sounded numb.

Roman thought he might throw up. He continued to stare at the floor. "I'm sorry I let you down. You've been very good to me."

Lance audibly sighed. "Christ, Roman. Look at me. *Roman.*"

Roman forced his eyes up. Lance didn't look angry. He looked sad. He scratched at one ear in a very unhuman like gesture. "Look. I'd be a damned hypocrite for telling you not to have a relationship with a full-blooded human male, and that's a fact. Truth is, as you recall, I didn't trust Tim when he first moved to Mad Creek either." He paused, picked up a pen, and tapped it. The rhythm reminded Roman of how Lance switched his tail when he was in dog form.

Roman waited, hoping.

Lance sighed. "I've had to work more closely with Matt since you've been out. It's not that I don't like him. But Matt is a DEA officer—you know that. So it's a bit tricky. Still… I'm sorry I put you in that position. I should have known you're too honest and good-hearted not to give your friendship wholeheartedly once you got to know a decent person like Matt."

Roman's heart fluttered with joy at Lance's understanding, though he still didn't know what Lance was saying exactly. "Sir?"

"I won't ask you to do anything like that again, Roman. But please don't quit. You don't have to have anything more to do with Matt in an official capacity if you don't want to."

Roman was so relieved. He couldn't help but break his stance and take a step closer to his friend. They hug-snuffled and Lance rubbed Roman's head while Roman drank in the smell of pack. But after only a moment, it felt awkward and Roman stepped back.

He rubbed his face with one hand and went back into his military stance. "Thank you, sir."

Lance chuckled. "God's sake, Ro! As if I would ever let you resign." Lance slipped back behind his desk and sat down. His face got serious again. "Just... one thing. You know, humans 'date' and it doesn't always last. It would be best if you didn't tell Matt about us right away, not until you two have been together for a while, and you're sure he's going to stick around. Because if you expose the truth to Matt and then he freaks out and leaves, it endangers the whole town. Does that sound fair, Roman?"

Roman considered it. He didn't want to lie to Matt anymore. But being with Matt as a man was one thing. Telling Matt he was Paco? His gut told him that would be a big mistake, at least for now.

"Yes, sir," Roman agreed.

"So he doesn't already know? You're sure?"

"He has no idea."

Lance looked relieved. "And also—sorry—if you have any more questions regarding... you know... uh... sex. With humans. Human male type sex. Activity." Lance shut his eyes and grimaced. "Maybe you can ask Tim. Or my mother. Or the librarian."

"Yes, sir," Roman said seriously.

"Good. And if you get to the point where you think the two of you are serious, and you have to tell him about us, please discuss it with me first."

Roman nodded.

Lance regarded him hopefully. "So you're still my deputy?"

Roman smiled. "Deputy Roman Charsguard. That's me."

"Oh, thank God! Now fill me in. I think I know what happened the night you were shot, but I want to hear the details from you."

\*          \*          \*

Roman told Lance about the night he was captured and escaped, about the red-haired man called 'Colin' and the big one named 'Big T'.

"I think I killed that man," Roman said with a flush of shame. "I'm sorry, Lance. He had a gun, and I didn't know how

277

to avoid getting shot again without.... Will the law come after me?"

Lance set his lips in a worried line. "I haven't heard anything about a body being found. If that man is dead, I doubt his cohorts would advertise the fact. After all, they'd been in the process of kidnapping and threatening *you*. I'll keep an ear to the ground, though." His blue eyes were bright under dark, brooding brows. "As for being sorry—it was self-defense, Roman. You had no choice."

Roman knew this was true, but still. "Yes, but I didn't like to do it, sir."

"I know that. I'm sorry you had to, but they would have killed you. I'm just grateful you escaped. You did the right thing, Roman. Now tell me the rest of it."

Roman finished his story. Then Lance brought him up to speed on the current operation. The red-haired man who had shot him had been identified as Colin Clery, a man from Los Angeles with prior busts for drug possession. He seemed to be running the operation. He and his men were busy setting up a pot farm in one of the quadrants northeast of town. And Lance was letting them.

"We've gotta do this carefully, Roman. I want every single one of them busted so hard and so thoroughly that they won't see the light of day for years. I don't want them ever coming back to Mad Creek again."

Roman agreed. "Can't we arrest Clery for shooting me?"

Lance looked awkward. "Well now, that's tricky. We'd need medical records—human ones. And you'd have to explain where you've been for the past few weeks."

Roman didn't like it, but he could see Lance's point. There were no records of the human Deputy Charsguard being shot or in the hospital.

"Don't worry, Roman. We'll get them on other charges, but we *will* get them. I promise you that." Pure malice sparkled in Lance's blue eyes.

It spiked Roman's blood, making him feel equally determined. "Yes, sir. What can I do to help?"

"The most important thing is you've gotta stay out of sight. If they see you, they'll know you survived and that they've been made. As long as you're not seen, you can work with Matt on surveillance. But you'd best not come into the office until this

279

is over. We can talk on email and the phone, or even meet out at your place when we need to. Do you think you were seen coming in this morning?"

Roman thought about it. But he'd shifted at the vet's clinic at the end of the street, and he'd had to borrow some clothes. He didn't recall seeing anyone on the street as he'd walked the short distance to the sheriff's office.

"No. I don't think so."

"Good. Put that hood up before you leave. Oh, and your truck is still M.I.A., but Charlie's going incognito in Tim's truck, so you can use Charlie's for now. Just don't be seen around town in it. Leesa has the keys."


After Roman left Lance's office, he paused. The door to the office he shared with Matt was open, as if in invitation. He stepped toward it on feet that felt three sizes too big, awkward and heavy. He was so nervous about seeing Matt again. Of course, he'd just seen Matt this morning, but that was as Paco. He had a voice now, but that didn't mean he had the first idea what to say.

All that worry was for nothing. The office was empty.

Leesa came up behind him and rested her chin on Roman's arm. "He had to go home."

"He did?"

"Yup. Luci called all upset. Their puppy dog, Paco, has gone missing." Leesa gave Roman the big, sad eyes treatment. "Poor things."

By which she meant Luci and Matt, of course. Roman felt guilty.

"Before he left, Matt said to tell you that he'd be back as soon as he could."

"Oh. Okay. Can I get the keys to Charlie's truck?"

"Sure!" Leesa went over to her desk and dug them out of the drawer. "You're leaving too?"

"Yes. Lance says I should work from home for a few days. I'm not supposed to be seen in town."

"Oh." Leesa smiled happily. "Well, I'm glad you're back, Roman! We sure missed you." She gave him a quick hug and skipped away.

Roman was glad to be back too. And he was glad the Mad Creek's Sheriff's Office was still home.

*       *       *

Roman was terrified. He sat in a truck outside his own cabin—showered and dressed in the nicest jeans and shirt he owned—and debated with himself about whether or not to turn on the ignition and drive to Matt's house.

His dog had been restless ever since Roman got back, pacing under his skin. The smell of the cabin was familiar and welcome, yet it had never felt so empty. His dog missed Luci and Matt. He didn't want to be alone.

Dogs were not solitary creatures, Roman knew this. But in the past few years, the pain he'd felt had made him want to withdraw and hide, the way an animal found a quiet place when it was dying. That had only made things worse. As a newly quickened, Roman had felt cut off from both dogs and men.

Then Lance had pushed his way in—with a job and a pack. That had been Roman's salvation. But now there was the possibility of more. So much more. But reaching out to take it... what if Matt didn't want him anymore? What if Roman gave himself away as not-human? What if he was bad at that kind of human intimacy?

*Are you a brave boy?* He'd been brave as anything, as long as James was by his side. Now he had to be brave on his own.

He started the truck.

# 16

## Roman's First Kiss

Matt was surprised when the knock at the door turned out to be Roman. He hadn't had a chance to talk to Roman that day after he'd gotten back from his vacation, and Matt had a lot of questions. But the timing sucked. It had been one hell of a day. First Paco had disappeared—and was still missing. Then a visitor had arrived unexpectedly this afternoon. Matt had his hands full.

So what did it say that he was still so fucking delighted to find Roman Charsguard on his doorstep? "Hey!" Matt smiled.

"Hello, Matt."

Roman looked at him strangely—his gaze vulnerable and... shy? He'd made an effort on his appearance too. His jaw was clean-shaven and smooth, and his dark crew cut glistened in the light. He had on a denim shirt, which fit him close around his chest and waist, and rather tight blue jeans too.

Wow. That was quite a package.

*Fuck.* Matt caught himself lingering in his appraisal. He hastily raised his eyes to find Roman watching him intently. "I came here to tell you something, Matt. That is.... I want to say that I—"

"Who's this?" Matt's dad came up behind him and clapped a hand on Matt's shoulder, looking out at their visitor warily, like he might be an enemy insurgent.

"Um, Dad, this is Deputy Roman Charsguard, my partner at the Mad Creek Sheriff's Office. Roman, this is my father, General Thomas Barclay."

"*Retired* general," his father insisted with false modesty. He held out a firm hand to Roman. "Always good to meet a friend of Matt's."

"Only retired since last year," Matt said. "Which no one in Washington yet seems to realize, apparently." The General was still on a dozen email lists and planning committees, to hear him tell it.

Roman's spine straightened, and he shook the offered hand in decidedly military fashion. "It's an honor, sir." His tone was full of sincerity.

"Thank you, son. You were in the forces?"

"Yes, sir."

"Well, come on in! Don't just stand there, Matt. Get the man a beer!"

The General could be charismatic as hell when he wanted to be. And apparently, he wanted to be with Roman. He put an arm around Roman's shoulder and pulled him through the house and out the back door where they had a fire going to fend off the chilly October evening. Luci, as usual, was bingeing on s'mores.

Matt fetched a beer from the fridge and wondered at his life. His father had just shown up a few hours ago with no explanation, but Matt was pretty sure he was there to push for Matt to make an honest woman of Luci. Now his biggest man crush, and a guy he hadn't seen in three weeks, had come around to witness that conversation. Fun times.

But really, why *was* Roman here? There'd been something at the doorway, Roman had been about to say something. Was it something about where he'd been? About why he hadn't contacted Matt? Something else? There'd been a warm look in Roman's eyes.... Damn. Matt wished like hell he could find out what Roman wanted.

But the General was in charge of the party now.

Out back, Roman was sitting in Matt's chair by the fire pit, so Matt grabbed another one from the porch and carried it out to the yard. He sat opposite from Roman on the other side of the fire, with Luci between them in one direction and the General between them in the other. Roman's eyes met his over the fire and they were brighter by far than the flames.

God, it was good to see him again. Matt's pathetic, unrequited love-lust returned in full force. So much for moving on. He held the beer out around the fire. Roman reached out his right hand to take it and winced. He switched to his left hand and took the bottle.

"What happened?" Matt nodded at Roman's right arm.

"Hurt it a few weeks ago. I'm all right," Roman mumbled with a slight blush.

"What unit did you say you were in?" the General prompted.

"Dad. He's not here for a grilling."

"I was in the Army, sir. B Company, 2-87 Infantry Battalion."

"You were in K-9, weren't you?" Matt said. If Roman was willing to talk about it, Matt was unable to resist bragging on him.

"Yes." Roman licked his lips nervously and drank beer.

"K-9! By God, that's been a good program for us," the General enthused. "Amazing what dogs can do. You a dog lover, Roman?"

"Yes, sir."

"So am I! So am I! I hear Matt's dog just ran away today. That's a terrible shame, isn't it?"

Roman's gaze met Matt's. "Yes, sir. That's a shame."

"I don't understand it," Luci sniffed, her eyes red. "Matt and I looked for hours today. We drove up and down the roads all afternoon. I'm gonna put up fliers in town tomorrow."

"He'll come home," Matt told her for the hundredth time. He had to believe that. They'd doted on Paco. Surely, he'd want to come back to where he'd been so loved.

"But what if he doesn't?"

"I'm sure it wasn't anything you did," Roman told Luci solemnly. "Maybe he just had somewhere else he needed to be."

*What?* Matt wondered. He was about to ask Roman how he knew about Paco. After all, Roman had been out of town, well... pretty much since the night Paco had shown up on their doorstep. But the General spoke up.

"Awful crime, shooting a dog. Any man who'd do a thing like that deserves to be horse whipped as far as I'm concerned. He was a fine-looking German Shepherd, too, from Matt's pictures. Good dogs, shepherds. I had one once myself. Smartest dog you ever saw. He could—"

The General and Roman talked about dogs. And talked about dogs. It went on for a good hour. Roman told them about the bomb-sniffing patrols he'd done with his dog in Afghanistan. That was a dangerous job, Matt knew. Not only was it possible a dog could miss a mine, but you were out in the open, a prime target for snipers. But Roman talked about those patrols as if they were fond memories.

Then the General went through pretty much every dog he'd ever had, the K-9 program in general, and a military service dog that was awarded for bravery last year. Matt watched them get along like a house afire, and couldn't help feeling jealous. Of course the General loved Roman. He was a man's man and he all but reeked of strength, obedience, and deference.

Roman was like his brother Mitch, Matt realized. The perfect man. The perfect soldier. The perfect son. He was the perfect everything that Matt had always tried to be—and failed. Matt was too soft-hearted to really enjoy being a bad-ass, and he was too much of a goof-off and comedian to be respectful. And he was definitely too gay. Even if the General didn't even know Matt was gay, he probably knew Matt was simply not manly *enough*.

Feeling like a third wheel, he excused himself to go into the house and get everyone more beers. He went into the small pantry to see if they had any bags of chips or pretzels. He felt someone behind him and turned to find Roman trying to fit into the small space with him. It was so strange, Matt laughed.

"Hey. What're you doing?"

Roman made no move to back out and let Matt out of the closet. "Matt." His voice sounded very grave.

"Roman," Matt said in turn with faked seriousness. "What's up, buddy? Did you come over to talk to me? I'm sorry about my dad. I wasn't expecting him."

"It's a privilege to meet your father."

"Okay, that's…." Matt took a deep breath. "Yeah. Thank you."

Roman still didn't move.

The pantry was so small, Matt had shelves pressed against three sides of his body. And in front of him, Roman's large—*toned*—body blocked the door. They were quite close together.

"Did you… need to talk to me?" Matt suggested. "We could step out front."

"I want to talk to you," Roman agreed, but he didn't move. He squeezed his hands into fists nervously.

291

"What is it?" Matt was starting to feel concerned.

Roman made a little noise in his throat and tilted his head. "That day... when you asked me if I was straight. I didn't understand. Sometimes I... I was raised differently than most people. Sometimes I don't catch on to things."

Roman hesitated. Matt's heart started to beat so loudly, he'd be surprised if it wasn't visible under his T-shirt. He bit his tongue and waited.

"I said 'yes' I was straight. And you thought that meant I didn't want to... that I didn't like you in the way that.... I mean, like humans like other humans. Not as friends...."

Roman's face was flushed now, an awkward blush crawling along his cheeks. Matt could have put him out of his misery, but he needed to hear Roman say exactly what he meant. Besides, it was rather adorable to see the tough guy flustered, and Matt was too in love with this moment to interrupt him.

"As a sex partner," Roman finally got out, turning redder. "I didn't mean to say that I didn't like you as a sex partner. Or mate. Because I think I would. Do." Roman looked down at his feet, though the pantry was so small he probably couldn't see them. "If those aren't the right words, I'm sorry. I've never done this before."

Good God in heaven, where had this guy come from? Not for the first time, Matt wondered if maybe Roman had been a little more damaged in the war than was obvious. He did have that scar on his head. But he was so intelligent in other ways. He was just... sweetly naive. How was that even possible with a guy who looked like Roman and had been in the military?

"As a boyfriend?" Matt suggested, his voice sounding gruff. "Is that what you mean? We could try being more than friends? Dating?"

Roman looked relieved. "Yes. That's what I mean." His golden eyes were like warm honey as he looked up at Matt hopefully. "If you'd like that. But if that's not what you want, I understand and I apologize for talking about it."

Matt smiled. "Yeah? Well, screw that."

Fate didn't bring two people together like it had Matt and Roman for no reason. Matt felt a bubbling exultation. *Thank God.* Roman liked him too. It was the best news in the world. Matt reached out a hand and touched Roman's cheek. Roman had the most beautiful bones. His jaw was smooth from the recent shave and his lips were wide and soft. He closed his eyes under the touch in a surrender that felt like more than the simple pleasure he'd seen Roman take in touch before. This felt erotic.

Matt couldn't resist. How could he? Since he'd first seen this face during that Coarsegold raid, so piercingly sad and resigned, he hadn't been able to forget it. He'd dreamed of this face. And since he'd come to Mad Creek, he'd seen so much more. Roman was often stoic, like any soldier. But he felt things, deeply, and when they showed on his face, there'd never been anyone more open. Fear, longing, embarrassment, anger, and happiness were easy to read there.

And now *want*.

Matt stepped forward, tilted his head up, and placed his mouth on Roman's.

The kiss started slow, with Roman tensed beneath him expectantly. He didn't pull away, so Matt pressed small kisses on Roman's closed mouth, lingering longer each time, and then letting the tip of his tongue be felt in the kisses too.

Roman pulled Matt a half step forward and wrapped his arms around Matt's waist. He kissed back, mirroring Matt's pressing of lips, enthusiastic but with his mouth closed, not trying to take it deeper. *Not knowing how to.*

Dear God, had Roman never kissed anyone before? Matt pulled back and stared.

Roman's face fell. "Am I doing it wrong?"

"No, darlin'. Just open your mouth a little." With his thumb, Matt gently parted Roman's lips. He kissed him again.

This time, when he played the tip of his tongue over Roman's slightly parted lips, he tasted wet sweetness and felt Roman's tongue tentatively stroke his own. Roman made a low growl in his throat and pulled Matt as close as he could, quivering all over. A heated surge of lust rolled through Matt's body, carrying away all thoughts of common sense. When Roman's tongue made a cautious foray deeper into Matt's mouth, he sucked on it teasingly.

One of them groaned, the sound loud in the small space, and Matt pushed against Roman's hips. Roman was erect—large and hard and so hot, Matt could feel the heat even through two layers of denim. *Oh, God.* Matt was going to die if he didn't have Roman right the fuck now.

"Matt?" Luci's voice, confused.

Stunned, Matt pushed back from Roman as far as he could go in the pantry. Roman stared at him, panting. One hand went to his right shoulder protectively.

"Wow. That was...." Matt cleared his throat.

"Good," Roman said earnestly.

"Hell, yeah. But we'd, um, better get back. My dad...."

Roman moved immediately to step out of the pantry. Then he went straight out the back door. Matt leaned against the open pantry doorway and wiped his hand over his face. *Holy shit.*

He'd just been making out. With Roman Charsguard. In his kitchen pantry. He wanted to whoop and holler, maybe jump up and give God a high five.

"So. Not straight then," Luci said, amusement in her voice. She was leaning against the kitchen counter.

Matt knew his face had to be glowing like a lightbulb. He shook his head, a grin creeping across his lips. "Saints be praised. My God, Luci, I really think this guy could be The One. Is that nuts? That's so insane, right?"

Luci's expression softened. "Oh, Mattie. I'm happy for you. But be careful tonight, *cariño*. Daddy's gonna figure it out."

"No." Matt straightened up. No, that didn't even bear thinking about. The idea of the *General* catching Matt and Roman kissing poured a bucket of ice water on his lovely afterglow.

Luci came over to pat his cheek. "He's beautiful," she said softly. "And he seems like a super sweet guy too. By the way, you? You have it sooo bad."

Yeah. He totally did.

 

 

\*                 \*                 \*

Matt had kissed Roman.

Matt had *sucked* on Roman's *tongue*.

Roman sat by the fire pit, a beer in his hand, pretending his dick wasn't hard enough to bounce rebar off of it. He got the feeling it would be wrong to talk about sex in front of Matt's Dad. And Luci too. After all, Lance got very nervous when Roman talked about it.

His eyes had a hard time staying off Matt, though. He stared at Matt's hands or his mouth across the fire and thought about what he wanted. Matt's dad, who was a *general*, a very important man, talked about Afghanistan, but Roman had a hard time paying attention to him now.

Then General Barclay started talking about Matt and Luci, and how they should get married. Roman was confused at first. But when both Matt and Luci put him off with roundabout excuses, instead of saying that they weren't mates, Roman understood: they were lying to Matt's father.

Why? Matt was an honest man, as far as Roman knew. Matt met his eyes over the fire and something in them warned Roman to be silent. Roman decided he needed to go. He felt like he was intruding, and he didn't understand the situation. He'd likely screw up if he stayed.

He stood. "I should get home. It was very nice to meet you, sir."

Matt's father stood up and looked at Roman. His face was not as friendly as before. "Good night, Roman."

"Good night, Luci," Roman said.

"Good night." She smiled at him, but she looked sad.

Matt walked Roman inside the house and to the front door. "I'm so sorry about that. The General... well, obviously he doesn't know I'm gay. It's complicated."

"Okay." Roman was still confused, but he wanted to trust Matt.

"Hey." Matt looked around to make sure they were alone. "I could come by your place later. If you'd like. If it's not too late when these guys go to bed."

"Can we kiss some more?"

Matt smiled. "Hell yeah."

"I'd like that." Roman thought he was probably grinning foolishly, but he couldn't help it.

Matt winked. "I'll be there as soon as I can."

\*　　　　　　　\*　　　　　　　\*

Roman paced in his little cabin, anxiously waiting for Matt. Matt was coming over to have sex. Roman wanted that very badly, but he was nervous too. He'd watched a few videos on his laptop with two men having sex. It wasn't difficult to find videos like that. Pretty much enter the word 'man' in Google, and you could take your pick.

The videos had been informative, mechanically, and they'd made Roman think about Matt real hard. But they weren't what he was hoping for, the connection he craved. Maybe that was something you couldn't see in a video.

There was a light *rat-tat-tat* on his door. Roman opened it fast, and there was Matt. He wore a brown corduroy coat with sheepskin lining, a dark T-shirt, and blue jeans. His cheeks were rosy from the cold. He looked so good, Roman's mouth watered.

"Hi, M—"

Matt grabbed Roman's flannel shirt in two fists and pulled them together, crashing his mouth down on Roman's.

300

Apparently, no talking was needed for sex, and that was fine with Roman. Yes, that was really good news!

Matt's mouth softened as he stepped into the cabin, pushing Roman back and shutting the door with his foot. Roman held his ground then, liking the feel of Matt pushing up against him. He put his hands under Matt's coat, on his back, and pressed him in even tighter. Matt's tongue did magic things in Roman's mouth and fireworks went off all over his body. His shoulder throbbed a little, but with all the pleasure zinging through his veins, it didn't matter.

*Oh God.* Every time he thought he'd experienced the coolest thing about being human, something more amazing would happen. Matt's body was solid, hard, and warm, and the feeling of it pressed up against Roman's body, while his cock was aching and his blood was boiling, was heaven. Matt's hands were on either side of his jaw, and he possessed Roman's mouth completely. His tongue was wet and sweet and sexier than Roman had ever imagined. Everything felt so good, he almost couldn't bear it.

He went a bit lightheaded and his knees went weak. Matt held him up as he wobbled. He broke the kiss. Matt's dark eyes were smoky and full of want. "Bedroom?"

"I just use the futon," Roman said, feeling stupid. He'd never minded the futon until now, but he wished he had a real bed for Matt's sake.

But Matt didn't seem to mind. "Then let's get that fucker set up!"

He went to the futon mattress and pulled it off the frame like it was on fire. Roman hurried to move the frame to its flat position and pull the mattress back onto it, and then Matt was casting off his coat and kicking off his shoes and crowding Roman down onto the soft/hard surface, and crawling on top of him.

"God, Roman. Feels like I've wanted you forever," Matt gasped, nuzzling into Roman's neck. His knees straddled Roman's hips and his hands were already working at the buttons on Roman's shirt.

Matt seemed to know exactly what he wanted and exactly what to do. So Roman relaxed, realizing Matt would lead them wherever they needed to go. As the last of his nerves fled, happiness bubbled up inside him. It felt wonderful to have Matt all over him like this, as if all his dry places were being watered.

"I didn't know I was allowed to want you at first," Roman said, wanting to be honest. "But I really want you now."

Matt chuckled, the vibration tickling Roman's neck. He raised his head. "Well, thank God you figured it out, Ro."

"I know!"

Matt's fingers had finished the buttons on Roman's shirt. He pushed the fabric aside and rubbed his palms over Roman's stomach and chest, his face intent. When he rubbed firmly over Roman's nipples, the feeling went right to Roman's dick and his hips shot up of their own accord. Roman whimpered.

"Yeah," Matt whispered, his gaze getting hotter still. His fingers drifted down to the top button on Roman's jeans. "Okay?"

Roman nodded enthusiastically. He raised his hips up again, though they only went up so far with Matt sitting on him. Matt shifted forward so he was sitting on the base of Roman's erection and Roman cried out at the feeling of friction and pushed up harder.

Matt smiled. "Like that? Me too. Only without clothes would be better."

And then Roman's pants were open and Matt, dear God, *Matt,* tugged them down enough to free Roman's hard and heavy shaft. He sank down and *nuzzled,* nuzzled and licked.

Roman couldn't stand it. He felt too much. He wrapped his fists in the futon's cover and pushed into the contact, a low whine/growl in his throat.

"It's been a while, huh?" Matt chuckled, and then he pulled Roman's erection upright with his hand and took it into his mouth.

Roman raised up on his left elbow and tried to pull away. The sensation was so good, so raw, so tender, and so *undeserved.* He felt like he'd explode—his emotions and his body and his mind all racing at full speed. But he didn't try to pull away very hard, and Matt didn't let him go. He grabbed Roman's hips and held Roman in his mouth. He sucked gently at the first few inches, his tongue rubbing the underside and shifting Roman's foreskin back and forth, soothing.

In a spreading glow, Roman's surprise changed into the sweetest, most intense pleasure he'd ever felt. He closed his eyes and flopped back on the bed. He blocked out sight and sound and even the clamor of his own brain, just wanting to *feel.*

Matt's mouth was hot and wet. It felt so much gentler, more maddening, more stimulating, *sexier*, than Roman's own hands ever had. His cock throbbed and grew stiffer, straining for more. Tingles broke out all over Roman's body, and his balls felt heavy and tight. Roman swallowed down the noises he wanted to make, worried they'd be too dog-like.

When Matt started to move his head up and down, sucking harder, Roman gasped. "Matt." He gently pushed against Matt's shoulders. Matt raised his head, his eyes half hooded and his lips swollen. Roman had never seen a prettier sight. "I want to touch you too."

"Yeah, Ro."

The fire between them burned hotter now, but slower too—the intense red of when the wood is truly, deeply being consumed, not the flash of a surface fire. Matt rolled to the side and removed all of his clothes, and Roman did the same. Roman sat up and looked at Matt lying on the futon on his back. He felt awe.

"Oh, Matt." His body was fascinating. He had broad shoulders, a slightly thickened waist, strong, wide thighs, and a member that jutted out from a triangle of dark hair, proof of his arousal. Roman felt shaky all over at the sight of him, at the idea that Matt was allowing him into this most intimate side of his life. Humans normally stayed covered up. They didn't share things like this unless they were mates.

Matt didn't say a word, but he pulled Roman down so they were lying side by side. Roman kissed him again, eager for the sensation of Matt's tongue on his. Matt's hands moved all over his body and Roman happily did the same. The kissing and touching were good, but when Matt began to thrust against Roman at the same time, that was even better.

Roman clung to Matt, unable to control his hands enough to keep petting him anymore or to find the breath to kiss. He buried his nose in the crook where neck met shoulders and breathed him in. That musky tangerine scent was powerful now, laying over Matt's regular smell of woods and sweat and a piney soap. Roman nosed in farther, inhaling Matt's skin, eyes rolling back in his head at the pleasure of the smell, of Matt thrusting against his cock. His thighs trembled and his stomach clenched. He was about to—

Matt stopped moving and Roman couldn't hold back a choked sob.

"Roman?" Matt sounded hesitant.

"Yes?" Roman's voice quivered.

Matt chuckled. "This is awesome, but I'd really love to… to fuck. I want to feel you inside me." His voice was unsteady too.

"Okay. Whatever you want to do, I'll try it."

Matt pulled back and took a calming breath, studying Roman's face. "Have you ever topped? With a man?"

Roman wasn't sure what that meant. He bit his lip.

Matt's expression softened. "Have you ever fucked a man, Ro?"

"No. But I want to try with you."

Matt looked relieved—and hungry. He kissed Roman hard and quick and got up. "God, I've dreamt about this. I brought stuff." He got a small tube and a condom packet from the pocket of his jeans.

Roman knew what they were going to do—the most basic joining there was. Despite having been ready to come a moment ago, and being rather disappointed when that friction had stopped, Roman was now very much interested in the new plan.

If he joined with Matt in that way, it had to mean something. Didn't it? Roman wanted it to mean something.

Matt tossed him the condom and put some stuff from the tube on his fingers. He reached behind himself, his gaze locked on Roman.

"Are you sure? This the way you want it?" Roman asked, picking up the condom. "Me mounting you?"

"Yeah," Matt said breathily. "Yeah, absolutely."

Roman sat up and fumbled with the condom, having a hard time opening the package, and then staring at the flat disc dumbly.

Matt came to his rescue. "I can't believe you're for real sometimes," he said, looking at Roman with wonder. He took the rubbery disc from Roman's fingers, placed it on the tip of his erection, and rolled it down, using his other hand to lightly tease his balls and send electric sparks shooting through his body.

"Ugh," Roman grunted. "Now can we?"

In answer, Matt pushed at Roman's chest, sending him down to the mattress. He climbed over Roman, held his cock, and positioned himself over the head. With his eyes on Roman's, and his mouth open and panting, he began to impale himself.

Roman locked his fingers around Matt's thighs and closed his eyes. He felt Matt's body—*Matt's body*—slowly take him in to perfect heat and friction. It was so, so tight. Roman opened his eyes. Matt's face was completely focused, his eyes closed.

Roman touched Matt wherever he could reach, wanting even more connection. He rubbed his chest, his abs, his thighs, and back up again. He wanted so badly to thrust, but he sensed he needed to wait for Matt's signal. His groin was hot and tight and poised on the brink of orgasm and he didn't want that.

And then Matt had all of him inside and his eyes opened. They seemed to glow as he took a shaky breath. "*Roman.*"

"Matt. What should I do?"

Matt rolled, pulling Roman along with him, and somehow Roman managed to stay inside him. And then Matt was on his back, thighs spread, bare feet braced on the small of Roman's back and Roman knew it was time to move.

He let instinct take over his body and love take over his heart. His hips pumped, pounding into Matt. He couldn't easily reach Matt's lips in this position, but he propped himself on his good arm and used the other hand to grab Matt's wrist, kissing the inside of it and inhaling Matt's scent, sucking on his fingers.

Matt made a lovely sound, and his feet pressed into Roman's back, urging him on. His breath filled with grunts and gasps and cries of Roman's name and *faster* and *like that* and *yes* and *Oh God*.

Everything inside Roman was tensing, tightening, drawing in, like a video he'd once seen of water pulling back before a tsunami. He could feel it building and it was more than just an orgasm. It was like the first time he'd shifted, that feeling of something huge taking shape and getting ready to burst out.

Maybe he'd become an angel this time, Roman thought. Or maybe something invisible inside him was changing, DNA rearranging one more time, cells multiplying. He could blush, get an erection, and even laugh. And now he was... he was...

*Love*, he realized, as his heart filled up with heat and light. Now he could love like a man, love a soul-mate, a body-mate. *Mate*.

Matt's gaze was on his, blazing and fierce. His cock bounced on his stomach with every one of Roman's thrusts. The hand Roman was kissing turned to take Roman's wrist and pull it down, wrapping his palm around Matt's cock. Matt's hand stayed over his, holding it steady so that it was the movement of Roman's hips that thrust Matt's cock in and out of their Roman's fist.

Roman loved touching Matt there. The wave rose up inside him and he couldn't stop it. "Matt!"

Matt groaned, squeezed Roman's hand hard around the head of his cock and convulsed. Hot, wet semen spilled out over their fingers and onto Matt's stomach. That musky tangerine scent intensified and it drove Roman wild.

He slammed into Matt one more time, wrapped his arms around Matt's thighs to hold him tight, and let everything inside him burst out. It was the best feeling in the world, and he hung on to it as long as he could. And then he collapsed on the bed and Matt held him close.

"Jesus, that was crazy," Matt said giddily, still breathing hard.

"It was?" Roman couldn't summon the energy to raise his head. "It wasn't normal?"

"It beat the fuck out of 'normal' in my experience." Matt moved, sitting up. Roman opened his eyes to find Matt looking at him thoughtfully. "You've never put on a condom before?"

"No."

Matt's lips pursed. "But you have had sex?"

Roman shrugged.

"God, Roman! How is that even possible? You're so good-looking. And you're such a nice guy."

Roman's glow began to fade and worry crept back in. This was the sort of thing he wasn't supposed to tell Matt, and he hated that. "I didn't have the chance when I was younger. And then I was alone a lot."

Matt shook his head, his expression bemused. "Someday you're going to have to tell me about this mysterious childhood of yours. I'm beginning to think you were raised in a nuclear bunker or something."

Roman smiled sadly. "Or something."

Matt lay back down and kissed Roman's jaw. "Well, it was fantastic. Take my word for it." He hesitated, then sighed. "Because of my dad and my brother... well, let's just say I haven't been open about my preferences. So most guys I've been with were quick hookups or maybe *could* have been something, except being in the closet tends to piss boyfriends off."

Roman listened carefully, knowing this was important. He wasn't sure what Matt was telling him. He braced himself. "So... you will marry Luci?"

"No!" Matt sat up and stared at him. "God, no. That's not what I—I guess what I'm trying to say is that... there hasn't been

313

anyone who... who was worth coming out for. But you...." Matt ruffled his own hair, acting shy. "I really like you, Ro."

Roman thought that sounded pretty good. "I love you, Matt."

Matt laughed in surprise. "Geez. You just lay it all out there. You're a crazy person. You know that, right?"

Roman frowned.

"Don't worry. I like your brand of crazy." Matt leaned in to kiss him.

"I hope you *do* like my brand of crazy," Roman said, thinking Matt hadn't seen anything yet.

Matt smiled in a puzzled way. He put his warm palm on Roman's cheek. "You're not like anyone I've ever met."

"You too." Roman sighed. "I've never been this close to anyone except James. He's the one in the picture on the wall. My best friend in the Army." Roman nodded toward the framed photo.

"You weren't close to your parents?"

"I didn't know my father. I remember my mother a little, but it's more of a feeling than a real memory."

"Jesus. That must have been tough."

Roman considered that. "The thing that was the hardest in my life was the day James died." His voice trembled. "But I don't want to talk about that."

They were lying on their sides. Matt put his arms around Roman and pulled him close. Roman nuzzled his nose into Matt's neck. It was warm there and now it smelled like both of them, and like sex, which was better than Matt's natural smell or even tangerines.

"Were you lovers, Roman? You and James?"

Roman was shocked. "*No*. It wasn't like this."

"Okay! I just wondered. I know you can love a friend as much as you can love anyone in the world." Matt rubbed his palm over Roman's buzz cut fondly. "I wish I didn't have to go, but I should probably get back to my place. The General's spending the night."

"All right." It was warm and delicious lying naked with Matt in bed. Roman didn't want him to leave. Maybe someday he wouldn't have to. That would be awesome!

Matt smiled at Roman and kissed him once more, lingering a moment, before pulling back. "Hey, I noticed you favoring your shoulder. What happened?" Matt reached up and touched the wound. It was already healed over, but the scar was bright red. Matt frowned. "Is this *recent*? What the fuck happened?"

"Not, uh, not real recent." Roman fumbled the words. "I just hurt the bone on my vacation so it's a little sore. It's fine."

Matt looked like he wanted to ask more questions, but then he shook his head. "Okay, big guy. If you say so. Well, I'd better head out."

He got up and put on his clothes. "I can let myself out. Good night, Ro. I'll see you tomorrow."

"Good night, Matt."

Matt gave him one more quick kiss and left. Roman pulled the covers onto the futon and curled up, feeling happy and—the thrum of anxiety in his veins took him by surprise—

feeling a little scared too. It was wonderful to have something so grand, to love someone and be with them. But it was worrying. Because Matt didn't know the truth about Roman, and maybe when he found out, he wouldn't want Roman anymore.

He didn't want to lose Matt the way he'd lost James. He couldn't go through that again.

But it was foolish to dwell on that now. He wanted to hold on to the memories they'd made and file them away for safekeeping. So he pulled the covers over his head and did just that.

# 17

## Who's The Alpha?

The General's visit did not end well. The morning after he'd arrived—the morning after Matt had made an excuse about forgetting something at work, and had gone over to Roman's and had the best sex of his life—on *that* morning, the General was a monumental pain in the ass.

Luci slept in. She was such a lightweight with beer, and she'd probably gotten stoned on s'mores too. Without her presence to buffer things, the General confronted Matt over breakfast, urging, haranguing, and cajoling Matt in turn about at least giving Luci an engagement ring.

Finally, Matt lost his temper. "That's not going to happen, Dad. Period. Things aren't like they were in your day."

The General stared at Matt with suppressed anger. One thing Matt had learned growing up—it was a hazard of his father's job that he was used to being obeyed. Matt thought he honestly tried not to order his family around like he did his

318

soldiers, but it was a struggle for him. Blatant dismissal really lit his fuse.

"This isn't even about Luci, is it?" His voice was cold.

"No, Dad. It's about me. Now can we please stop fighting? I see you a few times a year, and this is how we spend our time. I've been promoted to a DEA agent now. It would be nice if you could be proud of me for one visit at least."

Matt's voice was bitter as bile, bleeding with the resentment he felt at never being good enough.

To his surprise, his father merely pressed his lips together and said, "All right, Matthew. We won't discuss it anymore today."

Matt sensed a warning in those words, as if *after* today he'd better watch the fuck out. But he didn't know what his father could do to force him on the Luci issue, so he decided he was being paranoid.

They ate the rest of breakfast in a heavy silence. And when the General said he'd be heading out, Matt wasn't surprised. He even hugged Matt before he left. But his eyes... his eyes were steely.

Matt didn't have time to worry about his father. The case they were working was too important. For some reason, Roman wasn't going in to the sheriff's office, but he coordinated with Matt via text. Matt picked Roman up at his cabin for a day of surveillance on the nascent pot farm.

It was a bit weird, when Matt had just been there mere hours before for very much non-work-related reasons, but he tried to stay focused. In truth, he was glad to have Roman back on the job. He felt more like a true work partner than anyone Matt had ever worked with. He filled Roman in on the new operation, on their six suspects, and what they'd been up to so far.

"The most important thing," Matt explained to Roman as they drove toward the site, "is that we can't be made. If they figure out we're on to them, this whole thing will disappear before you can spit sideways."

Roman, in the passenger seat, frowned. "I don't think I can spit sideways."

Matt swore Roman was either the most sheltered guy he'd ever met, or his sense of humor was Sahara dry. "No? Can you say 'Bob's your uncle'?"

"Bob's your uncle. Is Bob your uncle?" Roman asked seriously.

Matt glanced at him incredulously. Roman burst into laughter.

"Was that a joke? Are you actually joking with me?"

"It was funny, wasn't it? Wasn't it funny?" Roman looked very pleased with himself.

"Hilarious. Goofball. Anyway, if they make us, our suspects will disappear fast is my point."

Roman winked at him. It was a little awkward, but it was a wink nonetheless. "I can be silent, Matt. Don't worry."

They parked Matt's Cherokee on a dirt road that was so overgrown, branches scrapped the top of the vehicle. But it was close to the area where the outsiders were building their little enterprise. From there, it was only a mile hike into the woods to a ridge that overlooked the camp. Matt had spent a lot of hours on that ridge with binoculars and a long-lensed camera taking photos.

This morning, he was reluctant to get out of the car. It wasn't yet eight a.m., and the guys they were watching were not morning people. It was nice having a private moment with Roman. Matt wanted to reach out and squeeze his hand or something, but no. It was already crazy enough that they were sleeping together. They had to keep work and after-work completely separate. He sipped his coffee from the diner instead.

"Lance has been pretty helpful about this," Matt admitted. "Charlie has been watching these guys when they're not here. I swear, Lance is on top of every move they make, including their shower schedule—or lack thereof. Which is good, because I won't get much help from the DEA until we have enough evidence for a sting."

"Lance is a good man and a good leader," Roman said firmly. "He won't let these men get away with anything in his territory. He's very protective of the town."

"He's like a pit bull. Yeah, I know."

Roman looked confused. "He's not like a pit bull at all."

God, the guy was priceless. "It's just a saying, Ro." Matt covered the fond exasperation in his tone by taking another sip of coffee. He was still crabby over his dad's visit. And he didn't entirely trust Lance. Protectiveness was all well and good, but why had Lance objected to the DEA being there, of all things? And Matt was still convinced there was something weird going on in town. But at the moment, he and Lance were on the same side and it didn't entirely suck. Especially since there was no doubt Roman really did like and trust his boss, and Matt really liked and trusted Roman.

He felt the weight of Roman's gaze. He turned to look at him. Roman's eyes were warm, and his face was so open it almost hurt. Jesus, the guy was such a contradiction. He could be so uptight and tough and regimented sometimes, and yet he had this wide open heart and soft underbelly that was so vulnerable it scared Matt.

Roman shouldn't be that open with guys. There were a lot of assholes out there. He was lucky Matt wasn't one. But Matt wasn't sure even he could be not-asshole enough to avoid hurting Roman.

Or maybe this was simply something Matt had never experienced before and never really thought he would—falling in love. Was that what Roman was doing? Was Matt? The thought was scary as hell and amazingly wonderful at the same time.

Matt gave a quick look around, but there was nothing but greenery and the mountains. "Hey, I guess during work hours we should... be careful. Stick to work. But I, um, I can maybe come over again tonight. If you want."

Roman's smile turned brighter by a shade. "I want you to come over."

"Okay."

It was too many damn feelings for this early on a workday. Time to compartmentalize.

Matt put down his cup. "Okay, Deputy. Let's saddle up and get into position."

"Yes, sir," Roman said.

*               *               *

Roman found working surveillance with Matt frustrating. They watched the group of men work in a clearing surrounded by woods. The clearing was fresh and raw, with piles of trees and brush they'd brought down with their equipment stacked off to one side.

Roman recognized the red-haired man who shot him. His inner dog itched to run down to the clearing and corner him. But no. That wasn't the way men did things. Men used strategy and law.

Matt took pictures with a really big camera. He said they had to wait for the DEA to approve a raid, and then the DEA would come with SWAT and arrest the men, just like they'd done at the raid in Coarsegold.

Roman couldn't fucking wait. He wanted to see the red-haired man—Clery—arrested. He wanted to *be there* to see it. Hell, he wanted to do it himself, take the man down, physically, preferably with a nice, loud, satisfying *thump*! But most likely, he'd have to be on the sidelines. And this time, he'd be in charge of himself enough not to run into gunfire and do something stupid. He hoped.

325

They watched for six hours. It was boring just watching the men like that. Mostly the other men worked and Clery typed away on his phone.

At the end of the day, Matt said he had to go into the sheriff's office for a while, and Roman said he had to go home, so Matt dropped him off.

Matt smiled when they pulled into Roman's driveway. "Be back later. Want me to pick up a couple of burgers at Daisy's?"

"Yes, please." Roman got out of the passenger side of Matt's car. He wanted to kiss Matt, but something in Matt's posture told him it wasn't a good idea. That was okay. Roman understood the difference between work time and play time, and he figured Matt was still on work time. He hadn't touched Roman all day, because they had been working.

That was smart, because Roman would touch Matt all the time if he could, and they wouldn't get much work done that way.

"See you soon," Matt promised. He drove away.

Roman cleaned his house and then showered and washed his entire body, really, really well. He set his little kitchen table with his mismatched glasses, silverware, and paper towels for napkins. And he made up the futon with sheets and a blanket. It was Roman's favorite blanket. Lily had given it to him. It had big, colorful stripes on it and it was fuzzy and warm. Blankets were awesome!

But when all that was done, Matt still wasn't back yet. Something had been bugging Roman all day, and he decided to give in and call Lance because it was important.

Lance answered his cell phone. From the sound of his voice, he was still at the office. His voice was softer when he was at home with Tim.

"What's up, Roman?" Lance asked. "How did today go?"

"Today went fine. Lance, I'm not a virgin anymore."

On the other end of the call, there was a coughing/choking sound. "Well... congratulations?" Lance said at last.

"I had sex last night. With a person. With Matt."

"Okaay. Good for you. I know you like him… So…"

"It was good. It was really good."

"Fine. That's fine."

"But I have a question about it."

Lance's voice got tight. "I really think Tim is a better person for you to talk to about this subject."

Roman didn't understand why Lance didn't like to talk about sex. It was such a pleasant thing to do, and seemed like you'd want to talk about pleasant things. "But Tim is full human, so he won't understand my question. I wouldn't ask you if it wasn't important."

There was silence from the other end of the line, then a sigh. "Okay, Roman. Go ahead."

"When you and Tim have sex, are you the one who mounts him?"

There was an odd sound from the other end. Roman realized it was the grinding of teeth. "Usually. Yes."

"Because when we had sex, Matt wanted me to mount him. And I don't know what that means. Does it mean I'm the alpha in the relationship? If so, what are my responsibilities? I don't want to… I don't want to do something wrong or stupid or… make a mistake."

Lance sighed. "It's not like that with humans, Roman. Someone can, er, take the bottom position in, um, sex, but not necessarily anywhere else. It doesn't mean you're the boss. You can even, um, switch around. It's just about what you feel like doing at the time."

That surprised Roman. "You can switch? Do you switch around? Does Tim sometimes mount you?"

"Hey, look at that! It's a pen. On my desk. For writing work things down. And numbers. I should really get back to work and write things down." Lance's voice was stretched tight enough to snap.

Was he embarrassed to admit that Tim sometimes mounted him? Was that a thing to be ashamed of? But Matt didn't seem ashamed about it when he'd been mounted. Roman was still so confused. "So… should I let Matt mount me if he wants to or not?" he asked, desperate to know. He didn't want to screw things up with Matt, and if there was one place he'd repeatedly screwed things up, it was in understanding human expectations.

"Roman, it's all fine! Okay? You can top, bottom, or do it sideways, it doesn't matter."

"You can do it sideways? Is that like spitting sideways?"

"Look! Just do whatever feels, um, good. In the bedroom. And it doesn't mean you're the alpha. Okay? Gotta go. Bye." Lance hung up.

Roman put the phone down, still feeling totally at sea. But Lance had said it didn't matter who mounted, so that was something, he guessed. He supposed he should be prepared for anything Matt wanted to do. Hopefully, Matt wouldn't think he was stupid if he didn't understand things right away.

But when Matt knocked on the door a few minutes later, Roman didn't have much time to worry. Matt came in smelling of the woods and crisp air, cheeseburgers and musky tangerines, and Roman's body went straight into sex mode.

Matt must have gone there too, because he put the bag with the burgers on the table and tackled Roman onto the futon.

They rolled around on the blanket, kissing and laughing, and Roman decided he shouldn't worry so much about screwing things up with Matt. That's what it meant to love someone and be loved back—you could do something wrong and it was no big deal.

"Eat first or sex?" Matt asked, even though he was already taking off Roman's pants.

"Sex, eat, then more sex?" Roman suggested.

"Perfect."

Matt sat up enough to pull Roman's jeans down and off, and his socks too.

"My feet are cold."

"Then let's warm them up." Matt waggled his eyebrows and picked up one of Roman's feet in both hands. He brought it to his mouth and sucked on a toe.

Roman grabbed the blanket in shock because a) if anything was dog behavior, *that* was, and Matt did it without any pause whatsoever! And b) wow, the feeling of Matt's wet, gentle sucking and tonguing around his toes went right to his cock and made it throb on his belly in jealousy.

"Matt!" Roman wasn't sure if he wanted to pull his foot away so Matt would go elsewhere, or beg for more.

Matt pulled off with a plop. "You're so much fun to tease." He crawled up Roman's body with an expression that was wonderfully evil.

"I want to do that to you," Roman said quickly, because soon he wouldn't be able to talk and he'd just follow wherever Matt led. "Not that, but the other thing. I want to put my mouth on your penis and taste you there." Should he have said *taste*? "Is that okay?"

Matt paused in his crawling. His eyes darkened and he leaned down to kiss Roman's chest, right between his nipples. "Fuck yeah." He sounded like he really liked the idea.

Roman started to get up, but Matt pushed him back down with a hand. "Let's try this," he said, his voice thick and sticky as honey.

He swung himself around and pulled Roman onto his side and then, *wow*, they were both mouth to lap. What a brilliant

332

idea! Matt was a genius. Roman got lost in the ripe, luscious tangerine smell and in exploring Matt with his nose and tongue, memorizing each scent and texture, from silky soft to hard, from furred to smooth, and every nuance of taste. They all immediately went right to the top of his favorite things list.

When the attention Matt was paying to Roman's penis became too good to focus on anything but pleasure, Roman sucked Matt in all the way and tried to imitate the motion, suction, and pressure that felt so amazing when Matt did it. He must have done all right, because Matt's groans made his mouth vibrate and his thighs started to tremble. They came almost at the same time. Feeling Matt's penis grow even harder and then pump into his mouth was amazing! It was the best thing ever, and Roman really was positive about that this time.

"You're pretty good at this for a greenhorn." Matt panted, turning around to flop down next to Roman.

That made Roman so happy he could hardly stand it. "I want you to like having sex with me. Because I like having sex with you."

"Well, I do like it. A lot. So shut up." Matt lamely bumped Roman's arm with his elbow. "Ready for some burgers?"

333

"Yes. I'm starving. And then we can have more sex."

Matt laughed. "You about killed me just now, but I have a feeling you'll be able to talk me into it."

In fact, Roman found that when the time came, he had no trouble talking Matt into it at all.

# 18

## Shot in the Heart

Matt came over every night that week. They had sex and ate and sometimes even slept. But on Friday, Roman had to tell Matt he had other plans. There was a pack meeting at Lily's place, and Roman had to go to that by himself.

Roman stood in a corner at Lily's house watching people arrive—almost everyone in groups of two or more. Even Granger, the friendly old mutt he'd traveled with to Mad Creek, had a mate now, an older dachshund named Princess. The two were inseparable.

Roman wondered if he would ever be able to bring Matt to the meetings. It felt so good being there, with all the pack in one place. The quickened were so open. It was easy to tell on each person's face how things were going with them, if they were well, if they were lonely or sad, or if they were full of happiness and excited to get up each day.

He watched the couples, like Lance and Tim, or Bill McGurver and his wife, Jane, with their baby daughter. They smelled of endlessness, of contentment, of having made friends with time and the passage of days. Funny how Roman had never understood that the way he did now that he had Matt.

Then again, Lily's mate—Lance's father—had passed away some years ago, yet Lily had that shining, endless contentment too. She buzzed around, talking to everyone. Though often, when she got done talking to someone, that person seemed less content than before.

She headed his way, and Roman tried to escape her, but he was too slow. "Roman! Don't you dare slink away from me!"

Roman turned to face her, straightening his spine. "Hello, ma'am."

"I hear you have a boyfriend now! Well, I'm just tickled pink for you! Though I'm not sure why you couldn't take up with any number of nice quickened girls in town. A strong quick like you with such good genes and a steady job too! It's almost not fair. You see what I mean?" She pouted.

"I'm sorry, ma'am," said Roman, not meaning a word of it.

"Oh, I suppose I'll have to forgive you! That Matt Barclay is a hottie. I haven't had a chance to get to know him, but Luci is very nice. Do you know Luci?"

"Yes, ma'am."

Lily looked around conspiratorially and leaned in to whisper. "Her parents think she and Matt are engaged, but that's just because she wants to be a lawyer. Matt's like Tim—he's gay. But I guess you know that."

"Yes, ma'am."

Lily nodded, satisfied her secret had been relayed successfully. She leaned back and resumed full volume. "Now I hear you've been having a lot of questions about sex. I don't have personal experience with gay sex myself, obviously, but I've watched videos with two men, so maybe I could—"

"Attention, please!" Lance banged a spoon on his beer bottle, shooting a withering look at Lily.

"Oh, good! Lance is going to say something!" Lily patted Roman's arm. "We'll talk later."

She scampered over to where everyone was gathered around Lance.

Lance huffed and rubbed his forehead, which ached with the relief of a narrow escape.

Lance spoke up. "Can I get a report on the movements of the strangers? Gus?"

Gus had been a bulldog and he was far older than Roman. He nodded his head, sending his heavy jowls quivering. "I've been on morning detail all week. They left the house between ten and eleven every day, all six men, taking the big white car and the truck both. Charlie follows them when they leave. They never came back before my shift ended at noon."

"Thanks, Gus. Who's next. Tory?"

Tory was mixed breed, a short man with black hair and a large, bristly moustache, of which he was very proud. "I'm on afternoon shift. On Wednesday the truck came back and the big dark-skinned man with tattoos went inside for ten minutes, then came out and left again in the truck. Otherwise there was no activity during my shift."

"Davey?"

Davey was a second-gen Doberman mix and one of their strongest men, in Roman's opinion. He was very reliable and smart too.

"They've been noticing us," Davey said, "but I don't think it's a problem so far. Last night two of the men came out of the cabin to smoke. I pretended to be following a scent in order to get close enough to hear them. One of them watched me and commented on 'all the fucking dogs around here'. He thought it was creepy."

Everyone laughed. Roman laughed too. That was funny!

"The other one commented that he didn't care as long as the dogs kept their distance. Those weren't the exact words he used."

"Did they say anything else?" Lance asked.

"They talked about how boring it was in Mad Creek and how they wanted to go back to L.A. One of them said Colin was paying them well, so the other one should shut up about it. They talked about driving to Fresno over the weekend to pick up some girls."

"Good work, Davey. But I don't want anyone risking themselves by getting too close."

"I don't think they'd shoot a dog unless it tried to attack or get inside the cabin or something," Davey said. "Roman was human when he got shot."

Everyone looked at Roman with sympathy, including Lance. "Maybe not. But even so, everyone be careful. I don't want anyone else hurt."

"How much longer will they be here, Lance?" Lily asked with a whine. "It's disrupted our class schedule, and whatever you say about it not being too dangerous, they're still strangers with guns. What if they take it into their head to try target practice at some of the 'strays' they see hanging around? Huh?"

Lance's expression was grim. "Believe me, Mother, I want them gone as badly as you do. But we have to wait until the DEA says we've collected enough proof to convict them. It shouldn't be more than another few weeks. Hopefully sooner."

"I don't mind covering a few hours a day." That was one of Lance's brothers.

"Me too," someone else volunteered.

That started a long discussion about the rotation. Roman hadn't been around when that was set up, so he felt like he shouldn't stick his nose in now. Feeling hungry, he wandered into the kitchen. Tim was already in there, filling a cooler with beers and cans of lemonade from the fridge. Tim's dog, Renfield, who was only a dog but a very nice one, was sprawled out on the kitchen floor.

"Hey, Roman!" Tim seemed happy to see him. Renny banged his tail on the floor.

"Hello, Tim." Roman brushed his back against Tim in a friendly way and gave Renfield a rub behind the ears. He sat down on a stool at Lily's kitchen counter.

Tim came over, handed Roman a cold lemonade, and leaned on the opposite side of the counter. "So how's it going with Matt? I hear things are heating up." Tim tilted his head, his face curious.

Roman couldn't help smiling. "Things with Matt are very good."

"So you two have hooked up, I guess?" Tim put his elbows on the counter and his chin in his hands.

"If you mean have we had sex, then yes. Matt wanted me to mount him, so I did. But Lance says that doesn't mean I have to be in charge all the time. We also use just our hands or mouths sometimes. I like that a lot."

Tim laughed and his face went a little pink. "Okay! Well... awesome. I'm glad you're happy. You like Matt a lot, huh?"

"I love Matt. He's my mate, like you are Lance's."

Tim's face did something a little strange, and Roman couldn't quite figure out what it meant. "Look, Roman... I'm thrilled for you. Only...."

"Only what?"

Tim looked reluctant to speak. "Well. Quickened are very, very loyal. When you guys give your hearts, it's a big deal. But with humans, relationships don't always work out. In fact, most of the time, they don't."

The idea made Roman feel cold inside. "Why not?"

"Well..." Tim chewed his bottom lip. "Humans tend to date a lot of different people. Sort of more like a bee and... and flowers. Or something." He frowned. "And sometimes humans have hang-ups too. Baggage."

"Baggage?"

"Yeah, like maybe someone broke their heart when they were younger, so they decided never to fall in love again. Or they like dating and having sex with a lot of different people, so they don't want to be with just one person...."

Roman was feeling colder and colder. Was Matt like that? Was he like a bee and Roman was just one of many flowers to him? Because that was not the way Roman felt. Matt was the only flower he wanted.

Tim put his hand on Roman's arm and stroked it. "God, your face! I'm sorry. Don't be upset. I didn't mean to put a lot of negativity in your head. I just worry about you, that's all. I'm sure Matt really cares for you."

"I met Matt's father. He wants Matt to marry Luci."

"And *that's* what I mean by 'baggage'." Tim's eyebrows bunched together angrily. "So Matt definitely is not out." He blinked, seeing the confusion on Roman's face. "I mean, he hasn't told his family that he's gay."

343

Roman rubbed behind his ears to soothe himself, trying to process what Tim was saying. That night he'd met Matt's father, well, he and Matt hadn't had sex at that point. But it had still been awkward and uncomfortable hearing his father talk about Matt and Luci like they were a couple. Would Matt never want his family to know he loved Roman instead of Luci? That idea made him feel small and unimportant.

"*Hey.*" Tim pulled Roman's hands down from his ears and gripped his hands. "I'm not trying to freak you out. I just think… Matt's going to have to man up and stand up to his father sooner or later."

"His father is a very strong man. He's a retired general."

Tim shook his head. "Wow. That's tough."

"He likes dogs, though." Roman thought it was only fair to point that out.

"Yeah? Well then, he can't be all bad. Roman, I like Matt. I really do. I just hope he treats you like you deserve to be treated. Because you're such a good person."

Roman wasn't sure what Tim meant by that exactly, what would qualify as 'Matt not treating him like he deserved'. But he

344

understood that Tim was protective of the pack too, in a different way than Lance, maybe, but protective all the same.

"I'd be happy if we could be like you and Lance."

Tim smiled. "You will find someone like that, Roman. If not Matt, then someone else."

Roman didn't want anyone else. "I'm hungry." That was always a good excuse to change the subject. And it was true.

"Well, go get some food, big guy. Lily outdid herself as usual."

"What did you bring?" Tim always brought the best food.

"The lettuce wraps with Thai chicken and rice stuffing. They're really good."

Roman's stomach rumbled. He went to find something on the buffet table that was wrapped in lettuce.

\*              \*              \*

It had been a long week for Roman, but a good one. His shoulder was improving every day, and he'd stopped taking even the aspirin Lance and Leesa kept pushing on him. Since he still wasn't allowed to be seen in town, Matt dropped him off at his place after work. They usually picked food up at the diner or made something simple at Roman's house. They ate, and had sex, both in large quantities, and not necessarily in that order. Sometimes they watched TV too. Matt liked to go home to sleep, though, because Luci was there, and he felt guilty leaving her alone so much.

It had been two weeks since Roman and Matt first kissed, and Roman had never been happier. He'd been happy as a dog—being with James, doing his work. But it didn't compare to being happy as a man. He was a man who was in love, had a home of his own, a job he loved, lots to eat, and a cool uniform too! The surveillance work they'd been doing lately was awfully boring, but at least he got to be with Matt while they did it.

On Friday morning, Lance radioed Roman to say he and Charlie had spotted a new truck driving into town. The red-haired suspect, Colin Clery, met the truck at the diner. He and the man driving the truck had eaten breakfast, then Colin climbed into the passenger seat of the truck and they drove out to the illegal farm site where Roman and Matt were stationed on the ridge.

Colin's men helped the driver back the truck up as far into the brush as he could get. Then they opened the back door. The truck contained hundreds of tiny little plants packed in white Styrofoam trays. Each plant was no bigger than a thumb in size.

"Bingo," Matt whispered, his voice thrumming with excitement and satisfaction. He handed the binoculars to Roman so he could see too, and he started taking photos with the long camera lens.

They'd watched all day while four of the men planted the seedlings in the ground. Colin was the boss, and he didn't plant, he just stood around ordering the others or talking on his phone. He smoked a lot of cigarettes.

"Perfect," Matt said softly. The camera he used made tiny *click, click* sounds.

They were lying belly-down on the ridge, and Roman leaned close to whisper in Matt's ear. "Does this mean we can bust them now?"

Matt nodded. "Soon. We'll see what Dixon says, but yeah. This is what we've been waiting for."

It turned out it wasn't going to be right away, though. Later that day, Matt dropped off Roman and went into the office to file a report and talk to Dixon on the phone. When he called Roman an hour later, he seemed pleased.

"Dixon wants to give it another week or two, give the plants time to root and get a little larger. Still, with the evidence we already have, we could take them if we had too."

"So one more week?"

"Probably. But... fuck, Roman. We have them by the balls!"

Matt sounded very happy. Roman was happy too, but his emotions had a violent edge to them. Like Lance, he wanted those strangers out of his town. But it was personal for Roman. They'd *shot* him. They'd tried to get him to betray his friends. He'd never forget what it was like to be in that room with the plastic on the floor, bound to the chair and helpless. He'd thought for sure he was going to die. And it wasn't even just that they'd done that to him—it was the fact that they were capable of doing it to others too. Lance, for example. Or Charlie. Or Matt. The thought of Matt being in that room, tied to that chair, made Roman's vision go red. His growl must have been audible over the phone, because Matt laughed.

"Calm down, Ro. Everything's on track. Hey, want to come over to my place for dinner? Luci texted me that she's made lasagna, and she would love to see you. Her lasagna is the best. You'll love it."

"Okay." Roman was pleased that Matt wanted him at his house and around Luci. That conversation he'd had with Tim had continued to bother him, and at times Roman couldn't help wondering if Matt was ashamed that they were having sex.

"Great. Come by around seven? Hey, thanks for all your help. We wouldn't have found these guys if it weren't for your lines. At least, not as fast as we did. I put that in my report, you know. All hail Deputy Roman Charsguard."

Roman smiled. "Thank you, Matt."

"See you later, Ro."

Roman arrived at Matt's cabin freshly showered and dressed in his best clothes. He carried a bouquet of flowers he'd gotten from Tim. He'd seen on TV where men gave flowers to women, and he wanted to thank Luci for inviting him for dinner. And maybe, too, he wanted to say he was sorry for taking Matt away from her so much.

Not that he really was sorry, but it seemed like a nice thing to do.

Tim had rose bushes in the front of his house, including the one Roman liked the best. The petals were a soft cream color, like milk, and the edges looked like they'd been dipped in purple ink. The rose had won an award, Tim said, and was named "Linda's Flame" after the lady who owned his cabin. Tim added in some lavender roses and tiny white flowers called Baby's Breath—which was a creepy name, Roman thought. When it was done, the bouquet looked beautiful! Roman was excited to give it to Luci and tell her all about the special rose.

When he got to Matt's place, there was an extra vehicle in the driveway, but Roman didn't pay much attention to it. He knocked on the door.

Matt opened it. He looked very tense. "Oh, hi, Roman!" he said loudly. He looked at the flowers Roman held and his cheeks got pink. "You didn't have to bring anything. Luci, Roman brought flowers for the table!"

Matt took the flowers and stepped aside to let Roman in. Something was wrong. Matt was acting weird. Roman stood awkwardly by the door, not sure what to do.

"Hi, Roman." Luci came in from the kitchen. She had on a short black dress that made her look very skinny. Matt handed her the flowers and they exchanged a look, then Luci stepped up to Roman and kissed his cheek. "I'm so glad you could come for dinner."

That's when Roman looked up and saw Matt's father, the General, standing in the doorway to the kitchen. His face was blank.

"Hello, sir," Roman said.

"Deputy Charsguard." Matt's father didn't smile or look welcoming. He turned around and went back into the kitchen.

It was all wrong. The very air in the cabin felt wrong. Time itself was wrong, jumping forward in brittle little bursts. It felt like that day Roman had woken up in Afghanistan and known he and James shouldn't go out, that day it had all gone to hell. Roman wanted to turn around and leave Matt's house, but he didn't know if that would be insulting. He didn't know how to behave that wasn't all about dog instinct. So he just stood there.

"Come on in," Luci said, taking his arm. She tried to look cheerful, but her face was all wrong too. "We're just about ready to eat."

Roman was afraid to look at Matt, so he allowed Luci to lead him into the kitchen.

The kitchen table was set with four places. General Barclay was already seated, drinking from a glass that had amber liquid in it. He watched Roman, but Roman could read nothing on his face.

"I didn't know you had a visitor," Roman said, the panic continuing to build inside him. "I should go."

"Nonsense!" the General said sharply. "Sit down. If Luci and Matt already invited you to dinner, you're the guest. I'm the one who dropped by out of the blue."

"Because Mad Creek is so close to everything," Matt muttered.

Roman sat down at the table. He finally looked at Matt, but Matt just gave him a small, bewildered shrug.

Roman had never had a more uncomfortable meal in his life. Luci served salad and bread and lasagna. She chatted about her classes coming up in the January term and asked Matt's father questions that he answered with a single word or two. No one else even tried to talk.

The lasagna was as good as Matt said it was, but Roman wasn't hungry. Something inside him was still telling him to get out, telling him there was danger here. He couldn't understand what that would be, though.

When Matt cleared the table, he dropped a big spoon on the floor and it made a loud clatter. Roman jumped in his chair.

"You have PTSD?" Matt's father asked him. He raised his eyebrows at Roman, like he really wanted to know.

"I guess I do, sir. But it's not very bad."

"Uh-huh." The old man's eyes hardened. "Amazing that. Since you weren't actually in the military."

"Dad?" Matt's voice was a warning. He all but threw the dishes in the sink and strode back to stand at the table, hands on his hips. He looked as confused as Roman felt.

Roman didn't understand what the General meant, so he said nothing.

"See, Roman, here's the thing. I have friends in high places. I looked for your service record. Then I had *them* help me look for your service record. Roman Charsguard doesn't exist. Not in the B Company 2-87 Infantry Battalion and, in fact, not anywhere in any damned branch of the entire goddamned military!" General Barclay's voice was cruel.

Roman cringed inside. He felt frozen. He'd never been talked to like that before. There was so much hate coming off the man. Why? Why was he so angry?

"Dad, stop it! That can't be true! Why are you doing this?"

"Shut up, Matthew. You should know the way this 'friend' of yours has lied to you. He's an imposter. There's nothing I find more disgusting than a man who'd try to co-op someone else's glory, pretend he's earned respect and honor when he hasn't. That's the lowest of the goddamned low."

"Oh, Matt," Luci whispered, upset.

Roman's eyes were fixed on the tabletop, where his white plate was stained with red. He didn't know what to say. He didn't know what to do. Why hadn't he realized this might happen? Why had he told Matt's father about his unit? Of course his name wasn't in the records. But nothing else the General said was true, only Roman had no words to say that and no right to tell him the one thing that could make sense of it all.

"*Roman.*" Matt's voice was insistent. Roman looked up at him. Matt stood at the table, his arms folded across his chest. His dark eyes searched Roman's face, a frown on his brow. "That's not true, is it? This is just some paper glitch. Right? Did you change your name or something? Tell him."

Roman stared into Matt's eyes. He saw doubt there and confusion. They held nothing of the warmth and affection they'd held only the night before, when Matt had had sex with Roman in his bed. Roman was alone.

355

He took a deep breath, not realizing he'd been holding it. His shoulder burned and stung, and his ear throbbed. He felt like he'd been shot all over again. No, it felt worse than that.

"I was there," Roman said, as steadily as he could. "I was in the 2-87 Infantry Battalion."

"Son of a bitch," the General huffed. "Then give me a social security number, military ID, something. Because you sure as hell weren't there as Roman Charsguard!"

"Dad, stop it!" Matt said, but his voice was unsure. It was like the snarl of a dog who'd already submitted.

Roman's heart drained of life. Matt was not James. James had picked Roman up and put him on his shoulders when he was hurt, risked his own life to try to save him. But Matt—Matt just stood there and watched him bleed.

"You don't believe me." Roman's voice sounded funny.

Matt's eyes darted to his dad. He spoke low. "Well, Jesus, Roman. Give me a reason to."

"I thought I already had."

Roman stood up. His body didn't feel like his own as he walked through the house and out the door.

*                     *                     *

Matt watched Roman go, confused and upset. Why had Roman lied? How *much* had he lied? And what the fuck was up with his father? When the door closed quietly behind Roman, it felt like something irrevocable had happened. And Matt wasn't sure he even knew what it was.

He looked at Luci, expecting to see sympathy on his friend's face. But she was staring at him like he'd just shot a bunny rabbit. She stood up abruptly, muttered something about idiots and karma, and stalked out of the room.

The leaden feeling in Matt's stomach grew a few sizes, like the cartoon Grinch's heart. He turned on his father. "Dad, what the hell are you trying to do? Why would you do that?"

The General growled back. "I'm trying to save you from so-called friends who are full of shit! That guy is a liar. He's not worth another minute of your time, Matt."

357

"What the fuck? I hardly ever see you. Suddenly, you're all invested in my life and investigating my friends? You can't just walk into my house and insult my guests!"

His father stood up and placed his hands on his hips. He glowered at Matt. Thomas Barclay was still an impressive man— fit, tough, with a salt-and-pepper buzz cut and brown eyes like Matt's, only his had zero tolerance for nonsense, joking around, or anything else that was essentially Matthew Barclay.

"I came here last time to see you and Luci, to see if I couldn't get you to make some goddamn progress in your personal life. And what did I find? I find that guy." The General jabbed a finger toward the door.

"You didn't seem to mind at the time. I thought you liked Roman."

"I did! Until you two came back from some assignation, and he was looking at you like you had chocolate genitals and gold pouring out of your ass!" The words were practically spat out in disgust.

Matt pinched his eyes closed and rubbed at them with one hand. Oh. Fuck. That's what this was about. His extremities went cold and numb even as he felt his cheeks heat up. He looked at the wall, embarrassed and at a loss for words.

"I always suspected you had *issues*, Matthew. But I hoped you were at least 'bisexual', if that's even a thing, and that you knew your ass from your elbow enough to man up and do the right thing with your life. I won't have it!"

Matt's throat closed tight with a bitter rage. He couldn't stop seeing the disappointment on Roman's face when he'd left, and the way Luci had looked at him like he'd failed big-time. Then there were the years, yes, *years* of so many lies, so much fear, so much inadequacy.

His voice came out soft and furious. "*You* won't have it? Really? Well, that's too bad, because I'm not bisexual, dad, I'm gay. G-A-Y, gay. And no, I'm never going to marry Luci, even if she would have me, which she's way too fucking smart to do. I like men. I like Roman, in fact. And thank you so much for fucking that up for me!"

The General's face twisted. "Jesus, kid, forget about him. He's a compulsive liar! I'll send you the records if you don't believe me!" He grabbed Matt's upper arms tightly and shook him a little. "You can fight this, Matt. You don't *have* to be this way. Maybe a psychiatrist—"

Matt ripped away and took several steps across the room before he did something he'd regret—like punch his father in the face. This was the moment. This was it—he was coming out to his father. He had to at least try.

He took a calming breath. "Dad. You say you always suspected. Why do you think that is? I've known since I was six years old that I was different. Yes, I do *have to be this way.* No one made me gay. This is who I am! And nothing is going to change that."

His father stared at him, his face devastated. He shook his head.

"Do you have any idea what it was like for me to grow up with you for a father? Knowing I'd never be the son you wanted? Or with Mitch for a brother? Do you know how much I idolized him? How much I wanted to be like him? He was the hero, Dad, the real deal, and so were you. I've spent my life trying to be worthy of your respect, to live with integrity. But no matter how many battles I fight, or how many people I save, or how many goddamn guns I strap on, it will never matter. Because *inside* I'm someone you can never love. I'm sorry the wrong son died, Dad."

Matt's voice cracked. He couldn't stand to be weak in front of his father, so he turned and stormed out of the house, grabbing his keys along the way.

"Matthew! Get back here!"

But Matt slammed the door hard, got in his car, and peeled out, tires spinning in the dirt of the driveway.

He drove around for hours and finally parked off one of the dirt roads near town. He tried calling Roman, but he didn't answer his phone. That wasn't a good sign. Matt didn't know what to think. It had been a disaster since his dad first opened his mouth. But what could Matt have done differently? He'd been completely derailed by his father's attack. He'd only asked Roman to explain. But the look on Roman's face.... God. Matt felt like shit.

His father had picked his attack perfectly. Matt had grown up worshipping military men like his father and brother. The idea of someone faking a military career to make himself look better made Matt physically ill. But could Roman really

361

have done something like that? The more Matt thought about it, the more he was sure it wasn't possible. Roman was so fundamentally honest, *decent*. He always said what was on his mind, even when it wasn't the best idea. And his behavior was very ex-military, even the way he thought about their strategy.

More to the goddamn point, Matt had fallen for Roman, hard. And Roman seemed to have fallen for him too. For the first time in his life, Matt had seen the possibility of a relationship that might last… forever. Had he been a fool? Was anything about Roman real?

No, he wasn't going to think like that. He needed to talk to Roman before he leapt to any conclusions, and fuck his dad. He tried calling Roman several more times, but there was still no answer. Finally, Matt shut it all out of his mind and slept for a few haunted hours. It was a technique he'd learned after his mother died, when it all got to be too much to bear.

When he got home in the morning, the General's car was gone. Luci came out on the porch in her robe and hugged him.

"Oh, *cariño*. I'm so sorry. But its good you finally stood up to him. I'm so proud of you."

Matt didn't feel very proud of himself right then. "When did the General leave?"

"Last night. He told me to tell you that he had a lot of thinking to do, and he'd contact you when he was ready to talk about it."

*Or never,* Matt thought. Fuck his life. He was screwed in every way possible. Not only had he possibly lost his lover the previous night, a guy he'd *really* liked, but he'd lost his dad too. And just when he was about to coordinate his first big sting operation. That's what you got for thinking you had everything under control. The universe was a cruel bitch.

"Come on, sad sack. I have coffee ready." Luci took his hand and pulled him inside.

# 19

## Preparing To Bite

Matt got into the sheriff's office a half hour late that morning. He'd driven by Roman's house, unable to stay away. Roman hadn't been there, and he wasn't in the office either. Leesa looked at Matt blankly when he asked if she'd heard from him.

Fine. If Roman didn't want to see him, didn't want to talk, then he'd just have to wait. Matt had some research he wanted to do anyway.

The General had sent him a link to a password protected website, which listed all the personnel in the Army's B Company by last name and year. His father was right, Roman Charsguard was not listed, or anyone at all with the last name of Charsguard.

Was it possible his military record had gotten lost or was hidden for security reasons? It was hard to imagine anything that could cause that, short of some super-secret spy scenario. But Roman was a deputy in Mad Creek. As strange as Mad Creek was, Matt highly doubted the CIA or FBI or anyone like that would bother putting a spy there.

Matt looked through the names again for the years Roman might have served. A name caught his eye—Sergeant James Pattson, KIA.

That was the guy Roman had mentioned, his best friend. How would Roman know that name if he'd never been in that battalion? Fuck. He needed to just talk to Roman. Where the hell was he?

There was a knock on his office door. Matt looked at his watch. Yeah. It was nearly 9:30. Time to get to the stakeout. Would Roman be there?

He opened the door to find Sheriff Beaufort. He did not look happy. Beaufort stepped into Matt's office, crowding Matt back into the room. Matt frowned. "What can I do for you, Sheriff? Something up with our suspects?"

"No. They ate at the diner last night and then spent the evening in their cabin. A couple of hookers drove up from Fresno, and it sounds like they had a wild time. Everyone is still sleeping it off over there this morning. There's been no sign of movement so far."

Matt nodded. "They'll probably be late arriving at the site today then."

Lance had an uncomfortable look on his face. He tapped his fingers on Roman's desk anxiously. "Uh, Roman called in sick today. So. Do you want someone else to go with you to the ridge? Charlie's still on the vehicles, but I could accompany you for part of the day."

Roman called in sick? Matt didn't like that. At all. He tried to keep his face neutral. "No, I'm fine alone. If I need anything, I can radio you."

Beaufort nodded. He looked like he was about to leave, then he paused. His fingers tapped Roman's desktop. *Tap. Tap.*

"Deputy Charsguard. Roman…. He's the best officer I've ever had. He's a fine man."

Matt felt a wave of seasickness as the floor shifted beneath his feet. Beaufort knew about them. Goddamn it. Matt felt like such an idiot. But at least Beaufort was gay. So while he might—rightfully—fault Matt's professionalism, getting involved with a colleague, at least his homosexuality wouldn't be an issue.

Matt nodded. "Deputy Charsguard has been extremely helpful since I arrived. I doubt we would have found this farm without him." There was more Matt could say. Roman had been tireless—out there hiking and searching the woods with Matt every day, his stamina seemingly unlimited, and then he'd worked a full day on Saturdays for Beaufort too.

Matt's stomach soured with guilt as he remembered all those hours.

*Give me a reason to believe you.*

*I thought I already had.*

"Roman..." Beaufort cleared his throat. "...he's, er, he's been through a lot. And he's not very experienced with, um, people." Beaufort studied the carpet, two bright red commas on his cheeks.

God, it was the Big Brother talk. How... incredibly awkward.

367

"Yeah. Um, look, I'd better get out there. I'll keep in contact and let you know what's going on at the site. Thanks, Sheriff."

Matt grabbed his jacket and escaped. He wondered if Beaufort already knew that Matt had managed to hurt Roman, and, if so, where he was likely to put Matt's dead body.

As he drove up the mountain toward the illegal pot farm, Matt wondered again where Roman was. Why had he disappeared? Why wasn't he answering his phone? *He's been through a lot.* Hell. Tonight. Surely Roman had to be home tonight. If it turned out there was a reasonable explanation for why his name wasn't in the records, and Matt needed to grovel, he would.

Please God, let there be a damned good reason for him to grovel.

\*                    \*                    \*

Talking to Roman that night turned out not to be an option.

368

That afternoon, Matt lay on the ridge above the illegal pot farm, hidden in the trees. He took photos with his telephoto lens, like usual. And like usual, those photos were uploaded directly to the DEA office via satellite.

It was a slow day on the site. After the big planting effort that had taken place the day before, only two of the bodyguard types and the dark-haired guy, identified by the DEA as Rufus Weaser, bothered to show up. They stayed for a few hours, checking on the plants and setting up some irrigation lines, then they took off again.

Matt radioed it in when they left, and Beaufort picked up the tail. But the relative quiet of the day ended at 4:05. Matt had hiked back to his truck and saw he'd had a call from Dixon at headquarters. The reception in the woods was spotty at best. He leaned against his truck and called his boss back.

"We're ready to move. The sting will happen at dawn tomorrow at their cabin."

"What? Are you serious? I thought you said it would be awhile."

"Yeah, well, the legal department says the evidence you've collected is enough—good work, Barclay, particularly on the photos. They were able to zoom in and positively identify all the plants they put in the ground as cannabis and the farm's on public land, so the lawyer's happy. We'll get plenty of evidence from the site to corroborate."

"That's good news."

"The governor has already signed off, and we have an opening in the SWAT schedule. So the regional coordinator wants to go ahead and move."

Holy shit. This was happening. It was good news, as far as Matt was concerned. Hell, it was fucking *marvelous*. There was always the risk that something would go wrong and the suspects would up and disappear. Matt would be relieved when this particularly operation was over and the men were behind bars.

*Maybe then I can go back to just regular patrols with Roman.* That sounded so fucking great. But Matt wasn't sure they'd be able to get back to those simpler days. Just thinking about Roman twisted him up so much it stole his breath away. He pushed it from his mind. He had work to do.

370

"Okay," he told Dixon. "So what's my role in the sting? Should I meet you there? You want Beaufort in on this too?"

"Yes, I want you there, but I'll be running the takedown. I'll need you to confirm we've got all the suspects in custody. And you can organize the search of the property once it's cleared. I'll call Beaufort to let him know what's going on, but this raid is entirely under the DEA."

"Sounds good."

"Oh, and I'll need a case file ready to be handed off. Bring a physical copy with you."

"Sure."

"We'll be setting up just out of sight of the cabin on Piney Top Drive. Be there at 0-500."

"I'll see you then."

Matt hung up, his body humming with excitement. He looked at his watch. Shit, this was going down in a little over twelve hours from then. His first instinct was to call Roman, let him know their work was about to come to fruition. But he'd

371

already left a half dozen messages, and Roman wasn't responding.

It was starting to freak him out. He wanted to talk to Roman. Surely, this thing with his dad wasn't so bad that he and Roman were just through, end of story. He couldn't believe that. But for every hour that passed with no word from Roman, Matt felt worse and worse.

Damn it, he had to focus on the task at hand. He had to get the file ready, and he had to talk to Beaufort. He had to keep his head screwed on straight and put his personal life on hold. That's the first thing you learned in the Marines, because if you were distracted, people could get hurt.

Matt closed his eyes, breathed deep, and did his best to let it go. There was an operation going down. He got in his car and headed, fast, for Mad Creek.

*         *         *

Colin woke up well past noon to the pound of earth-moving equipment. It took several minutes to realize the bulldozer was only in his head. Damn tequila. That shit was evil.

He rolled out of bed and took a cold shower, hoping to jump-start his system. In the bathroom mirror, he looked like crap. He had bags under his eyes and two big purple hickies on his neck. The sight of the bruises made him smile, though. The girls had been hot the night before, and his rank and file had been happy. You gotta let the guys blow off steam once in a while, and they'd had a lot to celebrate. Deputy Roman Asswipe had never shown up, and the local law had been non-existent since then. Colin had seen three different men and a woman going in and out of the sheriff's office—he watched it whenever he went into Daisy's diner. But they'd never bothered him, and he'd never seen anyone up around their site. Hell, they were so far in the middle of nowhere he doubted coyotes could find them.

Add to that the fact that they'd gotten the plants in the ground this week, and Colin was pleased. It was all going well. *So* well, in fact, he was considering doubling down, starting more acres. The big question was if he should keep clearing land around his current plot, or add a new location. Even with their camouflage tarps, a larger farm had the potential to be more visible by satellite. On the other hand, two locations would add a lot of work. Oh, the decisions of the rich and not particularly famous.

He ignored Jaycee, the pink-haired hooker, who was crashed out on the couch, and grabbed his keys. He'd drive into town and have a nice, long breakfast at the diner, flirt with Daisy, and think about his options. Rufie, Sam, and Xerses were at the site today, but they didn't need him there. He had a package to pick up from the post office too.

"Hi, Colin!" Daisy brought a menu over to his booth. She attempted a smile, but her lips trembled.

"Hello, doll. How are you today?" Colin was always up for charming Daisy. He was playing a long game there.

"Good." Daisy nodded, but her head bobbed too frantically to be natural.

"What's the matter? You look nervous."

"Me? Nervous?" Daisy tittered. "Huh-uh. Nope. Not nervous. So did you want lunch or dinner?"

Colin checked the time on his phone. It was nearly 4 p.m. Fuck. He'd lost the whole goddamn day. "Chicken sandwich and fries, doll."

"Of course!" She hurried away without asking if he wanted anything else. She came back and plopped a Coke on the table—his usual—smiled nervously again and went back into the kitchen.

Whatever. Maybe she was having personal issues. It wasn't Colin's problem. He sipped his Coke and watched the police station across the street.

Rufie said each tiny plug they'd planted could grow into a plant that would yield two pounds of pot. Given the street value of $2500 to $3500 per pound—and Colin had the contacts in L.A. to get the higher price—that meant he could make $14-20 million on what he had planted already.

Which was a lot of fucking money for a boy from Ohio that casting agents didn't wanna know. Fuck you, Tom Cruise. But what Colin really hoped for was that marijuana would be legalized. Being rich *and* legit—that was the ultimate goal. He wanted to be in a position where no one could take this away from him. With the money he'd earn this year, he could buy a big piece of property, grease some palms to get a license, maybe build his own huge, decked-out cabin. Then, when the lawmakers got their shit together, he'd be ready to grow the stuff on the map. That would be a good—

Across the street, a man emerged from the sheriff's office. Colin had seen him before. It was Sheriff Beaufort. He wore his uniform too tight and was good-looking in an obnoxious way, like he was right out of central casting for cop assholes. That was fine, though. Let the sheriff ride around looking cool in his sunglasses and chatting up the locals. Colin didn't give a shit, as long as he stayed out of their way.

Besides the sheriff, there was a dorky-looking deputy with the original name of Charlie Smith. The guy was skinny and all gawky limbs and a big nose. And then there was the DEA guy, Matt Barclay. He was the one who worried Colin. But there were a hell of a lot of woods out there, and with their camouflage they'd be hard to find by air unless someone knew just where to look.

The sheriff walked around to the driver's side of his vehicle and then looked right at the diner, right at Colin, who was sitting in a booth at the window. Beaufort smirked at him, then got in his SUV and drove away.

Colin frowned.

"Want a refill on that Coke?" Daisy asked, putting his plate in front of him.

"Yeah, thanks, doll."

Daisy took his glass away as Colin pondered that smirk. He'd never actually met the sheriff, and surely Beaufort didn't know who he was. Colin looked around the diner but didn't see any other obvious recipient of the smirk. Maybe Daisy had been behind him or something.

Colin ate his dinner, put some bills on the table, and left to get to the post office before they closed at five.

The guy who ran the post office, Fred Beagle, was busy weighing about forty million boxes for an older lady. Okay, there were four boxes, but it was still annoying. Colin hung back, looking at the bulletin board.

Jesus. Small towns. There were fliers for classes in English, reading and writing, basic finances, driving lessons, and personal grooming, all meeting various nights of the week. There were grief counseling sessions and cooking demonstrations. There were roommate notices and job listings. All of it had a strange intimacy about it, like everyone in town knew everyone else. Most of the listings were handwritten and just had first names on them like 'at Lily's place' or 'talk to Gus'.

Colin shook his head in puzzled amusement. Just then Fred Beagle's sharp voice caught his attention. He'd been droning on to the lady with the boxes ever since Colin walked in, but suddenly his words triggered an alarm.

"—first thing tomorrow. Before the sun's up. Isn't it exciting! Lance said we weren't needed, but heck, we've been watching those guys for weeks, and I'd like to see a big SWAT operation in real life! Wouldn't you? There's a whole forest behind that cabin on Piney Top, and I might sneak up there to watch it from the trees. What do you think? Is that a bad idea? They wouldn't notice, 'specially if we were wearing our fur suits."

"I don't know, Fred," the woman said doubtfully. "There might be a shootout. You wouldn't want to get hit by a stray bullet. If Lance said we should stay clear—"

Ice water poured through Colin's veins, starting at the crown of his head and descending in a frozen wave of dread.

He hunched his shoulders and quietly slipped out of the post office. He walked casually to his car, even though he wanted to run. His fingers clutched the cell phone in his pocket, and he was dialing as he pulled out onto Main Street.

"Rufie? All of you get your asses back to the cabin *now*. We've got trouble."

# 20

## By The Throat

After Roman left Matt's house, the General's words of condemnation still ringing in his ears—*liar, imposter, lowest of the low*—he didn't know what to do. He couldn't bear going in to work the next day. He didn't want to see Matt. He hadn't been going into the office anyway, since they were still hiding the fact that he was alive. But he didn't want to meet up with Matt for surveillance either. So he sent a text to Lance saying he'd be out the next day.

Then he drove home, changed into warm hiking clothes, tied on his boots, and stuffed his backpack with water bottles and protein bars. He needed to disappear. He drove to one of the northernmost points he'd explored, an hour's drive from town, and set off into the woods.

It hurt. It hurt almost as much as losing James had hurt. Roman wished he could cry to let out some of the pain, but he never had cried human tears. His eyes remained stubbornly dry. Tim had been right after all—it was easy for humans to fall into a relationship and fall out of one too. At the first sign of a challenge, Matt had doubted him.

*Come on, Roman, you can do it. I know you can do it!*

James had never let Roman down, never left him alone, never deserted him by word, look, or deed. But then, they hadn't been lovers, and Roman had been a dog. Maybe it was easier for humans to be true to a dog. Dogs never had to say anything, so they never had to lie. And there were a lot less ways to fail when you were a dog. It was so much less complicated than being a man.

Maybe Roman deserved Matt's doubt. Maybe he was the one who had failed. After all, he hadn't told Matt the truth about himself, so he had lied in a way. He just didn't know which of them had first let go of the rope that bound their hearts together, or when. But his inner dog was miserable, grieving, abandoned by the second person he'd truly loved.

He walked through the night and into the dawn. He wanted to change into his dog, give in to the animal all the way and try to forget his pain, but he couldn't. His shoulder was much better, but still sore. He didn't want to hurt it again. Plus, he couldn't ignore his duty. What had happened was not Lance's fault nor the packs. He should keep his cell phone in case Lance really needed him. But the only person who called was Matt. Roman didn't answer it. He was hurt and he didn't want to talk to Matt. Plus, he had no idea what to say. He couldn't tell Matt the truth.

The sun was at midmorning when his phone rang again and this time the display said 'Lance'. Roman answered.

"Where are you, Roman? What's going on?" Lance sounded worried.

"I left a message about a sick day. I need time alone. I'm sorry."

Roman stood on a rocky trail and looked down on the tops of pine trees. A red squirrel regarded him curiously from the safety of a high branch. Roman didn't even want to chase the squirrel. Boy, his dog was really feeling low.

"Did something happen?" Lance asked tensely.

"Yes. But I don't want to talk about it." Roman wanted solitude at the moment, wanted to curl up in the corner, his back to the world.

Lance huffed. "Does this—does this have something to do with Matt?"

Roman didn't answer.

Lance growled, low. "Okay, Roman. But if you're not feeling better by tomorrow, we *are* going to talk about it."

"Yes, sir." Right then, today was the only thing Roman cared about.

"And you call me if you need someone, okay? You know we're here for you. Me and Tim both."

"Yes, sir." Roman hung up and started walking again.

He ate some late berries for lunch and took a nap by a small waterfall in a patch of warm sunlight. The woods were so beautiful in the fall. He liked the yellow aspens the best, with their small round leaves that shimmered in every breeze. And he loved the contrast of soft, dark green pine needles against the burnt orange of oak and the red of maple. The birds and animals were busy everywhere in the brush. In the summer, they were often quiet in the heat of the day, but the cooler air and the oncoming winter kept them working all morning and afternoon. The woods had never felt so alive.

Slowly, Roman started to feel better, the pain in his chest easing bit by bit. But then he thought about how nice it would be if Matt were here with him to see this. And that made him feel sadder than before.

He sat on a peak for a while, appreciating the rolling view. He decided it was time to go home. He'd lost some muscle while he was sick, and his legs were very tired. He started walking back. He'd almost reached his truck when his phone buzzed again. He pulled it from his pocket hoping to see Matt's name. But the display read: *Lance*.

"Hello?" Roman answered.

"Roman? Goddamn it, I need you *now*. The suspects are escaping. We need to move on them right away!"

"I can be in town in an hour." Roman started to run.

\*                    \*                         \*

Matt was organizing the file for his hand-off to Dixon when Sheriff Beaufort burst into his office. He was white as a sheet.

"They know."

"What?" Matt stood up at his desk.

"Colin Clery and his men. They know about the bust. I have someone watching the cabin, and they're packing up right this minute."

"Shit! How'd they find out? It wasn't like we discussed it on police radio. Unless you...." Matt didn't want to accuse Beaufort outright, but he couldn't imagine how else the suspects had found out.

Beaufort shook his head angrily. "It doesn't matter now. What matters is, they're about to move. They're running around loading the truck and the Caddy. They'll be long gone by the time the DEA gets here at sunrise."

"I'll call Dixon," Matt said, frustrated and angry. He needed to report this. Dixon would give him orders on what to do. But what *could* they do? There were only a few of them, and the DEA wouldn't be able to move up the raid any significant amount of time, not with so many pieces to coordinate. They'd probably have to call it off.

"Look," Matt said. "We have photographs of them, and we've ID'd two of the suspects. The DEA can put out a warrant for their arrest. Eventually—"

"No." Beaufort's tone was ironclad, surprising Matt. He took another look at the sheriff. Beaufort stood there in the small office with his feet braced apart and his arms folded. He wasn't a tall man, but in that pose, he looked like a colossus, especially with those burning blue eyes and set jaw.

"No?"

"*Hell. No.* We can hold 'em on Piney Top. There's only one road up to those cabins and that lake is surrounded by deep woods. We should be able to hold 'em there until the DEA gets here in the morning. I'm not letting those assholes out of my territory so they can slip back in whenever they feel like it, or tell others about Mad Creek." Beaufort was practically bristling with rage. There was a sense of goosebumps or raised hair or something that radiated out from him.

Damn, he was intense.

"But there's only four of us," Matt said slowly, his mouth dry. Part of him wanted to agree with Beaufort, *forward men, once more into the breach* and all that. He didn't want to lose these suspects either. He knew there was a chance they'd never be found once they got out of town. But practically, the idea didn't make much sense. "And you and Charlie don't have SWAT or military training." Roman did. But Matt didn't want to see Roman on the firing line. The very idea made his gut twist up.

"We can do a blockade, down the hill from the cabin. Block off the road with three or four vehicles and hunker down behind them with guns. They won't be able to get past and we'll have a good position."

"What if they have bigger fire power? A rocket launcher? Grenades?" Matt had seen some of the arsenals they'd confiscated after raids, and he'd been up against some heavy-duty shit in SWAT. It was sickening what your average citizen could get their hands on, much less guys with lots of money and crimes to hide.

"We'll cross that bridge when we come to it. I'm not going to back down without a fight."

Matt shook his head. As much as he didn't want to lose his suspects, he didn't want to see Lance, Charlie, or Roman hurt either. This could be a bloodbath. "It's too risky. We should report this to Dixon and let the DEA handle it."

Beaufort stepped closer to Matt's desk, put his palms on the top of it, and leaned over into Matt's space. Good Lord, his eyes were like laser beams.

"Let me rephrase this," Beaufort said, enunciating clearly. "Those men are on my territory. I, my deputies, and my town, are not letting them escape. I *am* doing the blockade. You want to sit here and twiddle you thumbs waiting for the DEA to show up, that's up to you. Is that perfectly clear, Mr. Barclay?"

Matt felt very, very clear about it.

It wasn't like he could prevent the town's sheriff from doing what he was going to do. He didn't have that authority. Matt shook his head in resignation. "I'll call Dixon and apprise him of the situation, ask him to move the time line up as much as possible. Where should I meet you for the blockade, Sheriff?"

Lance nodded once. "Good man. Piney Top Drive. Get there as soon as you can. I'm leaving now."

Matt banged into his cabin, scaring Luci, who was working at the kitchen table. "Matt?"

"Can't talk. We've got a bust. Just came home to change."

He stripped quickly in his bedroom and put on his bulletproof vest from SWAT underneath a black DEA shirt and jacket. He strapped on his firearm and grabbed some extra rounds. His blood was pumping hard, the way it always did before battle. There was a chance he wouldn't survive the fight.

"Mattie, you're scaring me." Luci stood nervously in the doorway to his room, her hands clasped together.

"It'll be all right," he told her, because that's what you say.

He grabbed his keys and went to push past her, but she grabbed his arm. Her eyes were bright with tears. "But what's going on? I thought you said when you were ready to move on your drug guys, the DEA would come out, and you'd just be watching."

"That was the plan, but something's come up." He paused long enough to kiss her forehead. "I'll call you as soon as I can, but it will probably be morning. Don't worry. Okay?"

He couldn't bear to look at her face again before taking off out the door.

*         *         *

Matt drove up Piney Top Drive at breakneck speed, his window open, listening for the sound of gunfire or car engines, for anything at all. But it was quiet other than his own engine and the occasional squeal of his tires. The road was twisty and uphill, and he wasn't sure if that gave them or the bad guys an advantage.

He rounded a curve and saw two sheriff's department vehicles, a post office truck, and another pickup truck parked on the road. They were still out of sight of the cabin where the suspects were staying.

Beaufort and Deputy Smith were there along with a fourth man Matt didn't know. There was no sign of Roman. Matt got out and approached the group. It was clear Beaufort had been waiting on him.

"Matt," Beaufort nodded at him. "This is Elliott. He was on a sharp-shooting team in school."

"Hello." Elliott nodded at Matt. He was in his twenties and he looked terrified. He had the pale sheen of a greenhorn before his first real shit storm in the Marines. He was on the frail side—healthy looking, but very thin, with red hair and freckles.

Jesus Christ, Beaufort was bringing in civvies with guns. This wasn't good. But it was Beaufort's operation for now, so Matt kept his mouth shut.

"What about Roman?"

Beaufort looked away. "He's here. I have him stationed out where I need him. Don't worry. Here's what we're going to do. We're gonna get in the vehicles and drive up the road until we're just within sight of the cabin. I'll be in front. When I pull my truck to the left, that's the spot. Charlie, you park across the middle of the road. Elliot, the post office truck will go in front of Charlie, blocking the right side and shoulder. And Matt, you park yours right up next to Charlie's. So we'll have three vehicles in the front line, blocking the road and shoulder, and one behind the middle for reinforcement. Got it?"

Everyone nodded.

"Then out of the vehicles and get behind them with your weapons. Charlie, you'll be with me behind my car. Matt and Elliot, you two will be behind the hood of Charlie's truck. We'll be visible from the cabin, but not that close. That's what we want. I'd prefer they stayed holed up in the house rather than get in their vehicles and challenge the blockade."

"And if they do? They've got pretty large vehicles," Matt pointed out.

"Then we fire," Beaufort said flatly.

It wasn't much of a plan, as far as Matt was concerned. It seemed like the four of them with their vehicles were not enough to hold back the men if they were well-armed and determined to get through. Where was Roman? Was he stationed closer to the house so he could report on their activity? They needed a lot more manpower. Dixon hadn't been happy on the phone, though he'd been hopeful that Beaufort could hold the suspects down until they got here. Now, seeing what they had to work with, Matt felt like it was a suicide run.

"Sheriff Beaufort, we don't have the resources for this operation. I have to advise you—"

"Matt!" Beaufort barked. He looked determined as hell. "I'm asking you to trust me, just this once."

Matt shook his head, but he shut his mouth.

"Are you in or out?" Beaufort demanded.

Matt felt no hesitation. "I'm in." No matter how ill-advised this blockade was, there was no way Matt was going to walk away from the fight and leave his friends to face it alone.

*Friends.* Beaufort and Charlie were friends, he realized. Beaufort was tough as nails but also gay, out and proud, which Matt admired like crazy, and so protective of his town. Everyone in Mad Creek loved Beaufort. And Charlie was a big dufus at times, but he was entirely sincere and tried so hard. When had that happened? When had they gotten to be friends? As for Roman, *his Roman*, he was out there too. No fucking way was Matt going anywhere without him.

"Lock and load." Matt put his shoulders back and his hand on his gun.

Beaufort gave him a feral smile. "All right then. Let's go."

They pulled the cars up fast. Matt was last in the line, and he swung a hard left and then right, getting his Cherokee as close beside Charlie's truck as he could. Then he got out, pulling his gun from the holster, and ran hunched over to the front of Charlie's truck. Elliot ran up and crouched beside him.

Matt looked over the hood at the cabin. There was no movement, but Matt was pretty sure that meant fuck-all. The white Caddy SUV was parked nose out and close to the cabin. It's back liftgate was raised—they were packing up the cars. The supply truck was next to the caddy, its back end facing the open garage.

"Two men ran inside as I pulled up," Lance called out, his voice carrying on the still fall air.

That was that then, Matt thought. They'd definitely been spotted already. Beside him, Elliot was tense, his rifle braced on the hood of Charlie's truck. The height of it had him squatting awkwardly.

"Elliot," Matt said, low. "First, relax. You don't want to fire first and make things worse. Relax and wait for the sheriff's command. Second, you can't shoot if you're not comfortable. Try getting on your knees."

Elliot gave Matt a relieved glance, as if glad someone who knew their shit was beside him. He went to his knees, but the hood of the truck was too high for him to see over.

Matt crept around Elliot to the front of Charlie's truck and pointed his finger at the fat bumper, mimicked the position he wanted Elliot to take and then moved out of the way. Elliot shuffled forward on his knees, put his rifle's barrel on the bumper and looked through the sight with ease. It was the right height and he could still be mostly concealed behind the truck. He looked at Matt and nodded.

Matt stayed at the hood. With his handgun, it was easier for him to crouch or rise up to fire. The cabin was still silent.

And then it wasn't. There was a burst of gunfire from a window of the cabin—*rat-a-tat-tat*. It sounded like a semi-automatic, maybe an Uzi. Matt ducked down behind the car and looked over to make sure Elliot had ducked too.

The fire continued, breaking the glass out of the windows of their vehicles and thudding into the asphalt and side panels on the other side. That gauge shouldn't be able to make it all the way through the car, not with the engine in the way. Matt hoped.

The gunfire ceased and there was the sound of motors revving. Matt peeked over the hood. Shit. Yes. The fire had been for cover. The supply truck pulled out of the driveway fast, rocking on its wheels, and the white Caddy was behind it. There were multiple people in each vehicle. They headed straight for the blockade at top speed.

Oh *fuck.*

"Shoot!" Beaufort shouted.

Matt braced his gun hand on the hood of the car and fired, aiming for the driver of the truck. One of the big men he'd seen at the site leaned out from the back bumper of the truck and fired. The supply truck's windshield shattered, but it kept coming, the driver hunkering low.

"Aim for the tires!" Matt shouted to Elliot.

A moment later, one of the truck's tires blew, but the vehicle wobbled and kept coming. The Caddy drove onto the shoulder, pulling out from behind the supply truck. Men fired out both back passenger windows, forcing Matt and Elliot to duck down and presumably Beaufort and Charlie too.

Matt braced himself for impact, but it didn't come. The shots ceased. He looked over the hood of the car to see the supply truck and the white Caddy stopped side by side on the road, facing the blockade. Four men were pointing guns at them from the vehicles' windows. And one guy... shit. The guy at the back of the moving truck held something on his shoulder that looked like a rocket launcher.

Matt kept his own gun braced on the hood, but he swallowed. They were deeply screwed.

To his left, Beaufort slowly stood up. His gun was in his hand, but he casually rested it on the hood of his truck. "You might as well relax, Clery," he called out, "because you're not going anywhere."

Matt gritted his teeth. At any breath, he expected Beaufort's head to explode in a sea of red. *Idiot.* Jesus, this was not worth it. They needed a lot more men—pros. He should have made Beaufort drop this crazy plan. He should have—

A man's voice called from the Caddy. It was the redhead, Colin Clery. "Move one of those fucking trucks or be roadkill. Your choice."

"Give me a minute," Beaufort said calmly. He dropped down behind the truck again. *What the hell is he doing?*

Matt decided he couldn't just stand by anymore. He was the one with SWAT experience after all. He did a crouch-run around his Cherokee to reach Beaufort and Charlie on the other side. Beaufort saw him and held up a hand. *Wait.*

"Five minutes. Then we're coming through!" The voice from the Caddy informed them, sounding pissed off. "One Mississippi, two Mississippi.... I'm watching the clock motherfuckers!"

Matt motioned to Beaufort adamantly, pointing at them and then down the road with swift jabs. *Withdraw.* Beaufort shook his head and held up his hand again—*wait*—and peeked over the hood. He seemed unafraid and, in fact, pissed off and defiant. Jesus, the lunatic was going to get them all killed.

Matt listened. There was silence except for the rev of the car engines in front of them. But... there was something. It wasn't a noise exactly, but Matt could sense something. He raised his head to peek over the hood.

The first thing that caught his eye was a dog. It was coming out of the trees on the side of the road, crouching low. It almost looked like a wolf, it was so big and furry, but its black coat had some spots of white. It was a collie of some kind. A huge one. Then movement caught Matt's peripheral vision and his eyes shifted. There was another dog coming out of the trees, and another, and another.

"What the fuck, Colin?" A man's voice, from the Caddy, carried in the weird silence. He sounded nervous.

"Shoot it," Colin said.

"Which one? They're all over the fucking place!"

"I ain't shooting no dog," one of the other men said.

These words registered on Matt's battle-sharp brain even while his eyes couldn't leave the spectacle in front of him. *What the hell?* Where were all those dogs coming from?

There were hound dogs and retrievers, a bunch of black collies, a few huge mountainous dogs with long shaggy hair, a great Dane, bulldogs, poodles, even Chihuahuas. It was entirely surreal, like an Alfred Hitchcock movie. A large German shepherd moved in from the flank, crouching low, ears back, eyes locked on the Caddy like a wolf stalking a rabbit. It moved to the head of the pack. There was an unmistakable air of command about the dog, which—

*Paco?* Holy shit, was that *Paco?* The top of the German shepherd's head and its chest were black, and his right ear... *his right ear was torn and scarred.* That was either the dog Matt had nursed back to health, or Matt was losing his ever-loving mind.

"Beaufort...?" Matt couldn't finish the question, even in his own head. Beaufort ignored him.

"You're surrounded, Clery!" Beaufort shouted confidently. "Surrender *now*. Put down your weapons or—"

Clery threw open the passenger side door of the Caddy, leaned out, and began to shoot the dogs.

He got off two shots. The first hit a large black collie, which jerked and yelped in pain. The second appeared to miss as the dogs scattered. There was a blur of movement and then Clery was out of the car and on the ground, a furry body on top of him, and jaws on his throat. His gun skittered away on the asphalt.

It was the German shepherd. *Paco*.

A sound left Matt's mouth and he started to move, but Beaufort clamped an iron hand on his arm and held him back. Clery screamed. The men who'd been riding in the back of his Caddy aimed guns at the writhing pair, but didn't fire.

"Shoot it!" Clery screamed, his voice garbled and gurgly as the dog squeezed his throat in strong jaws.

"Can't, Colin! I'll hit you too!" one of the gunmen called out.

The rest of the dogs crept closer, teeth bared and growling, looking ready to rip apart the suspects. Christ, there had to be a hundred of them, with more on the other side of the moving truck too. Where the fuck were they all coming from? This was *insane*.

"Clery?" Beaufort's voice rang out.

There was silence other than the almost subsonic threat of a hundred growls and the harsh, panicked pant-sobs from Clery, who was still on the ground. Clery 's men had their guns aimed at the dogs, but seemed leery of firing into them.

"This is how it's going to go," Beaufort went on, his voice rigid with command. "You're all going to surrender your weapons. Put them on the ground. Then my men are going to handcuff you, and we'll all head down to a nice, safe cell in the sheriff's office in town. It's either that or I tell the dogs to attack. It'll take my friend there about five seconds to rip your throat out, Clery. But the good news is, the excruciating pain won't last long because *you'll be dead.*"

Paco's growl intensified and he shifted slightly. He must have bitten down a little harder, because Clery's hands rose and pinwheeled in the air.

"Stop! Stop!" Clery shouted, terror in his voice. "Fuck! I give up! Put your weapons down. Do it!"

Maybe the men really gave a shit what Clery told them to do, or maybe the threat of the dogs was frightening enough that they were ready to surrender anyway. But almost instantly, their weapons clattered to the road. Hands were raised.

"Get out of the vehicles and line up facing us, hands on your heads," Beaufort ordered.

The men didn't look happy about getting out of the cars with the dogs there, but they did as asked. Two, four... five men, plus Clery, who was still on the ground with the dog on his throat. They faced the blockade and put their hands on their heads. The low growling from the dogs continued.

"Charlie, Matt, go cuff 'em," Beaufort said, low. "Clery too."

Matt didn't want to get any closer to those dogs, but he wasn't going to be a coward now. He kept his handgun out and ready and fished in his pocket for zip-ties. They were right where they were supposed to be. He slowly followed Charlie around the blockade and approached the suspects. The dogs in their path parted for them like they'd been choreographed. Matt spared a few quick glances around, but none of the dogs were looking at, or growling at, him. Sweat slid down his back. He liked dogs, yeah, but this... this was terrifying. There was something very funky here, and he had no idea what to make of it.

No way one man could train or control this many dogs. What the fuck was going on?

Charlie kicked a weapon farther away and started zip-tying the hands of the guy at the end of the Caddy. Matt was drawn, like a moth to a flame, to Clery. He had to know for sure.

The shepherd on top of Clery didn't raise its head as Matt approached. He holstered his gun and slowly reached for one of Clery's hands where it lay on the road, shaking. The dog's head was down, but it suddenly shifted, letting go of Clery's neck and backing off far enough that Matt could reach across Clery's body and get the other hand. The dog stood with its teeth bared and its eyes fixed on Clery, still growling viciously, as if daring him to move.

Matt zip-tied Clery's hands together and then his feet as the dog held Clery in terrified stillness. Finally, Matt was free to look at the dog. He stared. Christ, it *had* to be Paco. The dog's golden eyes met Matt's, intelligent and wary. It *was* Paco. Matt would know him anywhere.

*His eyes.*

*His torn ear.*

*The fresh-looking scar on Roman's shoulder.*

*Roman is here. I have him stationed out where I need him.*

*Matt would know him anywhere.*

Stunned, Matt jolted back and landed on his ass on the road. "Pa—Pa—Pa...." His mouth wouldn't work.

The dog licked its lips, whined anxiously, and turned away. It trotted off into the forest, limping on one leg.

"Ro?" Matt whispered.

"Matt!" Lance's voice was sharp. "Get up and help Charlie with the others. Now!"

Matt's training kicked in. They had suspects still unsecured and firearms lying all over the place. He stood and was about to move when Clery spoke to him, half whispering. "Barclay! It's this fucking town, man. *This fucking town.* They're a bunch of aliens or something! I swear to God. Just get me the fuck out of here!"

Matt glanced down at him. Clery's eyes were wide with horror. His throat was intact, but Matt could see the outline of every tooth, purple in the flesh, several puncture wounds trickling blood.

Matt didn't respond. He went to zip-tie the rest of the men.

# 21

## An Inconceivable Truth

Matt knew. Roman was pretty sure. The look on his face after he'd put the zip-ties on the red-haired man wouldn't leave Roman's mind. His face had been pale, shocked, accusatory, horrified, hurt.... So many emotions—and all of them bad!

Roman played it back in his mind, but he couldn't see how they might have done it differently. Lance hadn't wanted the men to escape. No one in town had wanted that. And they hadn't had enough strength to hold them without the pack. The pack had never done anything like that before, working together as dogs. It had been awesome—and frightening. There could have been widespread injuries. As it was, Lance's brother, Lonnie, had been shot. He was going to be okay, according to Bill McGurver. But Roman knew just how bad a gunshot wound could be and how painful the recovery.

Roman shifted back alone under a pine tree, his shoulder hurting like hell. He found the pack gathered nearby in the woods, excited and wanting to talk about what had happened.

None of them had been aggressive in their former lives, and they were shaken but proud of how they'd stopped the gunmen, how they'd helped the town. But Roman couldn't share their joy, not with Matt's face in his mind.

He drove back home, took a shower, and put on jeans and a comfy sweatshirt. He loved sweatshirts. They were like wearing a blanket, and right then he needed all the comfort he could get.

He should call Lance, warn him that Matt probably knew about them and ask if he should come in to the office. Deputy Roman Charsguard could reappear now that the men were in custody. And maybe Lance needed help booking all the suspects. That's what he *should* do, but all he wanted to do was see Matt. His heart hurt and part of him was terrified.

He was about to call Lance when a car pulled up out front. Roman looked out the window. It was Matt. He got out of the driver's side of his Cherokee and stood looking at the cabin. He looked determined, like he was gearing himself up for something.

Roman's heart grew cold and heavy as a stone. He opened the door and stood stiffly in the doorway. He felt like he wanted to run away and hide, and go to Matt and beg forgiveness, both at the same time. He wished he could get advice from Tim or Lance. He had no idea how to handle this, what to say or do.

Matt walked slowly toward the cabin. His feet sounded like they weighed a hundred pounds each as he came up the steps to the porch. Roman moved aside, and Matt came into the cabin. He paused after he crossed the threshold. Neither of them said anything. Matt turned and placed a hand on Roman's cheek and stared into his eyes, looked at his face, at his shoulders, at his scarred ear.

He grunted. It was a low, bewildered sound. He stepped away from Roman, paced a few steps, stopped, glanced at Roman, paced again.

Roman found his voice. "Did everything go okay? With the arrests?"

Matt shook his head, as if the question were unimportant. He waved his fingers. "Yup. They processed the suspects and put them into the jail cell at the sheriff's office. Dixon and a transport vehicle from the DEA will arrive in the morning to pick them up. We'll have to comb over their cabin and the farm."

"That's good."

Matt nodded, but he still didn't look at Roman. He paced back and forth a few more times, ran a slightly shaking hand through his hair, and gave a bitter laugh. "You know, I've never before in my life thought I was going mad. I mean, it's just an expression, right? *I must be losing my mind.* Tonight, I really fucking think I am."

"You're not crazy." Roman couldn't stand to see Matt so freaked out. He felt nervous and sick to his stomach, wanting to make it better but not knowing how to. "Matt...."

Matt had glanced at the photograph of Roman and James that was on the wall a few times since he'd come in. Suddenly he swiveled and went right for it. He took it off the wall.

"Matt, don't," Roman pleaded, but he made no move to stop him. Matt slid the photo out of the plain wooden frame it was in. He looked at the back. He choked out something that was half laugh and half scream.

Roman knew what was written on the back of the photo. He'd looked at the words so often, they were written in his heart. *James and Roman, Afghanistan 2012.* Matt would recognize

'Paco' now, even if the photo had been taken before Roman's ear was shot.

"You *were* in the 2-87 Infantry Battalion, weren't you?" Matt's voice was choked. " You were in K-9 *as a dog*."

The words broke something inside Roman, the way they were spat out, the disbelief and anger in them. Matt knew, and Matt hated him now. Roman, his eyes on the floor, turned and walked out of the cabin. He started jogging, heading into the woods. He had to get away, or he would break into a million pieces.

"Goddamn it!" Matt caught up with Roman before he made it into the trees. He pulled hard on Roman's arm to stop him in his tracks. Roman stopped, but he kept his eyes on the ground. He wouldn't fight Matt. He would never hurt him.

"Don't you fucking run away this time. Talk to me!" Matt pleaded. "For God's sake, Ro! What the hell is this? Is it the whole damn town? It is, isn't it? It's the whole fucking.... I can't—" His words broke off, along with his voice. He grabbed a hold of Roman, arms around his waist from behind, and clutched hard, like Roman was the only life jacket in a stormy sea. Matt's forehead ground between Roman's shoulders. He was shaking.

Roman was so relieved that Matt still wanted to touch him. Touch was good. Touch could heal anything. He felt bad for Matt. He knew how shocking and difficult this had to be for him. Roman's desire to flee ebbed away. He put his hand over Matt's, which were clasped painfully tight at Roman's belt buckle.

"Matt, don't be angry or afraid. It's not so bad," he tried to explain, his voice low and shaky. "Today—it was only to stop those men from leaving, because Lance was afraid they'd come back or tell other people about Mad Creek. Everyone here is a good person. The people in town—they're the nicest people you could ever meet. We don't hurt anyone. We just want to live here in peace. Don't be upset."

Matt breathed hard into the back of Roman's shirt. "You're Paco, aren't you? And James Pattson, he was your handler in the army."

Roman nodded slowly. Part of him felt like he was betraying Lance and the pack, telling Matt the truth. But there was nowhere left to hide, and he wanted Matt to understand so badly. "That night I came to your cabin… it was the closest place to go, and I knew you'd help me. Clery shot me. He caught me sniffing around at the Piney Top cabin. I'm sorry, Matt. I wanted to tell you, but it's the town's secret, not just mine."

Matt let go and stepped away. His face was incredulous, but at least it wasn't angry now. "Jesus. How did I not see it? The way you disappeared when Paco was with us. Charlie, sniffing around the woods." Matt waggled his fingers. "Lance with his weird, protective personality. Leesa. Fucking *broth*. That guy who peed on a fire hydrant in the street...." Matt laughed and it was a scary sound. "You're all dogs!"

Roman flinched. It didn't sound like a compliment when Matt said it. "Not all of us. There are full-blooded humans in Mad Creek too. Bill McGurver. And Tim."

"Dr. McGurver?" Matt sounded curious despite himself.

"Yes. He's married to a quickened named Jane. They have a little girl. She's real sweet."

"Quickened?"

"That's when a dog can become a man. It only happens to dogs who had a very strong bond with a human, like I had with James. But some quickened are born that way. If their parents were quickened, they will be too, like Lance. He never lived as a regular dog, but he can change into one."

Matt wiped his hand over his face. He still looked shocked. "Christ. So Lance's partner, Tim, he's human too?"

"Yes. He's like you. He moved here, and he didn't know anything about the quickened."

"Do Dr. McGurver and Tim both know about...."

Roman felt a little indignant at that. "*Yes.* They know. And they love their partners anyway. They would never hurt the town by telling outsiders."

It sounded like an accusation. And it was, and a heartfelt plea too. Roman suddenly felt the edge of the knife they were standing on. He felt like he was sliding down that wet, steep tile roof from the training course, his nails unable to catch hold. Terror. He closed his eyes, swallowed. "Matt, please. You don't have to... to... like me anymore. But please don't tell anyone. If you do, Mad Creek could be destroyed—me, and Lance, and everyone else in it. I don't care about myself, but I care about them. *Please.*"

Matt was silent. When Roman opened his eyes, Matt was looking off into the woods, his face sad. He shook his head a little, as if arguing with himself in his head.

He straightened his spine and glared at Roman. "That's why you didn't tell me? Roman, I don't know what the hell to think right now. But I know this—I would never hurt you, or the town either. You need to believe that."

"Thank you, Matt." Roman felt such gratitude and sorrow too. Was this good-bye? His dog wouldn't hear of it. Roman took a step and moved against Matt, bending down to rub the top of his head against Matt's chest. "I love you. I'm sorry I'm not the man you wanted."

Matt made a choked noise. His arms went around Roman, and he squeezed them chest-to chest in a desperate hold. "Listen to me. When that bullshit went down with my dad, I felt so…. I don't want to lose you, Ro. I mean that with every bone in my body. Just… give me a minute to think. Okay?"

"Okay." As long as Matt was touching him, Roman could wait forever.

\*             \*             \*

Roman's words had hit Matt in the solar plexus like a roundhouse kick from a bull. *Don't tell anyone. If you do, Mad Creek could be destroyed.* That was true, wasn't it? He could destroy Mad Creek. If he reported this, and in the unlikely case that anyone actually believed him, the military would descend on Mad Creek like locusts, probably in full hazmat.

Wow. That image chilled him to the bone. He would never do that to Roman, and not to the people—people*ish*—who'd been pretty damn swell to him since he'd arrived. Okay, so maybe Beaufort hadn't been so nice, not at first, but at least now Matt understood why.

Holy hell, though, he was still having trouble wrapping his head around it. Dogs could become 'quickened' and change into people. And somehow he'd stumbled into an entire secret community of them. And he'd fallen in love with one!

*Was* in love with one. He was surprised to find his feelings for Roman hadn't lessened one iota. If anything, they'd dug in deeper, like living roots resisting being torn out. He'd loved Paco, had felt the dog's incredible spirit, and that spirit

416

was in Roman too. Matt had sensed it from the start. Now that he knew the truth, there was an almost terrifying need to protect Roman from all the crazies who would rip him apart if they knew the truth. Christ, no wonder Lance was so tense all the time!

The photograph of Roman with James in Afghanistan burned in his mind. James had loved Roman too and somehow... made him a real boy? How did that even work? Matt had a million questions, but he was pretty sure it wouldn't have happened if Roman hadn't been an extraordinary dog possessed of a strong spirit and a good heart. A *great* heart. Matt could hang onto that if nothing else.

And it seemed like love was some powerful shit, because his deepest, gut feeling was that he didn't give a rat's ass if Roman changed into a dog, or a lion, or a fucking kangaroo, as long as he hadn't lost him.

"You're still you, aren't you?" Matt pressed Roman closer to convince himself the solid weight was real.

Roman sounded bewildered. "I don't know how to be anything else."

Matt couldn't help but laugh. "I know. You're so 'you' you could be your own postage stamp. But seriously, Ro, please talk me down from this ledge. Because right now I don't know if the moon is green cheese, or Canadian geese secretly run law firms in Alberta, or what. This is hugely fucking with my head. Like—can all dogs become people? Is Tom Brokaw actually a cocker spaniel?"

Roman hugged Matt tight and laughed. "I haven't smelled this Tom Brokaw, but if he doesn't live in Mad Creek, he's probably all human. Not many dogs can change, Matt. When I was out in the world, I only met one other dog who could, and he helped me find this place." Roman sighed. "I'll tell you everything I know, but Lance or Bill or Tim can answer your questions better. Up until two years ago, I was just an Army dog. I only became human after... after James died."

Matt drew back and searched Roman's face. "Christ. I knew you must have had a weird upbringing, but I had no idea, did I? Maybe we should go back into the cabin and you can tell me what you know. I hope you have beer. Or whiskey. Or Quaaludes. Shit, this is strange."

Roman looked hopeful. "I have champagne. I bought some after our picnic because I liked the bubbles. And this is a celebration, isn't it? Can we celebrate?"

How could Matt resist that face? "What the hell. We caught the bad guys, I haven't lost you, I came out to my dad, and I just learned there's magic in the world. Champagne it is."

They went inside the cabin. Roman got out the champagne, and Matt opened it and poured them both a glass. They took the bottle and glasses over to the sofa.

Then Roman told Matt a very strange tale. It was about a German shepherd who was born a dog, had a handler named James, trained hard, and was shipped to Afghanistan to sniff for bombs and work as a military dog. He told him about how close he and James had been. And when he got to the part where James died, his voice filled with so much pain that it brought dampness to Matt's eyes.

Roman told him about the first time he'd turned into a man, and how he'd escaped the K-9 facility. He told him about finding Mad Creek, and how they'd given him a home. He said that when he got to Mad Creek, he'd been lonely, lost, and barely

419

human—until he started working for Lance and had gotten to know the pack.

Matt listened. A tiny part of his brain was still saying *this isn't possible, he's pulling your leg*, but he knew it was true. Every word. When all other possibilities are eliminated, what's left, no matter how improbable, must be the truth. The weirdest thing, though, was how the 'weird' faded. He'd once read something about how strong smells only register in your nose for the first five minutes or so, then you essentially stop smelling them. This seemed to be like that too. Only a few hours into this inconceivable idea, and already, as Roman sat there telling his story, Matt's brain was nodding along like it was normal.

More than normal. Precious. A goddamn miracle. Roman sat only a few feet away, baring the sad treasures of his heart, laying them out for Matt piece by piece. And for every piece of himself that he bared, he stole a piece of Matt in return.

"I wanted to tell you about us," Roman said, when his tale had run up against the present. "But Lance said I should wait. That relationships with humans don't always work out, and it's very dangerous for humans to know about the quickened."

"So...seriously, no one outside of your... species... knows? The government? Doctors?"

Roman shook his head no. "I told you, there are some humans who know, but they're all part of the pack. No one outside knows. Lance says if the government finds out, they might put all of us in cages to be studied or... maybe even killed. People get scared of things they don't understand."

Matt rubbed his hands over his face. "He's right. I'll talk to him. He'll probably freak out that I know, but I'll make sure he understands that I'm not going to tell anyone. You believe that, Roman. Right?"

Roman nodded, his eyes completely trusting. Matt had no choice but to scoot over and pull him into a hug.

"So... Tim and Lance are a mixed race couple then?" he asked with a slightly hysterical laugh. He rubbed his palm across Roman's buzz cut.

"Yes. Tim didn't know about the quickened when he moved to Mad Creek. Lance was suspicious of him—"

"You don't say."

"—so he hung around Tim trying to make sure he wasn't a threat. And they fell in love and became mates. They're so lucky." Roman pulled back a little to look at Matt.

Matt felt a sharp ache in his chest at the open question on Roman's face. *Mates.* Jesus. Matt's emotions were bouncing around like ping-pong balls in a dryer right then. And probably he shouldn't make any big decisions while he was still in shock, but he knew one thing for sure.

He took a deep breath. "I'm sorry if I ever hurt you, Roman. I want to be with you. Do you think we could give this whole relationship thing a shot, see if we can figure it out? You know—your side of the fridge, holding hands in public, what I need to know about the upkeep and maintenance of an ex-military K9-sheriff's deputy-super hiker? Because... I love you, Ro."

Roman studied Matt's face intently, as if trying to see if he meant it.

Matt smiled. "And I'm a selfish bastard. I've always wanted the best. Trust me to find the most extraordinary guy in the world."

422

Roman didn't say a word, but his enthusiastic kiss was answer enough. And when they found their way to the futon and made love, there was nothing between them—no lies, no baggage, and not the slightest trace of doubt.

## Epilogue

### *Six months later*

"What are you selling, rocks?" Matt huffed as he grabbed another large box from the back of Tim's truck.

"That box has onions. You can take something lighter. Wouldn't want to cause your sciatica to flare up or anything," Tim replied sweetly as he grabbed another box himself.

"I've got your sciatica." Matt hoisted the box above his head to show off his muscles. He waggled his hips as Roman passed him, heading for the truck to grab another box of his own.

Roman smiled to himself as he picked up an open box of red, yellow, and orange peppers. Tim and Matt had become good friends, which was strange because the shy gardener and the ex-SWAT guy didn't seem like they'd have anything in common. But they both had quickened for partners, and maybe that was enough.

Then again, Tim was less shy these days and Matt had changed too. Since they'd started dating for real, and Matt had come out to his father, he'd mellowed. He acted less serious now, more playful and silly, more... himself. His true self. He was happy. Roman was happy too.

When Roman got to Tim's farmer's market table with the last box, Tim and Matt were setting up the green and brown canopy over the table. It read "TIM'S MAD VEGGIES".

Lance stood there, jiggling his keys in his hand. "You call me if anything happens today."

Tim raised his eyebrow. "What's gonna happen? It's the first day of the Mad Creek farmer's market, not the start of the zombie apocalypse."

Lance looked around suspiciously. "Farmer's markets attract people."

"That's sort of the point, yeah."

"People could include strangers," Lance muttered, still looking around.

"Hopefully hungry strangers who like vegetables." Tim started stacking big golden ball-shaped things. Roman wasn't sure what they were called, but the things Tim grew always looked so yummy. He was a good gardener.

"Your balls look real nice," Roman said politely.

At the end of the table, Matt choked and went red. Roman shot him an exasperated look. Matt thought about sex constantly! Roman only thought about it in the moments when he wasn't thinking about food. Which, admittedly, was still a lot.

"I'm going to go check the parking lot," Lance said worriedly. "I'll be right back." He strode off.

"God, he's ever more protective than usual. What's up with that?" Matt asked Tim.

Tim smiled a secret smile. "Reasons. He'll get over it. I hope."

"Okay, Mr. Enigmatica. So what can I unpack? Please don't say 'balls'. Also, not broccoli. I have a restraining order out against the stuff."

"Maybe cucumbers are more your speed," Tim told Matt with a secret wink at Roman. He kicked at a box at his feet. "You can stack them at the end of the table."

Matt went behind the table and pulled the box open. He whistled. "Wow. You grow 'em big."

"That's the way we do things here in Mad Creek." Tim looked at Roman, laughter in his eyes. "Isn't that right, Deputy?"

Roman wasn't sure he got the joke, so he just nodded. "Yes. We grow things big. How can I help, Tim?"

"You can keep Lance out of my hair today. That would be amazing. So how do you like your new place, Ro?"

"It's the best house ever!" Roman *loved* his new home. Luci had gone back to Berkley before Christmas, and he'd started spending a lot of time at Matt's place. Then Minnie at the real estate office found them a cute little cabin on a lake that was the same price Matt had been paying, and it was closer to town too. They'd decided to move in together, make it their 'couple house'. Roman loved swimming in the lake, even though it was only the beginning of April and the water was cold. He loved hiking near the cabin with Matt. And, more than anything, he loved the fact that he belonged with Matt now 24/7.

He even loved the fact that the tiny cabin he'd lived in for two years was now occupied by another newly quickened, a bull terrier named Simon. He hoped Simon found as much happiness in that little cabin as Roman had.

427

Charlie walked up to Tim's table, his arm slung around his girlfriend, Penny. "Do you have any bacon?"

Penny giggled. "Honey, Tim doesn't sell bacon! He sells fruits and vegetables!"

"And flowers." Tim put a big bunch of spring flowers into a vase on the table. "And herbs."

"And roses," Roman added, though Tim didn't have any roses today.

"But not bacon?" Charlie sounded bewildered, as if he couldn't understand Tim's life choices.

"Go see Bowser the butcher, Deputy." Tim pointed down the aisle. "But before you go...." He plucked a pink flower from the bunch and handed it to Penny with a smile.

Penny made a delighted face. "It's pink! I love pink!"

"And it looks very pretty on you, Penny," Tim said cheerfully.

"Thank you so much! You're the nicest, nicest, nicest!" Penny and Charlie wandered away.

Roman silently thanked his lucky stars he'd never dated Penny.

"Hell, the whole town is here," Matt noted. It was true. The park was getting more crowded by the moment. "And these cucumbers are ridiculous." Matt held up a foot-long specimen. "You could put someone's eye out with this thing."

Lance strode up to them, looking tense. "Parking lot's all clear. Why are you waving a cucumber around, Barclay?"

Matt put the cucumber down, looking sheepish.

"Thank God. I'm so glad you checked that, babe," Tim said in a distracted voice. He patted his pockets. "Got my keys, my register cash.... I'm all good. Wish me luck! Not that I'm trying to get rid of you or anything, but having the entire sheriff's department and the DEA hanging around my table probably isn't going to sell vegetables."

"Not DEA for long." Matt picked up a red tomato and bit into it. His grin was a bit seedy.

Matt had been thrilled to be accepted into the forest service, and he started his new job in only one month. Roman would be sorry to not have him in the sheriff's office all the time.

He loved that they spent all day together. But if Matt had stayed with the DEA, he probably would have been transferred out of town eventually. With the forest service, he was in Mad Creek for good. And Matt was happy about the change in career too. He said he'd rather spend his days building something up than tearing shit down.

Anything that made Matt happy made Roman happy.

Lance, however, was definitely not happy with the change. "I swear, Barclay, if they put another damn DEA agent in my office...! I can't go through that again."

"I told you, they won't! I'll be stationed in the area, I have DEA experience, and I won't cost the agency a dime. Besides, I've convinced Dixon that there's nothing strange going on in Mad Creek, and that you guys are on top of the drug threat. It's all good. Don't worry."

Telling Lance not to worry was like telling a baby not to spit up, but Roman kept that to himself.

Matt started twirling a cucumber, and Lance growled low and deep at someone who walked a little too close to Tim's table. Tim looked at Roman desperately, begging with his eyes. Tim was asking Roman to take charge. And Roman realized he knew just what to do.

"All right, Lance, Matt!" He clapped his hands together. "The market's about to open. Lance, I think we should put a car at the end of the hill coming into town. That'll have to be you, because Charlie's on duty here today, and Matt and I have to go check out a satellite image that came in last night. Could be trouble."

"We do?" Matt frowned and putting down the cucumber.

"Yup. It'll be a good hike in, so we won't be back until dinnertime. Can you handle the road patrol all day, Lance?"

"Yeah," Lance grumbled, though he didn't look happy about it. He leaned over the table to kiss Tim. "Call me if you get the least little weird vibe from anyone. Promise?"

Tim looked around. Roman followed his gaze. Lily was in the distance walking over the top of a table, a red streamer in her hand. Gus the bulldog was sniffing with the focus of a wine connoisseur at a tree, and Penny was jumping up and down excitedly in front of Bowser the Butcher's table. She looked like she was on a pogo stick.

"If I see anything weird, I call you. Got it." Tim's eyes twinkled with laughter. He kissed Lance again. "Now go on. I've got produce to sell."

As Roman, Lance, and Matt made their way through the tables to the parking lot, Roman was suddenly overwhelmed— the beautiful day, so many beloved friends who enriched his life, the town, Lance, Tim, and Matt, oh Matt....

*You're the best dog in the world.*

Roman wasn't really the best. James had just said that because he'd loved Roman so much. But he was the *luckiest* dog in the world, that was a fact. No, he was the luckiest *man*.

He felt a tightening sensation in his throat, like someone was squeezing it with a warm fist. His neck prickled, his eyes grew hot, and there was something wet on his cheeks. He stopped, touching his face and looking at his fingertips. They were wet.

Matt stopped and stared at him. "Ro? Are you okay?"

Roman showed Matt his fingers. His chest shuddered and his vision blurred with water.

"Oh, Ro. What's the matter?" Blurry Matt looked very concerned. He stepped close.

"I'm too h-happy," Roman said, in as gruff a voice as he could manage.

Matt laughed. "Oh no! Not the dreaded 'too happy'! Well, enjoy this moment, because sooner or later—"

There was a loud *bing-bam-crash* from behind them. Roman turned to see Tim's canopy collapse.

"Lily!" Tim shouted.

"What? It was crooked!" Lily shouted back.

The pressure in Roman's chest eased, and he wiped his face. "It's okay. I'm good now."

Matt shook his head. "And I thought my parental unit was bad. Come on, Ro. Let's go chase some foxes."

# THE END

# About Eli Easton

ELI EASTON has been at various times and under different names a minister's daughter, a computer programmer, a game designer, the author of paranormal mysteries, a fanfiction writer, an organic farmer, and a profound sleeper. She is now happily embarking on yet another incarnation, this time as an m/m romance author.

As an avid reader of such, she is tickled pink when an author manages to combine literary merit, vast stores of humor, melting hotness, and eye-dabbing sweetness into one story. She promises to strive to achieve most of that most of the time. She currently lives on a farm in Pennsylvania with her husband, three bulldogs, three cows, and six chickens. All of them (except for the husband) are female, hence explaining the naked men that have taken up residence in her latest fiction writing.

Her website is http://www.elieaston.com.

You can e-mail her at eli@elieaston.com

Twitter is @EliEaston

Read Lance and Tim's story in "How to Howl at the Moon".
Available in ebook. audiobook, and paperback format.

Made in the USA
Lexington, KY
30 July 2016